Time of Wonder

MAISIE HAMPTON

ROBERT HALE · LONDON

ISBN 0 7090 6637 6

Robert Hale Limited
Clerkenwell House
Clerkenwell Green
London EC1R 0HT

2 4 6 8 10 9 7 5 3 1

Typeset by
Derek Doyle & Associates, Liverpool.
Printed in Great Britain by
St Edmundsbury Press Ltd, Bury St Edmunds, Suffolk.
Bound by WBC Book Manufacturers Limited, Bridgend.

Time of Wonder

For Frederick and Sarah

My thanks are due to Peter for supplying the quills,
to Lois for ideas, advice and encouragement,
to Val for help and the final reading,
and last but not least
to Sue Curran for her valued guidance.

My gratitude to Allanagh and Hal for timely help,
to my dear sisters,
and to friends from Cotswold Writers' Circle
for support through all vicissitudes,
and thanks especially to my own Canadian *ancien combattant*
who listened to every word and sustained me throughout.

M.H.

Chapter 1

Hampshire, southern England. Late August 1811.

Fog. Above, beneath, beside and around, a vaporous void isolated the two riders on the muddy track to Whitchurch. It was curiously cold, curiously silent and the muffled land loomed endlessly before them.

Esmond Aumerle, Marquess of Lydney, had little liking for the weather. He was becoming impatient. ' 'Pon my soul, Tom, this mist is the very devil. I recognize nothing. Have we yet passed Monkshaven?'

'I think so, My Lord,' answered his outrider.

Esmond felt his mare's withers shiver against his knee. Had she sensed something ahead in that pallid mass? Suddenly, a bell broke the silence and tolled across fields behind them. Esmond smiled. 'There's the answer, Tom. Monkshaven church, to be sure.'

They picked their way in silence. Tom, studying the ground, frowned. 'I think we've company on the road. By the spread of puddles and ruts in the mud, I'd say it's a carriage and pair in front of us, My Lord.'

'Others setting out for Whitchurch, no doubt.'

They pressed forward now that the bell had made their position clear, and the light brightened as they approached a grove where tall trees held the fog at bay.

Esmond looked across the chord of a long crescent bend. Despite the sparse mist that hung between the trees and under-

9

brush, he could discern a black coach lumbering along about a quarter-mile in front of them.

'You were right, Tom. Is it a local coach? Can you see whose it is?'

Tom narrowed his eyes. 'I think it's the Andursley servants' coach. The earl permits it to go to Whitchurch about once a fortnight for victuals and staff who've errands in the town.'

Esmond suddenly halted as he saw a hunched horseman emerging from the mist ahead of the coach and cantering hard towards it. 'Look beyond the coach, Tom,' he said softly. 'That rider's coming on fast enough to collide with it!'

Tom reined in beside him. Concealed by a roadside thicket, they watched as the rider, muffled in black, slowed and brandished a pistol at the coachman. The coach came to a shuddering stop. Esmond could imagine the protests of the occupants at the crude commands of the highwayman.

'It looks like Cap'n Pitch, My Lord,' whispered Tom. 'Surrey must've got too hot for him. He's never worked Hampshire. Is he alone? I see no accomplices.'

Esmond smiled. He possessed talents perfectly suited to challenge the likes of Cap'n Pitch. 'We've four pieces to his two. Let's pitch into this Cap'n Pitch.'

By this time, passengers had emerged from the coach and were standing in line beside it. The robber, by the threat of one pistol, held the coachman aloft on his box.

'By jingo,' muttered Tom. 'He knows what he's about. He's forced the steward to give up his bag.'

But Esmond was not looking at the booty or Cap'n Pitch. His eyes were drawn to a young lady, cloaked and hooded in grey, who had alighted from the coach. Standing apart, she was a study in composure. He wondered, was she employed by the Buckland family at Andursley? Despite the distance he marked her stately bearing and pale face tantalizingly hidden by the hood. Her presence added impetus to his rescue plan. Watching the coach, they primed and charged their pistols.

Esmond said, 'To cut across isn't wise. The low brush hides marshes. Let's follow the grass edge to deaden the sound of our approach. Then we'll put the bays to a gallop and rush him.'

'He'll be off when he sees us, My Lord. Let's hope he drops the booty.'

'Come, we'll roast this bird,' said Esmond quietly, guiding his horse to the verge in front of Tom.

Rounding the bend, as the rear of the coach came into view, they spurred the bays to a gallop with Tom at full yell and both flourishing pistols. Cap'n Pitch hesitated then spat curses as he prepared to depart. In the mêlée, he dropped the bag which the steward rushed to retrieve. The coachman joined in the shouting but ceased when the coach-horses became skittish, and he climbed down from the box to calm them.

But Cap'n Pitch had not finished his business. Caracoling his horse, he looked back and raised his pistol, aiming at Esmond who was in the forefront and closing fast. Then, a startling thing happened. The grey-cloaked lady made a sudden movement, and a closed parasol clove the air as true as a dart. Missing the highwayman, the parasol struck the rump of his mount which ran amok, colliding with Tom. Tom's horse reared, spilling him into the undergrowth where he lay motionless, while Cap'n Pitch careered off towards Monkshaven.

Esmond immediately dismounted and threw the reins to the coachman to secure his horse. He ran to the spot where Tom lay outstretched in a clump of wild Michaelmas-daisies. The young lady from the coach was already kneeling at his side, the steward and his helper standing above her.

Sitting on his heels the other side of Tom, Esmond watched her hands loosen Tom's stock. After feeling his joints and placing a hand on his forehead, she said, 'He's slightly stunned, I think. No bones appear to be broken. He fell well, if fall one must, though I saw his wrist doubled beneath him as he went down.'

Esmond nodded, feeling suddenly awkward and clumsy. He could not think of anything to say to this brave young lady. He struggled to regain his composure, concurring with her opinion while marvelling at the cultured quality of her voice. He found it much to his liking, and her unruffled assumption of charge in the matter impressed him. She looked up, and her hood fell back.

He was confronted by a heart-shaped face in which every curve and line bespoke a quiet, artless beauty. Her ebony hair was lustrous under a lace half-cap with frills, which shaded a countenance of dazzling purity. Large, deep-green eyes gleamed through long black lashes, and two wild dimples played upon her cheeks as she extended her hand.

'Circumstances do not allow for proper introductions, My Lord Marquess. I recognized the armorials on your saddle cloths. We're all in your debt for your timely appearance.'

Esmond was entranced. He felt that only the two of them existed at that moment, the others seeming to fade into the surrounding mist. Gathering his wits, he leapt to his feet, bowed and clasped her hand.

'Madam, I would say my debt to you is the greater, for had you not despatched your parasol, I'd surely have a ball lodged somewhere in my person.'

'Aye,' said the steward. 'There might've been a lot more woe in the attempt. The earl will be told of it all, My Lord.'

Her hand fluttered in his like a captive sparrow, but he could not release it until he knew who she was. He looked askance at the steward, who quickly added, 'Miss Smith is your saviour, My Lord.'

'Miss Smith!' he exclaimed.

'Miss Prudence Smith,' she added. 'I live at Andursley and am honoured to serve the earl and countess as companion to the Lady Caroline Buckland.'

This explained her elegance and the deference of the other staff. But why was she travelling in a house-servants' coach? A lady of breeding, such as she, warranted appropriate transport. Reluctantly he released her hand as Tom stirred and opened his eyes.

Addressing the steward, Esmond said, 'I suggest that Tom is

settled in your coach to The Roebuck Inn some two miles hence, where I'll take a room and have a physician attend him if necessary. I'll be your outrider through the woods in case Cap'n Pitch comes back.'

They agreed. Miss Smith resumed charge and attended to Tom, taking part of his stock and binding his wrist in a sling. She then beckoned to the two stewards and they, with Esmond, carried the semi-conscious Tom to the coach. The stewards elected to ride on the box.

She remained outside the coach, peering within to see that Tom was comfortably settled. Esmond, noticing her parasol still lying in the road, made haste to retrieve it. He was surprised by its quality. He shook it to remove some debris whereupon it opened slightly and he saw inside a silk lining embroidered with peacocks' eyes of iridescent blues and greens. The gold handle bore an engraved name, 'S. Mulcaster. S'.

Curious, he thought. 'Mulcaster S'. must mean 'Mulcaster Smith'. All the possessions of that family had been dispersed throughout the sale rooms of the southern counties these last three years. The parasol's present owner had given her name simply as 'Smith', and the initials did not tally. Purchased at auction, he concluded, as he approached Miss Smith once more.

Raising his hat and bowing, he presented the parasol with a flourish. 'Miss Smith, your weapon returned. I confess I'd not thought a lady with a parasol could be as lethal as any sword-toting wag. I take the warning. It's as harmful a dart to one's person as is Cupid's to the heart, is it not?'

He smiled, then playfully gestured and sighed. She reacted to his gallantry with reproachful eyes and ladylike indifference, but graciously took the parasol and accepted his hand to aid her into the coach. Catching her eye through the window as she replaced her hood, he bowed again, seeking to ameliorate his flippancy at first meeting. She returned a modest smile which pleased him, for he read in it the pardon he sought.

Turning, he strode back along the track to fetch Tom's horse, now quietly grazing the grass verge, and hitched it to the rear of the coach. Then, mounting his own horse, he waited while the coachman joined the two stewards on the box. The coach surged forward as did Esmond, its armed protector.

Trotting alongside he thought how strangely the day had progressed, this ordinary Tuesday whose mists had parted upon a new and exciting scene. He smiled to himself. It had been some time since he had been so instantly charmed by a young lady. Tom's injury was slight, insignificant for a veteran of the siege of Dunkirk, and that artful skirmisher was no doubt relishing his coach ride attended by one so fair. He thought that a future call upon his distant neighbours, the Earl and Countess of Andursley, would be appropriate, it being incumbent upon him to corroborate the mishap to their servants' coach. He had certainly met their daughter, Lady Caroline, but could recall nothing about her.

Of course, a visit to Andursley might afford another glimpse of the intriguing Miss Smith. He realized that his desire to see her might present difficulties since, in the normal course of events, his path would not cross that of Lady Caroline's companion. After the morning's encounter he was determined his acquaintance with Miss Prudence Smith should not end in that sylvan glade. He held secret to himself a grudging gratitude to the rogue, Pitch.

His mind turned to the present and his appointment with Mr Landis Fittiwake in his repository and auction rooms at Whitchurch. Fittiwake's note had been vague, suggesting he attend him at an early opportunity to learn 'something to your advantage'. He was certain it must concern the porcelain figure he had left with Fittiwake for valuation.

In the coach, Miss Prudence Smith, relieved that Tom and the two servant girls were settling to nap as best they might, endeavoured to collect her thoughts. The marquess could never know the depth of her gratitude for his intervention in the robbery. The highwayman's next move would certainly have been the removal of personal valuables. Though she neither wore nor possessed jewellery, stitched to her petticoat was a bag containing five guineas which she had painstakingly saved. She had already lost everything through deceit and fraud – her father, title and position, her family home and possessions. She found herself trembling at how close she had come to losing again everything she possessed. That it was still intact was due to the elegant gentleman now riding alongside the coach.

She had heard of him, of course. The *bon vivant* Marquess of Lydney, darling of the ton at the spas and Almack's. He was to be seen and heard in the Prince Regent's coterie and in parliamentary circles. His demeanour exuded confidence; the manner of speech, flirtation and patronage formed by the principal clubs of St James's which counted him a valued member. A man of taste and talent, she had heard. In the House of Lords he had stood for Mr Wilberforce, speaking in favour of many a good cause – and yet, there had been whisperings. No defence of his reputation was ever proffered as nothing positive was known against it. But there were rumours. . . .

She turned to regard him at leisure through clear patches in the blurred window. His fair locks curled beyond the confines of his low-crowned hat, and he sat the bay so straight and strong that his black cloak hardly moved from the haunches of his mount. His face in repose was handsome, lean in contour. When he had returned her parasol she was stirred by blue eyes sparkling in merriment, and a cocked eyebrow lent a jaunty humour to his countenance. She tried not to be impressed but it was easy to see how irresistibly pleasing he could be to the many young ladies with whom he had been associated. Wistfully, she knew that she could never hope to entertain and be entertained by such as Esmond, Marquess of Lydney.

Enlarging a peephole with her glove, she pressed her face to the window to better her view. He was nearer than she had thought, and she glimpsed a fine leg in mud-spattered doeskin and black top boots. On a tan saddle cloth she saw again his Aumerle family blazon of a silver shield with three blackbirds, above which a helm and coronet were mantled in like colours. She withdrew to her corner, reminded of the trappings of her own family now reduced to ornament without the substance of property.

A cough from Tom made her realize he was now fully conscious and regarding her. Had he been witness to her scrutiny of the marquess? She hoped not, and enquired as to whether his wrist was comfortable enough.

'It's simply a wrick, ma'am, but I was knocked silly in the fall. When we get to the Roebuck a pot o' grog will put me to rights, and I've no doubt My Lord'll join me in it.'

She said, 'How can we ever thank you for the rescue? The robber took advantage of the mist and scarcity of travellers for pickings however slender. In reality we're poor prospects.'

'He was content with the steward's bag of cash, no doubt.' He leaned towards her. 'How is it that a lady such as you, ma'am, are a passenger in this coach?'

She coloured. 'Opportunity, sir. The family is visiting all day and I was excused. I knew the servants were going to Whitchurch and felt it best to join them, as I've some haberdashery to purchase for Lady Caroline. I'm glad I did join them, for had I been alone with a driver only for protection, I fear things would have been worse for me.'

There was a silence. Then Tom gestured outside. 'He loves this sort of adventure, the marquess. Very courageous gentleman. And quick thinking on your part, ma'am, if I may say so. Lucky we were on hand. He should've been in his coach, 'specially with the weather being how it is, but he'd rather be mounted.'

'You're both to be commended,' she muttered, wishing to hear more about the marquess but not at her prompting.

Relishing the opportunity to talk about his master, Tom continued. 'He's much maligned, you know, ma'am. He's supposed to have claimed that he's a "twice-only" man. He meets a young lady once, then again, but never a third time! If a third time, it's serious.' Tom grinned. 'He doesn't remember saying such a thing, but it's grist to the mill of the gossips.'

She did not comment. Tom was airing the very matter she had heard about the marquess. Her silence was taken by Tom as a signal for further confidences.

'When we were in London last, there was a lampoonist's rhyme circulating. No one laughed at it more than the marquess himself:

The bane of life would seem a wife
According to Lord Lydney.
If he meets her thrice he won't think twice –
'Marry me, I bid thee!'
Thus doth the bane go on the wane.
Assuredly, Lord Lydney,
You durst not falter at the altar –
But do you have the kidney?'

Tom chuckled while Miss Smith, thinking to have heard enough, looked from the window again. The woodland was giving way to an open aspect of the road and the lights of The Roebuck could be seen through the fog.

As they drove into the yard, the landlord of The Roebuck came out eagerly, summoning the ostlers, then hesitated when he saw the lowly coach.

The marquess dismounted, bounded back to the coach and opened the door. He smiled on noting Tom's recovery. 'Come, Tom, the coachman and stewards wish to be on their way. We'll stay here and freshen ourselves. If you object to that, I'll take your place and you can ride protector.'

Tom clambered from the coach. He bowed to Miss Smith as he withdrew to unhitch his horse, his haste doubtless spurred by the thought of the comforting grog to come.

The marquess leaned inside the door, removed his hat, and took her hand. 'You've brightened a gloomy day, Miss Smith. God grant when next we meet it'll be as pleasant.'

Her heart glowed at the prospect but, knowing it to be impossible, she merely inclined her head in acknowledgment. 'Thank you again, My Lord,' she said, wishing she did not sound so cold and ungrateful.

He did not seem to notice and smiled into her eyes with a roguish expression as her hand rested in his clasping hold. Still engaging her, he shouted instructions to the coachman and stewards, then bent and kissed her hand.

'I'll look for you at Andursley,' he whispered.

Withdrawing with a sweeping bow, Esmond clapped his hat on his head and closed the door. He strode alongside holding her gaze until the coach picked up speed and left the yard. For some moments he stood in the road watching as the coach vanished into the trees.

'Miss Prudence Smith,' he murmured, before turning to the welcoming innkeeper, 'a name to remember.'

Chapter 2

WOODSMOKE hovered amid black beams in the front room of The Roebuck, smarting to the eyes and pungent to the nostrils. Vying with the tavern odours of tobacco and ale, the smell of kidney stew lingered so strongly that Esmond could still taste it, despite having taken nuncheon an hour since.

Standing by the chimney breast he gazed into the fireplace. After the exciting events of the morning, he felt composed and ready for his appointment in Whitchurch. He kicked the fire to life. 'Landlord!' he called sharply.

The landlord entered promptly. 'My Lord Marquess?'

'I'll leave my man here while I ride on to Whitchurch. Attend him when he rises and keep another room for me. Be sure to warn travellers that Cap'n Pitch is abroad in these parts. He was in action this morning.'

'So your man has told us, My Lord. I've already sent a message to the squire and he'll alert his runners.'

'Good,' said Esmond, moving to the window. 'Please ask the groom to bring out my bay. The mist has gone but it'll settle in again tonight.'

'It's the season, My Lord,' said the landlord. 'We'll place more lanterns at the roadside in case it closes in earlier.' He shouted through a hatchway whereupon a stripling entered with Esmond's cloak, hat and crop. Esmond donned them, threw the lad a coin and left to seek his mount in the yard.

He reckoned to be in Whitchurch within the hour. The road was clear and allowed him to give the bay his head. Soon he was over-taking wagons and gigs on their way to the town.

He had time to spare before his appointment and walked his horse to The White Hart in the hope of spotting the Andursley coach. The inn yard was full of activity as the Oxford to Winchester coach had just arrived. He passed through the yard and found the Andursley coach standing in a lane where ostlers were washing down the horses. The ostlers ceased their work as he approached and halted by the coach.

'Is the coachman of this carriage nearby?' he asked.

They nodded and called into the adjacent stalls whence the coachman appeared, beaming in recognition.

'My Lord Marquess!'

'Where's the steward, Coachman?'

'Shopping in the town, My Lord.'

'When are you to start back to Andursley?'

'As soon as they return, in an hour or so, My Lord.'

Esmond dismounted and, leading his horse, took the coachman aside. 'I don't think it wise to tarry too long. The mist will be coming up and the gentleman we met this morning may try his hand again. Tell me, is it your custom to travel lighted and guarded?'

'Lighted, My Lord, but guarded, no. It's never been necessary on a local run.'

Esmond frowned. Uppermost in his mind was the safety of the passengers, especially Miss Smith, on the return journey.

'Can you handle a firing piece, Coachman?' he asked.

'Bless you, My Lord, indeed I can, and after this morning's incident, I've got it in mind to ask His Lordship the Earl to so equip us in the future.'

'Could you handle this, d'you suppose?' asked Esmond, producing one of a pair of pocket pistols, barely as long as a man's hand.

'That's a short barrel, My Lord, with a large ball and a hair-trigger that folds flat. I've fired one such before.'

Esmond smiled, then continued, 'It's without a guard and deadly as an asp. Obviously you're acquainted with the weapon and I'll lend it to you as security for your return. Keep it hidden and give it to Lord Andursley in safekeeping for me.'

The coachman gingerly took the weapon and its accessories, examining the wooden butt with its silver shield. 'It's most generous of you, My Lord,' he said, placing the pistol carefully in the pocket of his benjamin. 'I'll travel easier with this as companion on the box.'

Esmond turned to go, then hesitated. 'Miss Smith is also still in the town?'

'Indeed yes, My Lord.'

Esmond nodded, remounted and left the yard of The White Hart. He rode slowly, reins gathered in one hand and his other resting on his thigh. He scanned the thronged streets hoping for a glimpse of Miss Smith. It did not surprise him that she was about her business, despite an escapade that would have had many of her sex groping for a vinaigrette. Though not actively searching, he fervently wished to see her. He wanted to express his admiration for her conduct that morning, feeling he had given scant praise earlier – wholly inadequate for someone who had undoubtedly saved his life. Devising appropriate phrases, he was fired by fancy and basked in a glow of anticipation at the sight of her.

But he did not see her in the town. Soon he found himself on a tree-lined road beyond the silk mill where a three-storeyed building housed Fittiwake's Repository and Auction Rooms.

From a window on the first floor, Mr Fittiwake clasped and unclasped his hands and looked with satisfaction at the several carriages in his yard. He turned to regard the crowded auction rooms from his office on the mezzanine. It was viewing day and he knew local gentry were there not only to examine his offerings, but also to inspect each other.

'A goodly throng,' he remarked to Mr Peploe, his assistant, who was checking the sheets of a well-thumbed catalogue.

'The clocks are of interest, Mr Fittiwake. The display of quarter chimers always attracts the ladies.'

'Quite so, but I wager the porcelain collections will be a supreme temptation to them. Which reminds me, His Lordship the Marquess of Lydney is due any moment, Peploe. Kindly fetch his piece from my cabinet and place it upon my desk.'

'Certainly, sir.' Mr Peploe took a key from his belt and unlocked a wall cabinet above Mr Fittiwake's desk.

'It was a ploy to suggest the marquess visit me on this viewing day. There may be pieces in our collection that take his fancy. Perhaps porcelain is a new interest of his, one he can well afford.' By this time Mr Peploe had carefully placed a linen-wrapped piece of porcelain upon the desk. Mr Fittiwake continued, 'His seat at Lydney Hall is the most delightful Tudor mansion on the Hampshire Downs, and it bears witness to the considerable wealth of the marquessate which has a bounteous rent roll and contented tenantry.'

'Then there's the ships,' said Mr Peploe.

'Ah, the ships, the famous Lydney line. What would Bristol do without them and, indeed, the rest of us, for our baccy and sugar loaves! Yes, Mr Peploe, we must tempt the marquess into collecting even rarer pieces than those he now possesses.'

Mr Fittiwake moved to the window again, taking a jade snuff box from the pocket of his plum silk waistcoat. He flipped open the lid with his thumb and extracted a pinch of the finest, which he inhaled with a practised flourish. A solitary rider entering the yard caught his eye.

'The marquess has arrived, Mr Peploe. Let us conduct him upstairs. I have much to impart, so leave us undisturbed.'

Mr Peploe preceded him to the ground floor and opened the main door. Mr Fittiwake stepped forward to greet Esmond and escorted him to the privacy of his office.

'Please, My Lord,' said Mr Fittiwake, ushering Esmond to a chair, 'would you care to join me in a drop of brandy?' Esmond nodded as Mr Fittiwake unlocked a tantalus and poured a generous measure.

Esmond seated himself and took a sip from the goblet presented to him. He savoured the smooth taste of the finest Nantes brandy, then asked abruptly, 'Well, Fittiwake, what have you brought me here for?'

Mr Fittiwake smiled and placed a hand upon the top of the linen-wrapped porcelain nearby him. 'I have heard from various museum trustees and all are very interested in the piece you have here, My Lord. You knew it was Meissen?'

'I did, indeed, from the crossed swords upon the base of it.'

'It would seem it consists of two figures—'

'*Two* figures?'

'—which can be separated to stand independently of each other.'

'Ah, so mine is incomplete.'

Mr Fittiwake nodded. 'It's the work of one Heberlein who was at Meissen in 1735 for that year only and has since vanished without trace. His figures are much sought after. If your single figure is joined by its companion piece, together they form one of the most provocative pieces ever produced.'

'Provocative?'

' "The Amorous Damozel" it is labelled,' said Mr Fittiwake evenly, fumbling among his papers.

Esmond smiled. ' "The Amorous Damozel",' he repeated, reaching for the piece on the desk. He removed the wrappings and placed it before him, levelling his eyes to the figure. 'Well, little gentleman, your companion must be found.'

Mr Fittiwake smoothed out the letter he had been seeking. 'I trust you'll not think me impertinent, My Lord, but I'm curious to know how you came to own such a piece, incomplete as it is.'

Esmond rose and walked to the glass screen of the mezzanine. For a moment he stood looking at the crowds in the auction room. Then he turned, cupping his goblet and staring into it as he swirled the brandy. 'A kinsman, Sir Clancy Reedpath, gave it me before he left for America some three years since. There's no liking between us, and the family is relieved he now regards America as his home. He must have known it was of limited value without the other figure. Yet, I'm wondering did he know at all? He had no appreciation of antiquities, being expert only at gambling and carousing, but—'

'But he must have been in possession of both pieces,' interrupted Mr Fittiwake, 'for this letter states, "In the inventory drawn up by the assessors of the Mulcaster Smith possessions, for the purpose of satisfying the debt to Sir Clancy Reedpath, "The Amorous Damozel" is described as follows—" '

Esmond's eyes darkened. The subject of Reedpath always threw a cloak over his humour. He stepped forward and reached for the letter. 'Let me read it myself, Mr Fittiwake. I've passed through dame school and am quite capable,' he said sardonically.

'My pleasure, My Lord.' Mr Fittiwake smiled nervously as he handed the letter to him.

Esmond read: *The piece extends to ten inches in height with* bocage, *and the individual pieces are some five inches in width. A gentleman with powdered wig and skirted coat of claret and gold, is in an attitude of obeisance, his hands elegantly posed, head raised, eyes closed and lips pursed. His gold-buckled shoes rest upon a green base, scattered with flowers. The right-hand edge of the base is shaped as an elongated 'S'.*

Separate from the gentleman, seated on a similar green base but with the elongated 'S' on the left edge, is the amorous damozel herself, her dark hair threaded with the flowers of the cornfield. Her pale-yellow gown is lace-trimmed with a deep décolletage. Her left hand cups an exposed bosom, her other hand is outstretched invitingly, and her head uplifted displays an exquisite expanse of throat and neck.

When placed together, with the 'S' shapes interlocking, it is clear that the amorous damozel is soon to be satisfied, for the gentleman's lips are poised to kiss the offered bosom and his arms to intimately clasp her waist.

Esmond seated himself again and regarded the porcelain gentleman for some moments. He had long admired this piece, created by the master craftsman, and now saw it as another victim of Reedpath's deceit. He felt strangely protective of the little porcelain fellow and resolved to unite him with his lost partner. He looked up.

'I must find this amorous damozel, Mr Fittiwake. I must complete this *ensemble galante*.'

'That's where we can offer a service, My Lord. I have people all over the country – a word in their ear—' said Mr Fittiwake, spreading his hands.

'I'd like you to undertake that commission for me, Mr Fittiwake. I had no idea of its rarity. Please wrap the gentleman once more and I'll take him back to Lydney with me.'

Mr Fittiwake rang a bell, whereupon Mr Peploe appeared and received instructions to prepare the piece for travel and bring it back to the office.

As soon as the door had closed behind Mr Peploe, Esmond remarked, 'The Mulcaster Smith possessions pop up regularly, it would seem. I've little knowledge of that family's debt to Reedpath. It would appear that he retained nothing, all was converted to cash.' He paused. 'Only this morning I came across a parasol, its handle engraved "S. Mulcaster S", which I presume to be Mulcaster Smith.'

'Indeed, so. It must have belonged to Lady Sarah Mulcaster Smith, Sir Edward's wife, sadly deceased. She was the daughter of the old Marquess of Hybullen whose ancient line ended with her.'

'And Sir Edward?'

'He died three years since, I believe. He had family, but they have vanished from public eye after the estate foundered under the debt.'

There was a silence. Esmond frowned, contemplating the tragedy of a family overtaken by such a disaster.

'But,' said Mr Fittiwake cheerfully, 'Some misfortunes can be other's fortunes. I'd like to get my hands upon the Mulcaster Smith library. Where that ended up, I do not know.'

Esmond smiled enigmatically, his blue eyes hard and mirthless. 'That's one thing, my dear Mr Fittiwake, you'll never get your hands on if it's in my power to prevent. The library in its entirety is safely joined to that of my own at Lydney. I paid Reedpath dearly for it. I couldn't bear to think of it being broken up.'

Mr Fittiwake was open-mouthed. 'How wonderful, My Lord. Though it's a loss to such as me, it does the heart good to know it was rescued *in toto*.'

Esmond nodded. 'It was at that transaction Reedpath included this porcelain figure. Whether it was for the sake of conscience – for the price he exacted from me was uncommonly high – I know not. Neither do I know what happened to its companion.'

'When a house is stripped, My Lord, there are many hands to help in it. It could have been pilfered, damaged or destroyed.'

'Then let's hope you will succeed in finding it,' said Esmond quietly.

He rose and went to the glass screen, where he was joined by Mr Fittiwake in watching the crowds milling below. He listened to Mr Fittiwake expounding his theory of placing the antiquities in separate rooms and not jumbled together as in other auction houses. He indicated the furniture, the clocks, the musical instruments, all in their separate places and, on the other side, the crystal, the porcelain—

Esmond followed the pointing finger until his eyes rested on the porcelain room. His heart raced as he watched an overalled assistant attending a lady clad in a grey cloak and hood. The features of that cloak and hood were etched into Esmond's consciousness. How could he not recognize the elegance of those shoulders under the drapery of grey, the folds of the hood hiding the face he longed to see! Spellbound, he watched from his cover as she held the pieces offered by the assistant. He noted her scrutiny of the marks on the bases. She seemed to be looking for something – a particular piece – but whatever it was that she sought, she did not find it. Gathering the hood about her, she threaded her way through the crowds and out of the room.

He wanted to rush to her side but something bade him remain. He clasped his hands behind him under the tails of his coat, sinking his chin into the white folds of his neckcloth, and watched her as she reached the front door. He did not cease his observation or relax his stance until she was out of sight.

He was sure her visit to Fittiwake's had nothing to do with her employer. It was personal to her. Was this why she had decided to travel in the servants' coach on the viewing day at Fittiwake's? Why was it solely porcelain that claimed her attention? She knew how to examine the pieces. How was it possible that a lady's companion possessed such knowledge or could contemplate the purchase of porcelain as displayed at Fittiwake's? She was a fascinating mystery to him.

His reverie was interrupted by the arrival of Mr Peploe with the wrapped porcelain figure. He thanked them both and placed the porcelain in a satchel. Then, donning his cloak and hat, he took his leave of them.

Esmond walked his horse back to the yard of The White Hart, hoping for a sighting of Miss Smith. The black coach was nowhere to be seen and he felt relief in the conjecture that it had already left for Andursley.

He took his time on the road back to The Roebuck where he found Tom, in the very best of spirits, holding forth in the tap-room on his exploits in the Napoleonic wars.

Quietly he withdrew to his room where he supped on hot pigeon pie and ale. He sat regarding the porcelain gentleman of The Amorous Damozel which he had set upon his table. As he drank his ale, he watched the candlelight flicker on the planes of the expectant little face, granting it a liveliness and enriching the claret colour of his gold-laced coat.

His thoughts turned to Miss Smith as he ran his finger along the edge of the base where the companion piece would fit. 'I'll make this pledge to the two of us this night, my little porcelain friend,' he murmured. 'I'll seek out not one, but two damozels – your amorous partner and the beautiful young lady who saved my life this morning. Alone, we're each but part of a whole.'

That night he slept fitfully, disturbed by dreams he barely remembered. Only in wakefulness did the vision of the lady in grey invade his thoughts, encompassing and clinging to him as mists at the extremes of the day.

Chapter 3

CAP'N Pitch was conspicuous by his absence on the journey back to Andursley, but he was present in the minds of all in the coach, thought Miss Smith.

'Well, I'll drink a toast to Lord Lydney and Tom this night,' said the head steward. 'Brave gentlemen. But I think you deserve the greater praise, Miss Smith. The earl shall know of it.'

'Certainly, he should,' she replied, 'if only to ensure the shopping coach has some protection in future.'

'Lord Lydney thinks we should have a guard. Did you know he sought out the coachy at The White Hart and armed him for our return?'

'I didn't know,' she said, quietly. Dare she hope it was out of concern for her own personal safety? Her commonsense told her 'unlikely' – yet her heart made her believe differently and she felt a glow in the knowledge.

As they passed The Roebuck, her gaze lingered in the hope of sighting again the gallant nobleman. The indigo mass of the inn huddled in its grove of trees, and roadside lanterns flickered in the gathering dusk.

She leaned back, closing her eyes. The Marquess of Lydney. After Lady Caroline's London season last year, the earl and countess made no secret of the fact that they regarded him as the most suitable beau for their daughter. He was a neighbour and they eagerly awaited the visits that should follow. But months passed without incident, despite invitations on their part which had been so courteously declined they had taken no offence.

She felt sure the marquess would call at Andursley to apprise the earl of Cap'n Pitch's attempt on his servants' coach. There was also the firearm lent to the coachman, a matter which assured a personal appearance. He had whispered, 'I'll look for you at Andursley', and the intimacy in his voice and expression kept entering her mind unbidden. The marquess might 'look' for her but no converse between them would be fitting. She sighed, opening her eyes. Once upon a time it could have been different. The head steward's voice broke into her thoughts.

'We are safely delivered home, Miss Smith.'

She heard the iron gates of the west lodge clattering as they opened, and the coach came to rest by the carriage house where staff waited to unload it. Grooms appeared and as they led the weary horses away, she saw the earl's coach standing within. The family was home.

She took off her cloak, patted her hair in place and smoothed her dress. Carrying a bandbox containing her purchases, she mounted the stairs to Lady Caroline's apartment and tapped on the door.

'Lady Caroline, 'tis I, Prue.'

'Oh, enter Prue,' came the response.

Lady Caroline reclined on a *chaise-longue* selecting sweetmeats from a bonbonnière. 'Take one, Prue,' she said, offering the box. 'They're from the Honourable Hartingtons, kin of Mama's whom we called upon today. They own the most remarkable greys. I'd love to spend weeks with them, the greys not the Hartingtons. Did you manage to find the blonde-lace?'

'That and more,' said Prue, declining the bonbons.

Seating herself at the end of the *chaise-longue*, she opened the bandbox. 'Look! Isn't this the perfect trimming for your new dress, rose gauze topped with lilac grosgrain? And for the new bonnet I chose jessamine. I bought Valenciennes deep lace and ribands of blue and cherry. There's weeks of sewing, Caro, but it'll be worth it.'

Lady Caroline looked glum as she fingered the trimmings. Prue smiled to herself. Caroline's reaction conferred no criticism of her choices: it was simply that Caroline favoured the sombre hues of riding dress. The countess had prevailed upon Prue to guide her daughter towards fashionable elegance and, by using gowns of gossamer white trimmed in colour, Prue had made some encroachment into Caroline's preferences. Her appearance improved sufficiently to attract compliments at soirées, and at Almack's assembly rooms in London there was no shortage of escorts. Prue worked hard in the background during that London season, enjoying Caroline's seventeenth birthday launch into Society. But this meant little to Caroline. In London, her ebullient spirit deserted her while pining for Andursley and her horses.

Prue rose and collected the ribands together. 'Do you wish me to attend you further, Caro? If not, may I retire? It's been a harrowing day one way and another. We were held up by a highwayman on our way to Whitchurch, but no doubt you'll hear all about it tomorrow.'

'A highwayman!' Caroline exclaimed. 'Did he rob you?'

'No. He was prevented by the Marquess of Lydney and his outrider coming to our rescue.'

'Well,' breathed Caroline. 'Of course you may retire, Prue, but do tell a little before you go.'

Prue recounted all to Caroline, playing down her own role but praising the marquess's bravery in the affair. The mention of his name promoted a wild thrill within her.

Caroline's eyes were bright with excitement. 'What an adventure for you!'

Prue smiled. She longed to go to her quarters and was finally released by Caroline. She placed the bandbox on a shelf in her workroom then climbed a narrow staircase away from the grandeur of the formal rooms at Andursley. A passage led to a wing at the back of the house which she shared with an elderly retainer, Mrs Biddy Phipps, who had served as nanny to Caroline.

The withdrawing-room was already candlelit. A table, dressed in a white cloth, was set for two with Biddy's tea caddy opened in readiness.

'I knew you'd returned,' said a voice from within a large cupboard. 'I'd been looking for the coach for hours. Did the pole break or the horses go lame, or what?'

'Nothing of the kind. A delay of a different sort and many errands,' said Prue, hugging the emerging Biddy, who tut-tutted indicating the condiments she was carrying to the table. Prue took the condiments and completed the setting for their meal.

Biddy sat in her wing chair, her white cap starched high in contrast to a black spencer and quilted petticoat. Clasping her hands in her lap, she waited for Prue to seat herself before saying, 'The baked rabbit can bide awhile. Tell me, did you see what you were looking for at Fittiwake's?'

Prue shook her head. 'No, Biddy. There were vases and figures from everywhere. I inspected several pieces of Meissen. There were items I recognized from the cabinet that stood in the upper gallery of Hybullen House. I had a mind to garner them all.'

'That's impossible, Prue. Be content to seek the piece you want most. One day it'll present itself. But, my dear, you've not told me all; there's a dreaminess about you. Something happened to cause it.'

Prue coloured. 'It's simply that I met – in the strangest of circumstances – that most handsome and eligible "twice-only" man.'

'The Marquess of Lydney?'

'He came to our assistance when we were held up by a highwayman. Mother's parasol played a part. I think I saved his life, for the robber's aim was certainly to his heart.'

'Prue! How did he respond?'

'With gallantry, of course, saying he will look for me at Andursley.'

'Now here's a kettle of fish!' expostulated Biddy, meshing her fingers.

Prue rose. 'Don't fuss, Biddy. I know my place after three years in the earl's service.' She paused, adding softly, 'Sometimes it hurts when I think that I could have had a London season. But I was cheated of that as surely as father was cheated.'

There was a silence.

Biddy said, 'My dear, your service years will not go to waste. By birth and breeding you're a noblewoman, yet you have talents in your hands, your mind and your heart which are valued at Andursley. Here you're safe, your previous connections unknown. Here you can await developments in peace, apart from your forays to Fittiwake's which may raise a few eyebrows. Leave matters to your brother and Lord Dartree.'

Biddy left to serve their meal from the adjacent kitchen. Prue wandered to the casement where a full moon flooded the country-side in blue light.

It recalled the moment on a moonlit night six years ago when she had looked from a window in her father's house. She saw the coach and four like a black blot hurtling along the drive, and prayed that it was bringing her father home. His visit to London had stretched into months, causing concern to Prue and James, her brother. They had rushed from the porch as the coach drew up. She remembered her father's white hands gripping the door as it opened, his collapse into James's arms, sobbing, 'Cheats – villains – all is lost.' Their domain was shattered and the moon had shone coldly on them all.

A touch on her shoulder made her start. Biddy led her to the table where their plates steamed with baked rabbit, onions and potatoes mashed in cream.

'Thank you, Biddy. I was thinking of that night at Hybullen.'

'Ah, I could tell.'

'It's the moonlight, beautiful and so cruel. Father's homecoming presaged our terrible losses, and the illness which took him from us though his mind was already fled. He insisted his gambling losses were due to fraud. Poor father, we didn't believe him until Lord Dartree came forward with witnesses willing to testify against Sir Clancy Reedpath.'

'Reedpath has much to answer for, but he knows it and remains abroad,' remarked Biddy grimly.

'If only he'd return, but we don't know how to effect it. James says it's the key to everything.'

They continued their meal in silence. Biddy, first to finish, rose and brought in a pie of stewed blackberries. Pouring cream over the portions, she said, 'Didn't Reedpath make you an offer of marriage? Why not accept? That may coax him back, Prue.'

Prue shuddered. 'Reedpath is loathsome to me. I detest that man! I long for the day when we can prove his chicanery.'

Biddy nodded imperceptibly, noting that Prue had toyed with her food. Was it the recollection of an erstwhile unmentionable subject, her father's ruin by compulsive gambling after her mother's death? Or was there something else on her mind?

That she was the most beautiful young lady in the county was Biddy's oft-expressed opinion, brushed aside by Prue with equal conviction. Biddy acknowledged that the lace cap, discreet style of dress, abandoning of the 'Mulcaster' in her name, lent credence to her role as companion to Lady Caroline. But she knew that Prue spurned the advances of young men, and suppressed her attraction and her desires.

'I wish the downfall of Reedpath wasn't your sole commitment in life, Prue,' Biddy grumbled.

'Not my *sole* commitment; there's also the porcelain suitor I seek,' she replied with forced frivolity.

Biddy shrugged. Could such commitments be diverted? Only by something stronger than Prue's will. Pray it may happen, for otherwise it is a pitiful waste, thought Biddy as she set the tea to infuse.

The story of Cap'n Pitch buzzed all over the estate the next morning. The stewards and coachman had seen the earl and related all. At breakfast the earl and countess could talk of nothing else and Caroline was party to it.

'Lord Lydney will be coming to collect his pistol,' spluttered the countess, 'with no formality, a card presented at the door. The very worst type of visit!'

'Why so?' asked Caroline.

The countess turned the full flush of her face upon her daughter. 'Because we shall have to be in a constant state of preparedness – you, in particular. No morning rides and afternoon drives for a week at least!'

'Mama!'

'You shall forgo the company of horses and prepare yourself to receive him.'

'Oh, Mama, it'll be like London all over again!'

Caroline looked helplessly at her father, but he excused himself with the comment, 'Be guided by Mama, Caro. It's only for a week.'

The countess continued. 'You'll have to spend your days appropriately attired: morning gowns, afternoon gowns, evening gowns; Prue will have all ready. Should he arrive in the early evening, the new promenade dress will be suitable for a walk in the garden with him. Your hair must be dressed formally and I'll ask Prue to be generous with the blanching powder as your colour is too high to be fashionable.'

'But,' protested Caroline, 'he's not coming to see me, he's coming to see Papa. If he should wish to see anyone at all, it should be Prue for she saved his life or prevented a serious wounding.'

'Nonsense,' snapped the countess. 'That's entirely by the way. Be grateful that it's necessary for him to come to Andursley at all, and take full advantage of it. Prue would agree with me.'

'Must it all start immediately, Mama? Prue and I were to go driving with Squire Harley and Richard in their new phaeton—'

'Immediately,' pronounced the countess, rising from the table. 'No horses for a week. Let's seek Prue and give her instructions.'

Prue was suddenly engaged in a whirl of activity for the beautifying of Caroline. The fussiness of her mother was enough to effect supreme indifference to the marquess and banish any pleasure in his company, Prue thought. She was vexed at the sight of Caroline in her lovely gowns, seated with head bowed and hands demurely placed, waiting for something to happen.

The next afternoon, Prue was returning to her room from the conservatory where she had been repotting a plant for Biddy. She saw in the yard a dark-blue coach and four bays attended by a liveried postillion. On the coach doors was the gleaming silver shield charged with three blackbirds. The marquess had arrived and was in the house.

So soon, she thought, wondering why sudden strong palpitations in her heart were accompanied by a shattering weakness in her limbs. She began to tremble and could barely hand the plant to Biddy for the shaking of her hands.

'You are sent for,' said Biddy, rescuing the plant.

Prue gulped, her mouth suddenly dry.

'In the salon,' Biddy continued. 'Compose yourself, Prue. Have some embroidery by you. It calms the hands and nerves.'

'Yes, Biddy. I will, Biddy,' she whispered.

Breathless, she whipped off her gardening gown and apron, donning a severely styled dress made of grey taffeta shot with green. Removing her lace cap, she replaced it with one of chiffon which revealed more of her hair. Then, from her workroom she collected a small embroidery hoop containing a kerchief she had started, and placed needles, scissors and lengths of silk in a matching reticule.

She took a deep breath, regarding herself critically in a cheval-glass. 'Come, Prue. He's only the man whose life you saved. It's he who should be feeling submissive in the circumstances.' Tossing her head so that the folds of the white chiffon flowed at her back, she reached the gallery where an usher preceded her, opening the door to the salon. She entered and remained on the threshold. She saw the marquess seated by Caroline, engaging her in conversation, the subject of which she could guess in observing Caroline's sparkling eyes and gestures. Prue felt a happy relief and softened her disposition towards him. The earl, beaming with pleasure, came forward to lead her into the salon.

The marquess rose at her approach. She had not realized how tall he was. His elegance impressed her. A blue square-cut coat with large silver buttons topped cream pantaloons over which were shining hessians tasselled in silver. His high-tied stock and tall collar bestowed an upright stance, while his fair hair was groomed forward in quiffs over his ears. Roguish blue eyes engaged her during the earl's introductions. She felt herself colouring as the marquess took her hand and punctiliously bent over it.

'The talented Miss Smith,' he smiled. 'I've been thinking that instead of archery, there should be a ladies' competition for parasol pitching. Would you enter such in my colours?'

'I'd gladly do so, My Lord, but the propulsion of a parasol requires motive behind it.'

'Heaven forbid you want me to produce Cap'n Pitch again to provide it!'

Prue smiled. 'No need for his presence, My Lord, the thought of him is sufficient.'

He moved nearer to her and placed his other hand over hers. She attempted to free her hand but was transfixed by his presence.

'I'm at a loss to know how to thank you, Miss Smith. My praise was inadequate in the extreme when last we met and I long to rectify the matter, honour dictates it. And as "Mine honour is my life, both grow in one"—'

' "Take honour from you and your life is done", slightly misquoting King Richard II,' interjected Prue, as she tried to steer the conversation towards the safe haven of literature. She was aware that the countess and Caroline were watching intently.

He laughed delightedly. 'Obviously you're familiar with the bard. I enjoy his histories in the main but no doubt you prefer a lighter mood.'

'I relish all his writings, particularly the sonnets, some of which I know by heart. They come new to me each time I read or recite them.'

'So, I'm conversing with a blue-stocking! But I wouldn't say that you lack the womanly graces of the ladies aspiring to the name. What other giants of the pen do you admire?'

'I've a liking for the great humorists of the last century.'

'Ah, Addison, Congreve and the like. In my copy of *Johnson's Lives* Congreve's wig is the tallest with voluminous curls under which he peers, daring you not to admire him.'

She glowed in common pleasure with him, warming to the subject. 'Their correspondence is entertaining. In one of Pope's letters to Swift, he touches on the millennium. He fancies we should all meet, divested of former passions, smiling at past follies, and content to enjoy the Kingdom of the Just in tranquillity. I should like that.'

He was silent for a moment and then said quietly, 'We're all capable of launching the ship of passion at some time or another, but I shouldn't think you'd have too many past follies to encounter if it would end thus, Miss Smith.'

She turned her head aside. 'Follies are bred by passion and deluding pleasures. They can rule the wisest and turn him into a fool.'

He nodded. 'For me, then, all life is folly.'

Facing him again, she replied in light admonishment, 'Then I must chide you for thinking so, My Lord.'

'I should read more humour, perhaps. Do you possess all those books?'

'Not now. But I once had access to all literary masterpieces.'

'Oh, how so?'

She hesitated. 'Er – in a previous position. A wonderful library,' she murmured.

'If you ever feel bereft of such, I'd be honoured to pass you my own books.'

'That's most kind of you, My Lord.'

'Speak only the titles and they'll be delivered to you forthwith.' He smiled into her eyes. 'I am made to adore and obey.'

She coloured. Overcome by his generosity and awed by a sense of affinity with him, she suddenly felt the time and place ill-fitting for continuance of their converse. She was aware that he still held her hand and fidgeted in an effort to withdraw it. But his eyes, fully concentrated upon her and sharply blue, cut a swathe through her attempt.

He said softly, 'You saved my life and I'm for ever in your debt, my dear Miss Smith.'

Protesting, she shook her head. 'I couldn't stand by and allow Pitch his way. It was simply an instinctive reaction, My Lord.'

'An instinct for good,' he said, steadily holding her gaze and prompting within her a strange excitement she had never before experienced.

He gently released her hand as the earl approached bearing two glasses of sherry. Offering the sherry to each of them, he said, 'A matter to celebrate.'

The marquess held his glass to hers. 'Many matters to celebrate and hopes for more to come.'

Thus they remained, Prue conscious only of the measured ticking of the lantern clock on the mantel in unison with the throbbing of her heart.

'Come, Prue,' said the countess in a voice sheathed in ice, 'I've placed a chair and stool for you there.'

When attending Caroline in the salon, it was customary for Prue to be placed directly behind her, but the Countess gestured to a chair in a window embrasure away from the company. Prue seated herself, grateful for the distance as she felt all could observe her discomfiture.

Facing the chimney piece with its great mirror and overmantel, she saw the marquess join the earl and engage in discourse, while the countess and Caroline chatted together. Prue took a sip from the sherry and placed the glass on the stool. Starting her embroidery, she tried to control her trembling fingers. For the first time in her service, the countess had made her place plain to her. She was merely an employee. She knew the countess had marked the marquess's praise of her, forcing speculation as to whether she would be permitted to accompany Caroline to any event involving him.

The thought of such exclusion evoked feelings of wistfulness, ushering in a sense of bitterness that the company of her social equals was denied her. She felt deprived of her rightful place and freedom to act according to her *own* will and not that of others. A sudden unhappiness imposed itself upon her, bringing to the fore the severity of her loss. Was the presence of the marquess responsible for this change in her disposition? His intensity overwhelmed her and made her uncomfortable under the scrutiny of the countess. She felt a tremor of fear. She must not lose control.

Prue lifted her eyes from her embroidery and caught the reflection of the marquess's face in the mirror. He had risen from his seat, continuing to chat with the earl while facing the overmantel. He was looking directly at her. She was held by his gaze. Then, turning to face the room, he maintained his intense regard of her over the rim of his glass. Their contemplation of each other went on for what seemed an eternity, though throughout she could hear his short responses to the earl.

Suddenly Prue was aware of other eyes glancing between them. The countess was noting his concentration upon her. Prue could not risk the displeasure of her mistress and felt driven to withdraw.

She gathered up her reticule and approached the countess. 'Ma'am,' she said softly, bobbing a curtsy. 'May I have your permission to retire?'

The countess turned her head away. 'You may leave,' she said stonily.

Prue turned to curtsy to the earl and the marquess, and made a step towards the door. Both gentlemen bowed and moved to escort her. The earl bent over her hand, then deferred to the marquess who bowed again, taking her hand and raising it to his lips. 'My profound thanks to you, Miss Smith.' Then, engaging her eyes as the usher opened the door, he whispered, 'Look for me.'

She felt the slightest squeeze of her hand, flashed him a fleeting smile, bobbed another curtsy, and hurriedly withdrew.

With what seemed an earthquake in her heart she returned to her room, wondering how she could recount all this to Biddy.

On his way back to Lydney that night, Esmond was ill-tempered. He knew it might have been difficult to isolate Miss Smith to himself, but had not anticipated the obstacles involved. His attendance on her had been cut to the limit and it kindled a greater determination to see her again.

They had been on the verge of a lively discussion which he longed to pursue. Dealing openly with folly, they had glossed over the subject of passion. The light in those green eyes and her glances gave the impression of an idea passing in her mind accompanied by a recognition of what was passing in his. It was amazing that she could present a manner so unruffled, yet plunge him into a world of inexhaustible fancy. She was distinctively different from any young lady he had met in the salons of the ton. Why was such perfection hidden in the wilds of Hampshire in a position of service?

He noted that the countess regained her affability when he later engaged her daughter in conversation. Must he then pay court to Caroline in order to see her companion? He always made the running in a flirtation but here he was hampered by custom and propriety. He had talked of honour which he would do his utmost to observe. He must not jeopardize Miss Smith's employment and the high regard she enjoyed at Andursley.

What was he to do? He wished to know her, to lift the veil of mystery she posed. 'Stratagems!' he shouted against the thunder of the coach wheels. Then, settling back in his seat, muttered, 'Contrivance and stratagems. I'll employ both to see her again and again.'

He had no choice. She had wrought a startling change in the substance of his dreams.

Chapter 4

'GRATITUDE', said Prue. 'His attention to me last night was born of gratitude.'

She had refused breakfast and was taking tea with Biddy. Her mind was filled with images of the marquess, his manly grace and the air of romance he presented. In the aftermath she felt a certain unease. Why had he singled her out for such intimate glances causing her withdrawal from the scene?

'Gratitude is a fine quality, especially in a gentleman,' Biddy answered, and then added, 'If it was solely that.'

'What else, pray?' demanded Prue, half expecting Biddy to voice her own fancies.

'In expressing his gratitude for saving his life, the marquess found you to be a young lady worthy of further attention.'

'Pho, Biddy! Further attention? Remember he's the twice-only man and I a mere lady's companion. It's highly unlikely our paths will cross again. There'll not be a third occasion.'

'Would you wish there to be?' asked Biddy softly, watching her closely.

Prue rose quickly to hide the flush mounting her cheeks. 'He's erudite and comely with an ease to trap one in the amber of his charm. It's no wonder that young ladies within his social compass are often mistaken as to his intentions.'

'I wonder if he harbours intentions towards Caroline,' Biddy remarked.

'That remains to be seen,' said Prue calmly, 'but for me a return to normality is needed so I'll go now to my tasks.'

With a fleeting smile at Biddy, she withdrew to Caroline's room. She was seeking escape. The marquess dominated her thoughts and there was no question of dalliance with her, Caroline's companion. He must surely seek fashionable titled ladies upon whom to bestow his favours. Her pace quickened with an acceptance of her circumstances, and her work that morning was brisk.

Prue saw that Caroline was happy, and the flaxen curls, recently cajoled into formality, fell naturally around her shoulders. After the visit of the marquess she had been released to her horses, and that afternoon Prue was to accompany her for a jaunt in the new open carriage Squire Harley had given to his son, Richard.

Prue took coffee with Caroline and was surprised when she remarked, 'The marquess questioned my father about you last night, Prue.'

'About me?'

'Papa said he wanted to know where to find lady companions such as yourself, and through whose agency had we found you. The marquess said he often visited households where the absence of suitable companions was deplored, and he felt he could be of use if he could confide the procedure.'

'That's worthy of him.'

Caroline smiled. 'But I think he had another reason. A motive hidden within the generality.'

Prue frowned. 'What do you mean?'

'Papa told him how Mama had met a Lady Wainflete in Bath on several occasions. She recommended most highly a gentlewoman who had lost her family and was in need of such a position.'

'That's exactly how it happened and how it usually happens, so his enquiry was satisfied.'

Caroline placed her empty cup upon the table and faced Prue. 'It would appear so,' she said. 'But I heard the marquess pursue the matter as if certain facts about you were necessary to him. Such as, how long had you been with us? Where could Lady Wainflete be

found? Did she reside in Bath? Were you related to Lady
Wainflete? Mama said that she'd not seen Lady Wainflete for some
time and thought you were a kinswoman who had suffered a
misfortune.'

'Is that all?' commented Prue, trying to suppress her bewilder-
ment.

'Not quite,' said Caroline with a sly smile.

Prue finished her coffee and rose to busy herself at the dressing-
table. 'Then what else, pray?'

'Papa gave a glowing account of your talents, Prue. I added that
your gifts weren't confined to salons, galleries and parlours. You'd
helped Mama in the flower garden, planned the Dial Walk, and
were daily in the greenhouse because Papa wished you to inspect
his exotic plants.'

Prue turned to face her. 'How tiresome for the marquess to be
forced to listen to a catalogue of such boring accomplishments.'

Caroline appeared to be enjoying herself. 'I think,' she said,
punching a cushion in emphasis, 'that the marquess has great interest in you, Prue. How did he address you – "the talented Miss
Smith" and "my dear Miss Smith"—'

'All in the cause of gratitude, Caro,' Prue said.

'Nonsense!' exclaimed Caroline, tossing the cushion at her. 'The
marquess heard it with meticulous attention. I was stopped by Mama
in going further, but I could have mentioned your dancing—'

Prue, her cheeks aflame, threw the cushion back at her, saying,
'Come, Caro, let's ready ourselves now and you'll have more time
with the Harleys.' Her soft projectile struck. A flush rose in
Caroline's face.

That afternoon the wind freshened. Her mother suggested that
Caroline decline the excursion to the abbey ruins. The countess's
strong urge to cancel was no match against Caroline's fierce determination to keep the appointment.

Prue said, 'I think, ma'am, we could venture if we were well
wrapped up, and I'd insist upon returning should the weather
become inclement.'

The countess hesitated. 'Then you shall be the arbiter, Prue.'

'I'll agree to that,' said Caroline eagerly.

The countess consented, and they both withdrew to dress for the drive.

Seated alongside Caroline, Prue was content to listen to her praise of the new phaeton and the 'good hands' of Richard driving the chestnuts so expertly. The squire was up beside Richard, ostensibly sharing the pleasure of the excursion but keeping an eye on his son's handling of the equipage.

The pace slackened as the Gothic arches of the abbey ruins came into view, and Richard brought the chestnuts round to cross a stone bridge over a swift-flowing river.

'Stop by the campanile,' directed the squire, 'the grass is shorter there for the ladies to walk upon.'

The phaeton halted and the squire stepped down. He assisted Prue and took the reins from his son. Richard leapt from the driving seat and lifted Caroline from the carriage in so caring a manner that Prue could not help but mark it. Caroline lingered with Richard, both stroking the soft neck of one of the horses. Inevitably their hands touched and tender glances were exchanged.

Prue, watching surreptitiously, wondered why she had not perceived the extent of their affection before this moment. She walked slowly towards the bridge. Were her perceptions the keener to recognize signs of attraction since her own had been tested by the marquess? She sighed pleasurably in thinking of him and his enquiries about her.

Looking back, she could see Richard aiding Caroline in balancing on a large stone which had tumbled from a parapet. She teetered along the top supported by Richard's sure grasp. As Prue watched them laughing together, she knew the countess would strongly disapprove.

Prue dallied by the bridge, then she turned towards the phaeton where she could see the squire inspecting its wheels. There was no sign of Richard or Caroline. She judged it expedient for the homeward journey. 'Then you shall be the arbiter, Prue,' the countess had counselled. It was not inclement weather that prompted a curtailment, but the growing attachment between Caroline and the squire's son.

As Prue approached the phaeton, Caroline and Richard appeared, breathless from a game of hide-and-seek in the ruins. 'May I take the ribbons?' asked Caroline of the squire.

'No, you may not!' laughed Richard, 'but you can sit beside me on the way back and I may pass them to you if you behave yourself. Is that fair?' The squire's approval spurred Richard to action and he lifted Caroline up beside him, while Prue found herself seated beside the squire for the return journey.

Squire Harley spread his portly but elegant self into the corner of the seat and, half facing Prue, said, 'I'm sorry to be such dashed poor company, Miss Smith, but today I'm suffering.'

'Surely Richard's driving isn't as bad as that,' smiled Prue.

'No, ma'am, it's not. But the fact remains, I'm suffering.'

Prue ventured, 'A touch of gout, perhaps?'

'No, ma'am,' he thundered, 'but it might as well be!'

'Then what?'

'A gumboil, a deuced gumboil, ma'am! Would you credit such a paltry thing could cause such a frenzy of face pain!'

'It must be like toothache,' said Prue sympathetically.

'Worse! A tooth could be drawn, but this –' he said, putting his hand to the side of his face, 'could last for days. Makes a dizzard of me. Plague on it!'

'Then you must await its progression for every day the pain must lessen.'

'So says my lady wife, Miss Smith. But, demme, it must be gone by Saturday else I'll be forced to the apothecary for a pennorth o' laudanum or such like.'

'What's important about Saturday?'

'The hunt, ma'am, the hunt! It's cubbing time.'

'Ah yes, the meet is at Andursley, isn't it?'

'Aye, and the field's bigger than last year, more gentry being at home. Among others, the Marquess of Lydney is coming and has arranged with the earl to stable two hunters and hunt-servants of his own. Richard will be giving me a hand, but as whipper-in he's the hounds to control. . . .'

The squire rambled on, caught up in his responsibilities as Master of the South Hampshire. But Prue had heard enough. Her concentration lapsed after hearing that the marquess was to be at Andursley again. She could not recall he had attended previous Andursley hunt meetings, for she would have remembered the excitement of the countess. It was possible he was in pursuit of something other than the fox and Prue's thoughts rested upon Caroline. If so, she would have to be tactful in view of Caroline's predilection for Richard Harley. She shifted uneasily in her seat, anticipating conflict between Caroline and her mother.

'Have you ever ridden to hounds, Miss Smith?' The question startled her and she stared dumbly at the squire. 'If not, you should try it,' he added before she could reply. 'I reckon you'd sit a hunter as well as anyone.'

She realized this was the greatest compliment the squire could pay her, and acknowledged it with a smile. She could not tell him that, from a closet window in an upper room at Andursley, she had watched the field gather and spread, relishing the sight of the splendid horses and colourful spectacle of the hunt but hating the cruelty of the conclusion. At Hybullen, her father had tired of persuading her to join the chase. But that was years ago and now she was simply an onlooker, and a secret one at that.

The next morning, Prue walked to the stables with Caroline to inspect the earl's hunters. They saw two splendid bays, which the grooms said were to be ready for the Marquess of Lydney the next day. They complained of one being a tetchy mount.

Caroline rose early on the morning of the meet, and was in excellent spirits as Prue aided her in dressing. Later, from her closet lookout, Prue saw her mounted, pert and pretty, chatting with other young riders from the vicinity. The countess rode alongside the earl in his cabriolet. Suddenly she put her horse to a trot to greet an elegant rider on a frisky bay. Prue recognized the marquess from his straight back and firm hands holding the reins taut. Try as she might, she could not take her eyes from him. Prue then saw the Master and Richard enter with the hounds, heard the piping echo of the horn and watched the field streak away to the first fence. She waited until she saw the marquess take it with ease, then left for the greenhouse where she had planned to do some potting.

She tied a long apron over her day dress, removed her lace cap and wandered through the gardens and shrubberies until she came to the pillared entrance of the greenhouse. She opened the door and closed it behind her. From a shelf she took a dibble and drew on a pair of linen gardening gloves. The potting section was in the temperate part of the conservatory and she took her time going through, inspecting the plants as she went.

Lately she had realized it was only in the garden and greenhouse that she could forget her worries and be at peace. As a child, she had been drawn to the crystal avenues of her grandfather's greenhouse, where the Hybullen gardeners encouraged her in horticultural arts. Those were happier days and she dared not think how the gardens had fared after Reedpath's plundering of Hybullen. But here in the Andursley conservatories everything thrived and she felt joy in being part of it.

Esmond was delighted with his temperamental mount. The bay bolted after the first fence and galloped far away from the field. Gradually he regained the mastery and, drawing slowly round in an arc, made for a copse which cautioned the beast and slowed his pace. As arranged, one of his mounted hunt-servants had given chase and trotted towards him. Esmond endeavoured to calm the bay before dismounting, and helped his man take the horse in tow.

'Bad luck, My Lord.'

Esmond shrugged. 'He's a bold jumper and would do well in a steeplechase. Take him away. I'll find my own way back to the house.'

He stood watching his servant lead off the lively bay. Then he removed his hat, tossed it in a ditch, and strode towards the glass towers of the Andursley greenhouse which he could see amid tall trees. Breaking through underbrush and hedgerows, he made sure his boots were muddied and jacket sufficiently soiled to suggest a meandering walk after a tumble from his runaway horse.

An opening in the estate wall brought him into the kitchen gardens which he skirted, seeing a turfed path leading to the main entrance of the greenhouse. There was no one about. He was following a hope that Miss Smith might be somewhere within, based upon a tidbit of conversation he had had with the family on his previous visit. His excitement grew at the prospect of seeing her. Would she be there? How would she react to him?

Quickly he opened the door and entered. Peering through luscious greenery, section by section, suddenly he came upon her. She was facing a bench, busy, with her shapely back turned to him. His heart thumped in his chest as silently he regarded her, isolating the moment to himself. Her hair was smooth and black but alive with colour and light. Despite the gloves, her hands moved with grace as she cradled cuttings and potted them, the dibble ringing against the pots.

Softly he said, 'How does your garden grow? Silver bells, cockle shells, and pretty maids?'

She whipped round, gasped and took a step back as she recognized him. Her expressions ranged through surprise, delight, then concern. She placed her hands against her cheeks. Unknowingly, she left upon them the potting-soil imprint from her gloved fingers.

He smiled, opened his coat and produced a kerchief from his waistcoat. He took her hands from her face and gently wiped the dirt from it. She appeared incapable of movement, the sea-green eyes fixed upon him.

'I hoped to find you here,' he said, with a final flick of the kerchief to her nose. 'I told you to look for me.'

'But, My Lord, the hunt—'

'My horse bolted.' He paused and removed the gloves from her hands. 'I have but minutes before I'm obliged to return to the house.' He took her hand and raised it to his lips. 'Do you see how difficult it is? I wish to know all about you, to be with you, yet everything conspires to keep us apart. You are Caroline's only chaperon, but the house, the county, the country, the whole world are your chaperons! Say you understand, and I pray you not to raise an objection.'

She frowned. 'And you have contrived this, simply to see me?'

He nodded. 'You must learn to adapt yourself to surprises such as this, for I'm bent on pursuing you, Miss Smith.'

She turned aside. Dismayed he saw her shoulders slightly shaking. Was she weeping? Then he would kiss her tears away. He placed his hands upon her arms and turned her towards him. Far from tears, she was silently laughing. Shaking her head in remonstrance, she said, 'You mustn't take such risks on my account, My Lord. Your attentions would best be directed elsewhere, to someone more worthy than a lady's companion.'

He stepped back and spread his hands, his face serious but his eyes bright. 'Then what am I to do? I know nothing about you except that you are not as you seem. But you seem to me perfection, despite the lace caps and pretence of maturity. Say, please, that I've engaged your interest.'

She was serious now, her eyes lucid. 'I'm flattered, My Lord, and have enjoyed our conversation, but you carry gratitude too far.'

'Gratitude is a crossroad. One direction makes obligation a pain but the other can lead to love.'

'You travel that road too fast, My Lord,' she cried, suddenly startled and stepping away. 'Are you not embarked upon a courtship of Caroline? She's more fitting to your station in life. I'm sure the countess has that opinion.'

'The countess, with her big eyes and large ears, should be thrown out of the window,' he said.

He gathered her hands in his and held her gaze. Time lapsed and in the stillness of those moments he took in every aspect of her face. His fingers twined in hers. 'I feel I know all that you would say,' he murmured. 'Do you feel that, too? And all the unspoken thoughts that pass between us. . . .'

'My Lord, please . . .' she pleaded.

He quashed a desire to hold her close as Prue withdrew her hands and turned abruptly to the potting table. 'Please, My Lord, you must go. You'll be missed.'

He stood behind her and whispered, 'I so enjoyed our talk together in the salon and long for similar opportunities.' Chidingly, he added, 'I'm disappointed you've not requested any books of me.'

'Perhaps you would select one for me, My Lord. I shouldn't wish for a melancholy book, nor a book of instruction in arts or crafts, but rather a book in praise of the natural world and its beauties.'

He laughed. 'That's a fine task to set me, 'pon my soul! Let me think. I've an anthology of poems that might please, or perhaps some troubadorial songs that are appropriate to our condition, being of longing and love in difficult circumstances.'

'The *natural* world,' she emphasized.

'What could be more natural, pray?' he argued.

She shook her head. 'I could be taking a risk but, nevertheless, I'll await the book you choose for me.'

He suddenly thought to pursue a matter that had intrigued him when he saw her at Fittiwake's. Casually, he said, 'I have a book on porcelain, but it's in the German language. Is that of interest?'

'I regret I'm not able to read German.'

Watching her closely, he added, 'But you are interested in porcelain?'

A blush rose to her cheeks. She hesitated. Then she faced him and was about to reply when a shout by the entrance shocked her into silence.

'Miss Smith! 'Tis I, Drake!'

Agitatedly she whispered, 'The head gardener! Please go. Your presence compromises me. Please—'

'Answer him,' he said.

She called, 'Yes, Mr Drake. I'm here preparing the carnations.'

She was flushed and looking askance at Esmond as Mr Drake,

approaching nearer, called out again, 'It's just that the door was left open and you're always insisting it's kept closed!'

Esmond gestured reassuringly to her. 'Your character shall remain unblemished, dear Miss Smith. Leave this to me. The door is the opening I was looking for.' So saying, he stepped forward to meet Mr Drake as he came into view. 'I'm the culprit. I was thrown from my mount and came upon the conservatory thinking it a short cut to the house.'

Mr Drake gaped in surprise, then bowed. 'My Lord, excuse my badgering manner. I'd no idea you were here. Are you hurt?'

'Just my pride that's injured.'

'I'm relieved to hear it. There is indeed a short cut through the south door, My Lord.'

Wishing to delay his departure for a moment more, Esmond asked, 'You know Evans, my gardener at Lydney?'

'Aye, I do, My Lord.'

'He'd be disappointed if I didn't inspect your rarest plant while here and carry the details back with me.'

Mr Drake turned to Prue, addressing her in a haughty manner which she found comic in the circumstances. 'Well, Miss Smith. What do you think is appropriate to his lordship's requirement?'

Struggling to regain her composure, Prue replied, 'I think his lordship should see the pineapple, Mr Drake.'

Mr Drake nodded eagerly. 'That's a good choice!'

Prue continued, 'In fact, you have some crowns available should his lordship wish to propagate pineapples at Lydney.'

Mr Drake enthused, 'The earl's forebears obtained a crown from the Ham House plant of the very pineapple that was the first to be grown in this country and presented by the royal gardener to King Charles the Second.'

Esmond brightened. 'Then I should like to see your pineapple, Mr Drake, and accept a crown or two for Evans. Meanwhile, Miss Smith, thank you for your patience at my blundering in and interrupting your work.'

Prue responded with a smile as she curtsied.

Esmond turned to Mr Drake. 'Shall we go?'

'With pleasure, My Lord,' replied Mr Drake, advancing to lead the way.

Esmond's eyes sparkled as, in passing, he seized Prue's hand and raised it to his lips. 'Thank you for the Merry Monarch's pineapple,' he whispered, in tones reminiscent of Mr Drake, 'but think well what else is appropriate to my requirement!'

Chapter 5

S HE gazed after him, rooted to the spot. The main doors of the temperate wing closed with a slam that boomed through the glass corridors. As silence reigned once more, she turned and gripped the bench. Did she dream it? Had the marquess stood beside her saying those unforgettable words? His mischievous smile and merry eye enraptured her. She was held captive in his charm, evoking feelings so unexpected that the gravity of the situation was slow to dawn. Gradually, fear took shape against the bliss. She felt hot, and brushed her brow with a trembling hand.

The merest whisper of scandal would mean dismissal without compunction. Her chances of obtaining a similar position with a good family would be prejudiced. All she could hope for would be employment in a tavern and, if the cause of her discharge became known, her character would be held cheap and subject to threat.

She straightened, tidied the bench, replaced the dibble and left the conservatory. Caution Prue, she thought. Hybullen House, empty and stripped, stood witness to her father's weakness and shame. Justice, and the clearing of his name was her avowed mission. Even if a partial restitution were achieved, she would have no need for employment.

Images of the encounter in the conservatory flashed before her. Never had she been so stirred. Serious dalliance had not entered her mind. Reedpath had offered for her and she shivered with revulsion in recalling her humiliation at his hands – those pudgy hands always reaching for her, his ogling, pock-marked face and foul breath. But the marquess? It was unthinkable.

Biddy was visiting on the estate, and Prue collapsed in the solitude of their retreat. The tea caddy was open, set by a single cup and saucer, with slices of marchpane placed under a muslin cover. She put the kettle to boil on the hob. A cup of tea would be calming in the circumstances. The singing of the kettle soon imposed harmony in her mood and a gentle return to reality.

Sipping the tea, her mind went back to her first sight of the marquess as she stood by the coach. The reason she was there at all was due to 'The Amorous Damozel'. Prompted by this thought, she rose and in her bedroom carefully unlocked and opened the bottom drawer of an oak chest. Cushioned by a quilted petticoat lay the porcelain figure of 'The Amorous Damozel'. She carefully placed it on top of the chest.

How lovely she is, thought Prue, as she touched the shining yellow dress, and how delightfully wanton. She gazed at the delicate lace of the plunging neckline, depressed where the damozel's dainty fingers exposed the pink stalk of her pretty bosom. She remembered the little courtier whose lips had hovered over it. His absence intensified her resolve to find him.

Suddenly she was aware of Biddy on the threshold, removing her bonnet and cloak. 'Biddy! There's tea in the pot. Let me pour some for you.'

'I'd welcome that,' said Biddy, leaving to hang her outdoor wear in the hall.

Prue busied herself, setting another cup and saucer and drawing milk. 'Come, seat yourself and I'll join you when I've put away 'The Amorous Damozel.'

'I hear there's to be a Fittiwake's sale where the porcelain is specially mentioned. But the venue is Winchester,' said Biddy.

Prue sighed. 'I can't travel to Winchester. I can but try the Whitchurch sale rooms when a viewing day coincides with the victualling run.'

After returning the porcelain to the drawer, she joined Biddy and both sipped their tea in silence.

Biddy sighed. 'I wonder, Prue, whether you'll ever come across the companion piece.'

'My worst thought is that it may still be in the hands of Reedpath.'

'He probably sold it to the dealers swarming around Hybullen at the time.'

'I hope that's so, Biddy. As soon as it's discovered to be incomplete, I think it will end up in a provincial auction room such as Fittiwake's.'

'Not in London?'

Prue shook her head. 'I think not, unless an expert recognized it as Heberlein's work and set himself the task of finding its companion.' She smiled. 'It's strange to think of someone in a similar search for my piece.'

'It was lucky she came into your hands.'

'On our final day at Hybullen, a carriage was waiting to take us to Harrogate. Father was already seated, a terrible vacancy in his face. I wanted to have a last look at the house from the church boundary. I asked James if he'd mind the short delay, and he decided to accompany me. We climbed the stile to the path which crosses the cornfield.' She paused, locked in memory. 'James found her by a stook, buried in the stubble, upside down and muddied. He picked her up, saw she was undamaged and gave her to me. Plainly it had fallen from the bag of a thief.'

There was a silence. Then Biddy said, 'One day you'll find the other piece, Prue, I'm sure of it.'

'Oh, Biddy,' she said, her eyes alight. 'I hope so. As a child I invented stories about those two at Hybullen. They were the personification of princes and princesses in fairy-tales.'

'I'd like to see the other piece,' said Biddy.

'He was handsome and very, very attentive to her,' smiled Prue.

She rose to clear the table and busied herself shovelling coal onto the fire. Replacing the shovel and standing upright, she continued,

'I didn't understand the words "amorous" and "damozel" until later, but the significance of one figure complementing the other has survived from the innocence of that first conception. I was distressed when they were apart, which sometimes happened when they were replaced in the vitrine after cleaning.'

She paused. Why am I feeling so shamingly emotional about the damozel and her lost lover, she asked herself. In her heart she knew the cause lay in the apparent hopelessness of their situation aligned to her own. She averted her face, knowing that her eyes were glistening with unshed tears of longing for her rightful place. The lost lover of the damozel and her own loss came together in obsessional hatred of Reedpath, the instigator of both. 'Wed me', he had urged in a voice quavering with expectation, 'and I'll wipe out the debt.' Anger surged through her at his gross presumption. She was repulsed by his crudity, and looked for a way to bring him to justice without sacrificing herself.

'Enough of reminiscing – it's bad for you,' said Biddy softly. 'Do you wish to hear what's happening in the house tonight?'

Prue shrugged in answer.

'The marquess is to join other local gentry in a feast of oysters and champagne. You'll probably be required to dress Caroline when they return.'

'I hope that's all I'm required to do,' said Prue, hoping Biddy would blame the stoking of the fire for the rising flush in her cheeks.

'Wouldn't you wish to attend it?'

'Perhaps.' How could she bear to see him after the morning's encounter, to feel his gaze upon her? She knew it would further unsettle her. She would dress Caroline and plead indisposition.

Leaving Biddy she went to her workroom to finish retrimming a gown for Caroline to wear that evening. She wondered as to Caroline's mood, knowing how she disliked such social affairs. But her doubts dispersed as Caroline returned from the hunt in cheerful spirits, excitedly anticipating the evening's events.

'Prue, I'd like your company tonight. It wouldn't be for long and to compensate, you may have tomorrow morning entirely to yourself.'

Prue's heart sank. 'Nonsense, Caro. I don't wish for compensation in time where you're concerned. It's just that all day I've felt a depressing languor and should prefer to withdraw early.'

Caroline turned to face her. 'I've a reason for asking you to come tonight – a reason which you must never repeat to Mama.'

Prue frowned. 'Is there some trouble, Caro?'

Caroline shook her head. 'Not really, but I'm concerned about Richard and Mama.'

'How so?'

'For the first time Mama is obliged to invite Richard to the evening festivities as a new official of the South Hampshire. She's always refused to invite him to other functions. Richard will be there with his mother as the squire is still troubled with gumboils.'

'I see,' said Prue.

'But do you really see?' asked Caroline passionately. 'Mama will insist on my being with Lord Lydney. Richard will be left with his mother and Mama is bound to ignore them. Would you attend them for me, Prue? Mama says it's my duty to be with the principal guest, but you may be sure I'll leap at any opportunity to free myself and join you.'

Having herself experienced the frigid hauteur of the countess, Prue recognized a situation that would give rise to awkwardness for Richard, and his presence could provide a barrier between herself and the marquess. 'You may be sure I'll see that Richard and Mrs Harley have an enjoyable time and are not unattended for one moment,' she said.

Caroline hugged her. 'Thank you, Prue. A gypsy told me I have a true friend in the shadows of my life, and I think you must be that friend.'

Prue held her at arm's length, smiling. 'Caro, the prospect of helping in your little scheme has vanquished my lowness of spirit. But what's this about a gypsy?'

Caroline turned to the dressing-table and started to brush her hair. 'Don't scoff, Prue, but there's an old gypsy who brings kindling to the west gate. She has the gift of prophecy, and I stole away to see her with one of the housekeepers.' Caroline's eyes widened as she added, 'It's surprising the things she knows about me – all my innermost thoughts!'

'How terrible!' laughed Prue, at the same time feeling that she should be more discouraging.

Caroline looked lovely in her evening finery, thought Prue. How could anyone ignore her glowing youthfulness? She was right for the marquess, she admitted ruefully, especially so far as her position was concerned. But Prue knew it was Richard Harley who gave the lilt to Caroline's voice and the light to her eye. Poor Caro, she thought. To have an adversary in an affair of the heart is one thing, but for that adversary to be a ruthless mother was another.

'The gown is beautiful, Prue,' said Caroline, regarding herself in the cheval-glass. 'Now go and prepare yourself. I'll await you here.'

Biddy was dozing by the fire when Prue returned. She crept into her bedroom wishing not to disturb her. The grey taffeta would suffice, she thought, topped with a sleeveless pelisse of black lace. Matching grey kid slippers were dusted off, and she decided to abandon her lace head-dress and wear her hair coiled at the back.

'So you've decided to risk the oysters after all?' Biddy called to her.

'To satisfy a particular request of Caroline,' said Prue, putting the finishing touches to her hair. 'Oysters are not my favourite dish and,' she added mischievously, 'I'm always afraid of swallowing a pearl.'

'It would be easier to find a four-leaf clover,' Biddy remarked, as she rose and unlocked a box that was always by her side. 'Here, Prue, are the best and largest pearls of the last century bequeathed to me by my old mistress. Wear them, my dear, and the ear-rings, too.'

Prue gasped at the sheen of the pearls, each the size of a large pea. 'Oh, Biddy, I couldn't. They are so dramatic and—'

'Ostentatious?' smiled Biddy.

'Well, yes,' said Prue, still admiring them.

'It's time you launched into a modest self-display. You've deprived yourself of that luxury for too long, and pearls would suit you. I can't see properly to fasten them for you, Prue, but take a candle to your mirror and do so.'

'Thank you, Biddy,' she breathed, returning to her bedroom.

Biddy was right. The pearls enhanced her gown and the pendant ear-rings dropped well below her jawbone.

'You're beautiful,' said Biddy.

'Tush!' Prue said, as she left.

She joined Caroline at the entrance to the grand salon, where wax-lights shone on displays of silver and glass. Liveried footmen, white-gloved and silent, moved among the guests, serving oysters on the half shell, oyster patties and other delicacies with champagne in flutes of finest crystal. The countess approached and bore Caroline away, presumably to join the marquess in a coterie of gentry gathered near the dais, where a string quartet played light music.

Richard lost no time in presenting himself to Prue and introducing Mrs Harley. All three circulated together, their progress halted many times as members of the hunt greeted them. Prue was thankful to be in such lively company.

Richard, with Prue and his mother on either arm, escorted them to a window embrasure set with upholstered chairs and a low table. Prue saw he possessed a sophisticated demeanour despite his youth and appeared to accept the dutiful absence of Caroline with resigned grace. Mrs Harley frequently expressed regrets that the squire was indisposed. Prue struggled to concentrate on their conversation, aware that the marquess was somewhere present.

'I trust the gumboils are not too painful now,' said Prue.

'One seems to go and another comes,' Mrs Harley replied mournfully. 'The apothecary has provided a mouthwash, but my husband swears it's only neat brandy that puts him out of his agony.'

'At least he got the hunt going,' said Richard. 'It turned out to be a good one – no quarry, but a superb morning and afternoon. Everyone had a good chase except for Lord Lydney.'

'Oh?' enquired Prue.

'His horse took off in the opposite direction. It wasn't until the last covert that he managed to catch up with us on another mount. It looked as if he'd been over twice the number of hedges and ditches by the state of him. Disappointing, no doubt.'

'No doubt,' echoed Prue. The marquess had covered his tracks well, she thought with relief, with none aware of his diversion to the Andursley conservatory.

Seated in the embrasure, she cast her eyes around the salon, surreptitiously watching for the marquess, when Caroline appeared and eagerly took the chair that Richard offered by his side. Engaged in chatting with Mrs Harley, Prue could not fail to note the lingering glances and furtive touching of hands between Richard and Caroline. Suddenly her heart ached for them.

Friends of the squire approached Mrs Harley, and whisked her away to join others of the hunting fraternity celebrating nearby.

Caroline said, 'The marquess was telling me of his bay hunter and I've offered to have the gelding here to try and break his bad habits.'

'You're very good at that,' said Richard slyly. 'In fact, I'm thinking of developing some of my own so that you'll be forced to correct mine,' he added with a grin.

Caroline giggled. 'I've already put most of yours to rights, Richard. But I was amused when the marquess told me the name of his wayward horse. It's Soumis, which in French means "obedient"!'

'Where's Lord Lydney now?' asked Richard. 'I'd like to commiserate with him for missing most of the hunt.'

'Oh, don't think he's disappointed. He said his adventures with Soumis this morning have endeared him to steeplechasing, traversing the country without hindrance of hounds or fox! But he's now withdrawn to the library for a business talk with my parents.'

61

Richard looked sullen at this. Prue could feel his anxieties in that direction, but Caroline cleared any ambiguity by adding that her father had been persuaded by her mother to invest in the marquess's shipping interests. Prue thought this a ploy on the part of the countess to involve him more deeply with her family. Dreamily, she regarded Richard and Caroline, obviously devoted to each other. Where would it all end?

'Why, Miss Smith!' came an exclamation from behind her chair.

Prue turned to see the marquess, resplendent in evening dress. He took her hand and slowly raised it to his lips. His eyes held hers intently. 'We meet again,' he said softly, as he released her hand.

He turned to Richard. 'I'm sorry your father is indisposed, but he must be assured that everyone enjoyed the hunt hugely.'

'He'll be pleased to hear that,' said Richard. 'But it didn't turn out too well for you, My Lord.'

'On the contrary. I've determined that Soumis is a chaser, which is of some value. No, I can't say it didn't turn out well.'

'You should change his name,' said Caroline. 'He shouldn't be called "obedient".'

The marquess smiled. 'That's a matter of opinion. Come, let's all take some wine and dessert together. Lady Caroline, allow me the honour of escorting you to the head table and perhaps Richard and Miss Smith will join us.'

Richard offered his arm to Prue and so they proceeded towards the dais. Prue's anxieties fled and joy flooded as the marquess's eye sought hers, but his decorum was impeccable, concentrating entirely upon Caroline and not neglecting her for one moment.

As they gathered for a hot beverage, the countess joined them. With hardly a glance at Richard and Prue, she drew the marquess and Caroline closer to her person.

'Come,' she said archly. 'Join me in my ante-room.'

Detaching himself with a slight bow, the marquess said, 'Alas, my dear Lady Andursley, I must beg you to excuse me. I should now take my leave from this pleasant gathering and return to

Lydney. Thank you and his lordship for your wonderful hospitality to the South Hampshire.' Taking her hand, he added, 'You may be sure I'll be at your call on our mutual business when necessary.'

With that he punctiliously bent over her hand and, with like grace, took Caroline's hands and kissed them both. He turned to Richard and shook his hand warmly. 'Many good wishes to the squire,' he said.

The countess appeared stunned by this peremptory withdrawal of the marquess. Finally he turned to Prue and, taking her hand, carried it to his lips. She felt the slightest squeeze, then a hard metallic object was pressed into her palm. His expression of geniality did not change. The countess accompanied him to the salon entrance, summoning servants to assist in his departure.

Clenching her hand tightly, Prue did not dare examine the item the marquess had placed in it. After his departure, the evening had to be endured rather than enjoyed. She longed to return to the privacy of her room but remained until Caroline displayed signs of exhaustion and asked to withdraw from the company.

Prue hastened to her apartment. Biddy had retired but a single candle burned in Prue's bedroom. In its circle of light she took from her hand a tiny silver patch-box, as used by gentlemen fops of the last century. With mounting curiosity she opened it. Within lay a piece of paper. She could hardly unfold it for the trembling of her fingers and quivering of her entire being. Written boldly in black ink, she read,

Prudence
I am being driven mad by you and this appalling situation. Could you not leave Andursley and reside where I may court you openly? If not, look for me in Bedlam.
Esmond

Throwing herself on the bed, she read the message again and again. Charmed by its content, bright and boundless hopes welled in her heart. She rose, clutching the note to her breast, and danced a little pirouette of delight. She slept little that night, disturbed by dreams that lit fireworks in her mind and, on waking, dreaded to greet the day.

Biddy was abroad early, raking the ashes in the grate and lighting the fire. Prue rose slowly, slipped on a morning robe and gathered up Biddy's pearls. Could she bring Biddy into her confidence and show her the marquess's note?

'Did you enjoy the oyster feast?' Biddy asked, setting the kettle on the hob.

Prue sighed. 'That's difficult to answer, in truth, but I return your lovely pearls, Biddy. Thank you for letting me wear them.'

Biddy waved a hand. 'They're yours to keep. I'll never wear them again and I've heard that pearls fret and become dull if kept too long in the depths of a box.'

'But these are valuable, Biddy, and were given you by someone of whom you were very fond.'

'Well now *I'm* giving them to someone of whom *I'm* very fond – and so it should be,' said Biddy brusquely.

'Thank you,' said Prue softly. 'They'll always remind me of the most extraordinary evening of my life.'

'That's a rash claim from someone who's not yet reached twenty-five.'

'I stand by it, Biddy. If you'd sit and listen, you'll understand why.'

Biddy turned. 'So the pearls did the trick. I wondered if they might.'

'What do you mean, Biddy?'

Biddy seated herself. 'I know you well, my Prue, and ever since you returned from Fittiwake's on the last occasion, there's been a certain quality about you – call it suppressed preoccupation – that I can but put down to a beau in the picture. That beau is the Marquess of Lydney. Am I right?'

Prue nodded. 'You're very perceptive. I only hope others are not so.'

'I've your interests at heart, my dear. Your life, past and present, has been shared with me these three years. I've prayed for something like this to counter your own will and direct your path away from revenge and Reedpath. Now, early as it is, I'll make us a cup o' chocolate and you'll tell me where matters rest.'

The dregs of chocolate had dried solid within their cups when Prue finished relating to Biddy the advances of the marquess, culminating in his note to her of the previous evening. Biddy sat engrossed until she read the note.

'Now here's a pretty kettle of fish, Prue,' she said. 'This means he's no intention of seeking Caroline's hand.'

Prue, exhausted in the telling, fell silent. Knowing Biddy's tender regard for Caroline, Prue felt unable to escape the ultimate confidence. 'Caroline's preferences do not lie with the marquess. She and Richard Harley are markedly fond of each other. It's the countess who's trying to make a match between Caroline and the marquess.'

Biddy nodded knowingly. 'Richard Harley is perfect for Caroline but her mother would have her the marchioness. Leave that as it may. This note places you in a difficulty for it's not possible to remove yourself from Andursley as he asks. You're dependent upon your employment until your position in society is determined. At the moment you've no status and no freedom to act.'

'I agree, Biddy. But somehow I must convey that to him. How shall I do so?'

Prue's helplessness imposed a silence upon them. At last Biddy said, 'For a twice-only man he's persistent. He's been associated with Lady Summerson and his name was linked with the daughter of Lord St Aubin. He was called out in another case, but all was settled amicably. There's expertise at work somewhere. His skills with sword and pistol win him bouts with fathers, brothers and uncles without a weapon being wielded. Perhaps the ladies concerned read too much into his attentions.'

'That may be so in my case.'

'You saved his life, Prue. In courting you there are difficulties.

It's no easy run and he's risking much. It'd be simpler for him to engage with a titled miss or tumble a wench. But he chooses a lady's companion who must worship at the shrine of respectability or she's done for. You're not the subject of gossip and I doubt that anyone here knows of these overtures on his part.'

'I think Caroline suspects his interest in me, and the countess watches and waits.'

'Somehow you must convey your position to him. Don't be tempted to express your difficulties in too extreme a fashion. His note carries a hint of desperation which may make him attempt to find you an abode himself, and that will never do!'

Prue realized only too well the implications of such an eventuality. Should she answer the note at all? Its content raised probable complications rather than possible hopes. Even those were dubious in the face of the marquess's past dalliances, as related by Biddy.

Taking up the pearls, Prue returned to her bedroom. Shining on the bedside table was the silver patch-box, encompassing in its brightness the assiduous charms of the giver. She stared at it for some moments. She knew she couldn't ignore his note. How was she to tell him he had posed a question she was in no position to answer?

Chapter 6

'YOU are the answer to a prayer, my dear Mr Bennet,' said Esmond. 'Your arrival here spares me a visit to Bristol which I have not the disposition to make at the moment.'

Mr Joseph Bennet beamed. The lenses of his spectacles flashed like golden guineas and the endmost hairs of his grizzled head glowed as a halo in the sun flooding Esmond's study at Lydney. 'I'm happy to accommodate you, My Lord. But I'm not here merely on business affairs. I bear a letter from your mother who asked me to deliver it into your hands which I now do.' So saying, Mr Bennet withdrew a sealed letter from an inner pocket of his coat and presented it to Esmond across his desk.

Esmond grimaced. 'Not bad news, I trust?'

'To tell truth, I'm not aware of the content of her letter and presume it to be a reminder that she awaits your pleasure.'

Esmond placed the letter on his desk intending to read it later. 'I'll prepare a reply for you to carry back to her.' He smiled. 'It's many months since you were here overseeing our interests. I've given instructions for your usual apartment to be readied.'

'It's always a pleasure to visit Lydney and, from a cursory look, all seems to be in order,' replied Mr Bennet.

'The shipping is going well. Captain Roper manages our fleet as if he were still in the Royal Navy,' smiled Esmond.

Mr Bennet nodded amiably. 'A worthy gentleman. I don't envy his task. Finding crews is difficult but the line has a good name, and I hear there are already applicants for the ship now on the stocks.'

'Our eighth commissioning built for steam and sail,' mused Esmond. 'I think Father would be impressed.'

'Most certainly, My Lord. He didn't doubt your commitment and ability for one moment. We all applaud your management of the shipping and the entire marquessate.'

'The inheritance was thrust upon me earlier than was fair. Without you, Captain Roper and the friends in the City, I would have floundered, Mr Bennet.'

'We're honoured by the trust you place in us, My Lord. Pray heaven it'll continue for many years.'

The sun was sinking. Esmond rose and gazed out of the window. After a moment he turned. 'There is one pressing matter. The Earl and Countess of Andursley have expressed a wish to invest in the shipping part of the business. Though I provisionally agreed, I'm unaware of the extent to which they wish to be involved and' – he shrugged – 'whether it's feasible, our being a family concern.'

Mr Bennet frowned. 'Andursley?'

'They're creditable, I believe.'

'We'd make enquiries to ascertain that,' said Mr Bennet. 'Meanwhile, we could draw up some options for them. Perhaps you'd wish me to deliver such to the earl and countess on my way back to Bristol.'

'That is a document I'd like to present myself.'

'As you wish, My Lord. We could work on it forthwith.'

'Excellent,' Esmond replied. 'Now you'll wish to freshen yourself after your journey. Join me in the salon ante-room in about an hour and we'll have a tipple of our own choosing before dinner.'

Mr Bennet bowed a withdrawal, leaving Esmond deep in thought standing by his desk. His first reaction to the earl's proposal to invest in the shipping line was one of irritation, recognizing in it the countess's hand to ensure a flow of contact between them. He had wished to ignore the interview, but gradually it dawned on him that this could be a two-edged sword for the countess. His visits to Andursley might now be justified on business grounds, averting the assumption that he was calling upon Caroline. He would simply have to tread carefully and seek opportunities to meet with Prudence.

She would have read his note by now. How would she respond? How *could* she respond? He wondered how he might communicate with her. The restraint imposed by her position at Andursley dogged his thoughts.

He seated himself again at his desk, took up his penknife, selected a quill and began to sharpen it. He must write to his mother and endeavour to explain his apparent neglect of her. He could not tell her that of late his mind was full of fancies about a young lady, unlike any that he had experienced before – fancies that he was unable to substantiate with an iota of intelligence as to her background. Smiling to himself, he could but say that she saved his life and had artlessly dominated it ever since.

A footman entered with a taper and lit the candle branch on the desk. Esmond then broke the seals and withdrew the crisp sheets of his mother's letter.

Melodon, Bath, 4 Sept.

To my son, Esmond, greeting
My love to you as I pen this, which the kind hand of Joseph Bennet is bringing to you. Many weeks have passed without a visit from you and I hope there's no impairment to your health. I'm now in Bath and the aunts are here. Both are in good spirits.

It's come to my mind that you are soon to celebrate the entry into your thirty-fifth year. I must raise a subject which concerns your future and the inheritance which has been bestowed upon you. Is there to be no one with whom to share your life? Names whispered to me in rumour are ever changing, there's no constancy in 'em! Are you the masculine version of that butterfly Nancy Summerson who flits everywhere but fails to alight?

*Reflect on this, and don't think I write in chastizing vein but
am compelled by love for you and the betterment of your life.
Be assured I am,*

your devoted Mother

Postscript. Captain Roper hears news of Cedric in America.

The subject raised by his mother was one he had tried to ignore.
In his many flirtations with ladies of superb lineage and fortune, he
had had no desire for commitment. The image of Prue came to his
mind. It would be premature for him to mention that there was
someone with whom he had every intention of commitment, if only
he could voice it. It was ironic that the pursuit of his ultimate choice
was peppered with difficulties, social rules he could not break and
proprieties he dare not ignore. As for the postscript, young brother
Cedric far away in Massachusetts, was the least of his concerns.

Inking his quill, he scrawled an affectionate reply to the dowager, saying he would be by her side ere long and that he was
looking forward to the celebration of his birthday at Lydney in
November. He sanded and sealed the letter and placed it in his
pocket. Then he snuffed the candles and left the study.

Mr Bennet proved pleasant company and a welcome diversion.
Sipping a dark red port, they discussed the Earl and Countess of
Andursley and the options they might offer.

'I think your idea of confining any investment to one vessel is an
excellent one,' said Esmond.

'Why not the new vessel?'

'That would allow time for the arrangements and is simpler to
apply. When is the launching to be?'

'Within a year. There's a consortium eager to back sailings on the
coaling run to Newcastle. These are frequent and of reduced risk
compared to Atlantic crossings. The returns would be sure.'

'Agreed. I think those are recommendations which the earl
would be foolish to disregard. What's the proposed name of the
new vessel?'

Mr Bennet pursed his lips and raised his eyes, pondering. 'Your grandfather directed that after the first three ships named for females of the family, those following should be named for the seven virtues. So we have *Faith*, *Hope*, *Charity* and the first of the cardinal virtues, *Justice*, so the new vessel is bound to be the *Lydney Prudence*.'

Esmond almost choked on his port. Placing his glass on the table and recovering sufficiently, he repeated, 'The *Lydney Prudence*.'

'A worthy name,' observed Mr Bennet.

'An *excellent* name,' said Esmond, his eyes bright with merriment. 'It's a particularly appealing name to me.'

Laughingly he reached for the letter in his pocket, giving it to Mr Bennet. 'By your kind hand to my mother.' He paused. 'Draw up a proposal for investment in the new *Lydney Prudence*. I'd like to present it at Andursley as soon as possible.'

'Tomorrow, My Lord, it will be ready,' smiled Mr Bennet, responding to the sudden good humour of the marquess.

Prue applied herself to her duties to lessen the 'suppressed preoccupation' noticed by Biddy. In Caroline's company she was bright and attentive, and there was a feeling of closeness as a result of the help she gave by entertaining Richard and his mother at the hunt supper. Since then Prue knew Caroline regarded her as a confidante.

After breakfast they withdrew to the music-room. Prue opened the Broadwood piano and, with Caroline, romped through a duet Prue had composed about a runaway pony. It was a jerky little tune which they endeavoured to play quicker and quicker, each testing the other for a livelier pace. Caroline was first to give up, laughingly lolling over the keys and dislodging from the rack a music sheet which fell to the floor. Picking it up she replaced it, suddenly serious.

'Do you see what this piece is called, Prue?'

'Yes. It's the "Tirano Amore", the tyranny of love.'

'Is love a tyranny?'

Prue frowned. 'It seems to be a paradox, for the very nature of love is unrestrained and tyranny seeks to oppress it.'

Caroline sighed. 'Then I'm the victim of a paradox. I suffer oppression, but not from love itself.'

Prue took her hand. 'Those are profound thoughts, Caroline.'

Caroline turned to face her. 'I'm so unhappy, Prue. Mama comes to my room, instructing me on what to say and how to behave to elicit an offer from the Marquess of Lydney. He's like a charming young uncle but his heart and mind are elsewhere committed. You recognize the oppressor, don't you Prue?'

Prue nodded, her heart beating fast. There was a silence. Then she asked softly, 'Who has your love, Caroline?'

'You're not blind, Prue. Richard and I are madly in love and moments together are few. Mama suspects something and that's why she discounts Richard in every respect.' Caroline paused and sighed deeply. 'There, now you know.'

'Oh, Caroline, I *do* understand,' Prue said, her eyes moist with sympathy.

'I'm always plotting to escape, even for a few moments with Richard. We write regularly to each other. Every week, when the kindling is delivered, I go to the west gate and give a letter to the gypsy who is our courier. From her I receive Richard's letters.'

'So it's not only prophecies you receive from the gypsy,' Prue remarked lightly.

'Those, too. She advises caution in all I do.'

Prue rose from the piano. How she sympathized with Caroline! How similar was her own situation! She so desired her status restored and her father's name cleared. Only then would she feel it appropriate to receive the marquess's advances. She wanted to help Caroline, but what advice should she give? To follow her heart could lead to disaster. She knew only too well the necessity for head to rule heart.

Caroline was slumped over the piano. Prue placed her hands on Caroline's shoulders and said gently, 'Caro, if talking helps, I'm here to listen. If I can do anything else, I'm ready to do it.

Richard is admirable in every way.'

Caroline raised her head. 'Thank you, Prue. You're my only comfort,' she said, slipping her hand over Prue's and guiding her to the piano stool. 'Come, let's play the "Runaway Pony" again to chase away our melancholy.'

They were well into the piece when the countess's strident voice was heard over the music. 'Caro! We have a visitor! His lordship the marquess wishes for a garden walk in your company. Prue, see that she is appropriately clad. He awaits you on the terrace. Join us there.' After these clipped instructions, she withdrew.

Prue and Caroline looked long at each other before rising and retreating to Caroline's room.

'Do you see, Prue?' hissed Caroline. 'She's always making such arrangements. This wasn't prompted by the marquess and now he has to suffer me again.'

'But he's called, Caroline, and it behoves you to welcome him. Hasn't it occurred to you that he might prefer your company to that of your parents?'

Caroline looked slyly at her. 'It's occurred to me that he might prefer *your* company.'

Prue coloured. 'That's hardly appropriate. Come, I have your promenade dress ready for you. I think a bonnet and matching short cape will serve.'

Despite Prue's chivvyings, Caroline suffered her dressing in silence. Then she said, 'Did you mean what you said about helping me?'

'Of course,' Prue answered, taking Caroline's gloves from the stretchers.

'It's kindling day today, Prue.'

Prue paused in her task. 'I see. Does that mean the gypsy will await you at the west gate?'

'It does, and I have a letter ready in my reticule. Would you accompany me, Prue? When we're out of sight of Mama's windows, you could entertain the marquess while I leave for a moment. Say you'll do it, Prue.'

'Perhaps it would be wiser if I were to deliver and receive your letters.'

Caroline shook her head. 'No. The gypsy wouldn't take them, nor would she release Richard's letters unless it's to me personally. We agreed on this for our own protection.'

Prue sighed and handed the gloves to Caroline. 'Then I'm prepared to do as you suggest but in an informal way. It will irk your mother if I accompany you, but I'll be pottering in the garden. Lead the marquess to the Dial Walk where I shall be and will remain until you return. It'll be safer for you to exit from there.'

'That's an excellent idea, Prue. I'll do as you say. Mama will probably return to her apartment and the Dial Walk isn't visible from there.'

Prue was unable to express to Caroline her gratitude for this opportunity. She would be able to see the marquess alone for a few moments, sufficient to answer his note.

Caroline gave a conspiratorial wave from the foot of the stairs as Prue left for her room. She placed a clean apron over her day dress, fastened a short green cape over her shoulders and tied a wicker bonnet with a matching riband over her hair. She made her way downstairs to a store in the yard from where she took a trug and trowel, thinking to dig up for resting some early dahlias adjacent to the Dial Walk.

She dallied on the way to her task, but quickened her step after she saw two men drawing a wagon of kindling to the wood-shed. The gypsy was already at the west gate and Caroline would wish to see her. She didn't know whether her rushing pulses could be blamed on the precarious plan for Caroline's rendezvous, or the prospect of seeing the marquess. Her face was aflame and her hands moist with excitement as she arrived at the Dial Walk.

There was no one to be seen. At the end of the walk, a hornbeam hedge grew in the shape of a bay. There the flagstones ended and a stone sundial stood before a wooden garden seat set in the curve of the hedge. The dahlia bed was on the far side of the hedge.

Throwing back her cape, she stooped to dig out the tubers to place in the trug, at the same time keeping a watchful eye on the Dial Walk.

'I've been deserted,' said a quiet, cultured voice from behind her.

He wore no hat nor carried a cane. His fair curls lifted in the breeze. His single-caped coat of blue worsted flared over white breeches and shining top boots. He reached out, assisting her to stand. Slowly withdrawing the trowel from her grip, which he dropped into the trug, he raised her hands to his lips, kissing them fondly, his eyes engaging hers in a blue crystalline humour.

'I'm doomed to meet you armed, if not with a parasol, then with all the implements worthy of Mr Drake. If I should pass through the Garden of Eden, should I look for you tending it?'

She gave a long, slow smile. 'I till the soil only when I'm certain no serpents are about their business, My Lord.'

'But angels are about their business, Prudence, for here we are together in this pastoral paradise. I came to deliver a business proposal to the earl and countess, never dreaming such an opportunity would come my way. But Caroline directed me here saying you would be awaiting me.' Her hands were still fast in his clasp, and he raised them again to his lips.

She trembled. 'I've read and pondered your note,' she whispered, 'and you're asking me to do that which is impossible.'

'Impossible? Haven't you kin that might accommodate you? Come, it's time to tell me of your family. I wish to make myself known to them and seek approval for the favours I long to bestow upon you.'

'Oh My Lord, could you delay a little?'

'Provided it's delay and not rejection, then I agree. Where you're concerned, my patience could have limits.' He paused. 'Could you tell me more on the matter?'

She turned away. She longed to tell him everything but something held her back. She could say only, 'My parents are no more. My brother is seeking restitution in a family matter. Until that is resolved, I'm dependent upon my employment at Andursley.'

'May I not aid you in this? I've friends at court. Perhaps an interview with your brother could be arranged.'

Prue nodded. 'I look to hear from my brother soon and shall suggest a possible interview.'

'You must do so, for I'd like to make him aware of my intentions.'

He took her hand and strolled slowly along the Dial Walk. She was silent, staring ahead. Then she murmured, 'I've wanted to tell you a thousand things.'

'I'll listen spellbound to your thousand things,' he answered lightly, swinging her hand.

She smiled, shaking her head in remonstrance. 'A delay is necessary. My present circumstance is temporary but its cause rests in a matter of injustice. When rectified it will result in the restoration of my father's honour. It is from that state I prefer to receive your favours. Your position warrants no less, My Lord, and it is due to the respect I hold for you and your family that I insist upon this course.'

He halted and turned to face her. 'I care nothing about your family honour or lineage, but acknowledge and admire your feeling. Though I could one day elevate you to a coronet and title, your very presence ennobles me and all in your vicinity.'

His voice was softly tender as he fixed her with a gaze of solemn intensity. She averted her face, appeared to sway and catch her breath. When she recovered, he saw a tear upon her cheek and her eyes shone green as willow leaves caught in a spring.

'You overwhelm me, My Lord, but could you delay a little?' she whispered.

Touched, he looked the consent she sought. 'I'll not cease to see you. I'll continue to seek occasions such as this,' he said, with vigour. 'But, let me add one thing: I could offer you sojourn or provide a house for you. I do not insist upon it and, in withholding such proposals, you must be aware of the respect I have for you. Your reputation is safe with me. You'll come to me on your terms, no less. But my eagerness could overtake discretion—'

'Have hope, My Lord,' she interposed. 'Hope is the heart's balm.'

A gardener with a wheelbarrow crossed the Dial Walk, causing Esmond to turn and retrace their steps to the hornbeam hedge. He walked with the keenest enjoyment, deeply sensitive to her and the happiness they shared. There was a voice in his head echoing from dreams dreamed over time. Since knowing Prudence he had felt drawn to her as a complementary companion where ideas and feelings, similar to his own, spread their wings in her head and heart. At the bend in the road he had met his ideal.

He led her to the seat next the sundial where he slipped her bonnet back over her head, the ribbon catching at her throat. Indefinable sensations flashed like lightning as her hair was revealed, sleek and blue-black. He drew her closer to his heart, beating in unison with hers. Slowly he moved to face her and knew he was going to kiss her. Tenderly he held her head between his hands and kissed each eyelid lingeringly. Then in a tumult of passion his mouth crushed hers in the fiercest and sweetest kiss he had ever known. She must be his – he loved her. His kiss endured until breath nigh ceased and his unsated lips moved to her ear.

'A token of our tryst, my love,' he murmured.

She gave a little choking sigh. 'There's wild charm in this, My Lord.'

'Esmond,' he insisted, his lips brushing hers again. 'My name is Esmond, Prue. Never more call me "My Lord".'

She drew back as gently he released her. Rising and helping her to her feet, he pressed her tremulous form close to him. 'Is your heart unoccupied, Prue?'

Dimpling, she answered, 'Possibly not.'

'Perfect faith is the groundwork of all passion, Prue. Retain it for me.'

They shared a long, tender look.

Suddenly, Esmond felt her stiffen. She drew away, grabbed her skirts and hastened to the other side of the hornbeam hedge. From there she called in a hushed voice, 'Esmond, the Countess is coming. I'm leaving to find Caroline.'

Her departure posed a dilemma for him. He was uncertain whether to remain, or plunge through the hedge in pursuit of her. Observing the countess walking rapidly towards him, he thought it best to face her.

'Where's Caroline?' the countess demanded, her eyes bright with annoyance and her mouth set in disapproval.

'She and Miss Smith are playing hide-and-seek with me,' he said in as disarming a manner he could muster.

'Miss Smith! She here, too? What's going on?' said the countess in a fluster. 'How dare she persuade Caroline to neglect her duties to you as our guest!'

Esmond smiled, offering his hand. 'Come, ma'am. Walk back with me and those girls will be baffled when they return and find me gone from here.' So saying, he took the countess's hand, placed it on his arm, and led her away from the Dial Walk.

Prue's flight had been prompted by a glimpse of the countess's lace head-dress bobbing over an adjacent hedge. Her immediate thought was of Caroline and the possible discovery by the countess of her visit to the west gate. By now Caroline should surely be on her way back, and it was imperative that she be warned of her mother's presence.

Prue realized she had left Esmond to cope with the situation without his knowing anything about Caroline's real reason for deserting him. She admitted this to be an advantage. Her anxiety over Caroline had momentarily swept aside the wonder of her interlude with him. It was useless telling herself that a dalliance was out of the question. She had wanted to bare her soul to him. The meeting had enhanced their attachment where she had sought to lessen it.

Esmond! His very name caused her limbs to crumple beneath her. Sobs of delight caught in her throat so that her panting breath could not be blamed entirely upon her present haste. She heard again the phrases that had burst upon her, charming and unexpected as sonnets performed by nightingales. For ever would she remember that foliaged place, and the taste of Esmond's lips pressed with tender passion upon her own. It was her first experience of an amorous advance and she relished her emergence from the shadows into the light of love. Her heart was full, her senses enravished.

'Prue!' It was Caroline coming towards her on the path, flushed and happy.

The sight of Caroline banished her rapture. She gasped, 'Caro, you must return to the Dial Walk immediately. Your mother is there. She's probably still with the marquess and wondering at your absence.'

Caroline was wide-eyed with dismay. 'Oh, Prue! You must come back with me and we'll concoct a tale together.'

'We'll have to take matters as they come,' Prue replied, replacing her bonnet.

To their consternation, the countess and the marquess were nowhere to be seen at the Dial Walk. Prue and Caroline hurried towards the house and caught up with them by the pond garden.

The marquess, on seeing them, called, 'So, you've found me at last! I'm the victor in our game of hide-and-seek!'

Prue and Caroline recognized the message within the greeting, and reacted with the pseudo indignation of being outplayed. They laughed in self-derision, but the countess was not amused. She fixed Prue with a look of venom.

'You were not asked to promenade with Lady Caroline and his lordship, and I see you are not dressed for it. Your garb is fit only for a garden worker and if you have been so engaged, I suggest you return to it immediately!'

'Mama!' cried Caroline. 'I asked Prue for the pleasure of her company!'

'She had no right to accede and should know better. Her government of affairs seems to be failing.'

Prue reeled inwardly at this outburst but with a calm demeanour replied, 'I'm sorry, ma'am, that you feel so. Indeed, I was gardening by the Dial Walk and shall return to complete my task.'

She bobbed a curtsy to the ladies and finally to Esmond, not daring to raise her eyes to him. As she left, she heard him coldly decline the countess's invitation to take some refreshment.

At least the countess had no suspicion of her meeting with Esmond, Prue thought, and she was thankful that Caroline's excursion had escaped notice. Still trembling, her mind in turmoil, she retraced her steps to the Dial Walk. She took up the trug and trowel and returned to the yard. There she hailed a gardener to place the tubers for storage.

'These dahlias are from one of the oval beds near the Dial Walk,' she said. 'Mr Drake would wish them to be labelled.'

The gardener frowned as he regarded them, then smiled as recognition dawned. 'They'd be the carmine ones, Miss Smith. Harrison's *Tempus mirabilis*.'

She stood still as in a dream.

Tempus mirabilis she thought. With Esmond's kisses imprinted upon her heart, she knew she was on the verge of her own 'time of wonder'.

Chapter 7

ESMOND was pleased to leave Andursley. He summoned Tom from the servants' kitchen and promptly began his return to Lydney. As his bay horse broke into a canter he gave but a cursory parting wave to the countess at the porch.

He was infuriated by the countess's treatment of Prue and deplored his helplessness to intervene. Added to intense exasperation was his failure to convince Prue that family affairs were but minutiae against the magnitude of his love for her. She had lit a fire in his heart and brain, sorely tempting him to make his declaration before all present that morning. But he had agreed to abide by her wish for delay.

He rode fiercely to distance himself from Andursley, but he could not flee the image of that shameful scene in the garden. He eased off to a canter and, looking back, saw that he had far outstripped Tom. In an open space nearby he drew rein to await him. He slowly circled to soothe his sweating mount and the quietude imposed a respite. His temper abated. Prue had said, 'Hope is the heart's balm.' He would give hope a helping hand and adopt a different strategy in the progress of his suit. Of one thing he was sure: he would cease his visits to Andursley.

But he felt a deepening anxiety about the difficulties confronting him. Prue's magnetic beauty made him wonder why there was not a queue of gentlemen paying her court. Her position prohibited it. A change in the venue of his courtship was essential.

He leaned forward to stroke the neck of the bay, feeling pleasure in the silky warmth. He must get Prue away from Andursley. How could he achieve it? To provide an apartment for her was out of the question. Suddenly he sat upright as he recalled his talk with the earl and countess about a Lady Wainflete. It was through her influence that Prue had obtained her position as Caroline's companion. Might Lady Wainflete be persuaded to invite Prue to Bath for a short stay, provided the lady still lived there? My dear mother, he thought, with her prodigious knowledge of spa society, should know the whereabouts of Lady Wainflete. He would depart for London at daybreak on the morrow, conduct all necessary business, then leave immediately for Bath and present himself in answer to his mother's letter.

Elated and eager to refine his new strategy, he guided his horse to the lane once more and saw Tom approaching at a trot. As he came abreast, Esmond smilingly taunted, 'Why so laggard? Was it too soon to be dug out of the cookmaids' haven?'

'Lor' lummy no, My Lord,' laughed Tom, indicating bulging saddle-bags, 'I've got enough souvenirs from the patty-pans that'll do me for the next sennight.'

'So you were well looked after?'

'They were all over me, My Lord. The coachy, the stewards and their wives – feasted, I was. Cap'n Pitch was useful for something, for they still hark back to his attack that morning. The coachy says he travels armed now with an outrider.'

'And so he should. But there was another rescuer, Tom, and I hope she enjoys their praise.'

'No doubt o' that, My Lord. Full o' good words, they are. I spoke with Biddy Phipps who shares quarters with Miss Smith. She's highly respected and a true gentlewoman who's had a muckle o' trouble.'

Esmond marked the comment. 'Biddy Phipps,' he muttered, spurring on the bay, 'a useful connection.'

He stared ahead in mute abstraction. Concentrating on his new strategy put from his mind Prue's humiliation by the countess.

Delight swept through him in recalling every aspect of Prue's countenance and every word she had spoken during their meeting in the Dial Walk. He had held her close and dared to pass his lips over her lovely features, culminating in a kiss of unsurpassed tenderness. It had been the most natural consequence, so blissful the shared moment. In all his life there had been nothing as bewitching. He was in love and longed to bind her life to his.

His reverie was interrupted by the shouts of the keepers opening the gates of the park. He saw his mount delivered into the hands of the grooms and, feeling no inclination to enter the house, strode out over the broad lawns of the park.

He walked on, engrossed in his plans, hardly aware of the distance he had covered. Turning, he looked with faint pride over the broad park, the distant woods and sequestered lake. In front of him were the vast wings of Lydney Hall. Strange that he had never before been struck by its emptiness, its lonely grandeur. With a shock he realized that his own condition was thus reflected. Abruptly, he turned to enter the house.

After a light refreshment, he retreated to the library where he chose a book which he carefully inspected before taking it to his study. There he sat at his desk, assembling paper and quills, and wrote a note to Biddy Phipps. Then he addressed a letter to Prue.

He told her of his proposed absence from Hampshire but that not for one moment would she be away from his thoughts. He pleaded with her to arrange that he meet her brother as soon as possible. Smiling to himself, he commended to her the book of Elizabethan poetry he had specially selected from his library and that she ponder the poem on page 21 by John Hoskins. He concluded:

You are a living poem to all that is graceful and beautiful in life. I rejoice that I have pressed that beauty and grace close to my heart. I've kissed you and touched you, and long to hold you more. I yearn to repose on certainty that we'll be together ere long, to have your eyes engage mine with that divine look that flows from the depths of your own feelings and finds the well of my own. In your every waking moment, know that I love you and when you sleep, dream it.

Your Esmond

After sealing the letter and enclosing it with that addressed to Biddy, he dallied by the carved oak mantelpiece. Set upon it, within a triptych of mirrors, was the lone porcelain courtier of "The Amorous Damozel". There he could be seen from all angles, the arms ready to embrace and lips to kiss, all posed to no account, a lover in a void. Esmond regarded the figure for some moments before murmuring, 'You're adrift too, poor fellow. We're alike, defective and incomplete without our damozels.'

At daybreak next morning, Esmond ordered the readying of the blue travelling coach and four. He then summoned Tom. 'Tom, I want you to call at Andursley and present the servants with a gift of venison. While in the game larder, select a brace of hare for Biddy Phipps. Deliver them with this wrapped book and note into her hands only.'

Tom took the book and note, and placed them carefully in his satchel.

'Her hands only, Tom,' Esmond emphasized.

'I understand, My Lord.'

'Then you may follow to my mother's house in Bath, but bring another horse along with you. You'll have much travelling to do within the coming weeks, so prime yourself.'

Tom grinned. 'I'll look forward to it, My Lord.'

Esmond then mounted the stairs to join Mr Bennet who was awaiting him in the study.

'My plans have changed,' said Esmond. 'I shall be in Bath sooner than I thought.'

Mr Bennet smilingly handed him the letter he had written to his mother. 'Then there's no need for this, My Lord.'

'No,' said Esmond, tearing the letter and tossing it in a bin. 'She'll be surprised, for I don't usually act with such immediacy in answer to her letters.'

'She may welcome the habit, My Lord,' said Mr Bennet with a knowing smile.

Prue hastened to the Dial Walk, her pulses racing. With a sigh of pleasure she sat upon the bench in the arbor and unfolded Esmond's letter that Biddy had handed to her. Reading it she felt again the tingling spell of his kisses, the sensuous joy of his nearness and the scent of him, vital, vivifying. His written words reinforced all her dreams.

Happily, she took up the book and turned to the page as he had directed. Interleaved therein was a slip of paper where Esmond had copied the last verse of Hoskins's poem on absence, re-casting it for his own purpose. Smilingly, she read:

> *By absence, this good means I gain*
> *That I can catch you*
> *(Where none can watch you)*
> *In some close corner of my brain:*
> *There I embrace and kiss you.*
> *And so enjoy you, and none miss you.*

She read it several times and, idling through the book, glimpsed poems by Donne and Campion. A sweet book, beautifully bound in calf leather with gold tooling, somewhat familiar to her.

Suddenly the pages fell back to the flyleaf, revealing an ornate bookplate. But it was not Esmond's. It was the bookplate of her grandfather, Henry Faulkoner, Marquess of Hybullen. She stared at it dumbly. A lump came into her throat as she recalled where the book had rested with others on the library shelves of her beloved family home. She closed it and cradled it against her breast. It was hers, hers! She hugged it tighter. How had it come into Esmond's possession? Had he obtained it from Reedpath? Did he *know* Reedpath? Had he been present during the plundering of Hybullen? Unanswerable questions tumbled one upon the other. With trembling hands she opened the book again and looked at the bookplate. She pictured the numberless volumes It had prefaced and drew her fingers slowly over it, tracing the well-known blazon of the armed falcon, the motto 'Holdfast', both mocked by Reedpath's destructive villainy.

She rose, still holding the book close to her, and walked slowly back towards the house. The shock of the bookplate had countered all her joy in the love letter. Pin-pricks of doubt would not be brushed aside. How *had* Esmond acquire the book?

That afternoon Prue joined Caroline by the lake, feeding the mute swans. Since the dressing-down Prue had suffered at the hands of the countess, Caroline sought her company at every opportunity, blaming herself for the incident.

Prue watched as the cob and pen left the shallows and merged into the glancing light of the lake. Distance lent charm to the water-borne white shapes and she envied the naturalness of their alliance. If only her own affairs were as simple. Doubts about the bookplate lingered. She longed for Esmond's presence to dispose of her uncertainties.

Her thoughts turned to her brother James. She had written to him, anxious to hear how matters were progressing in their case, and suggesting he visit her as soon as possible. She would then tell him about Esmond.

Weeks went by when grey and featureless days came one after the other. To Prue it seemed that the withdrawal of the sun was coincident with the absence of Esmond. Her spirit floundered. Doubts about the bookplate surfaced constantly. She had discussed her fears with Biddy and together they decided that Esmond must have come across the book in the general dispersal of contents. Consoled, she found pleasure in repeating his name and had committed to memory every word in his love letter and the poem.

'Do you think James has received my letter by now, Biddy? I've suggested that he lodge at The Roebuck Inn should he come.'

They were sitting in their candlelit withdrawing-room, Prue with Esmond's book in her hands and Biddy gently stroking a kitten curled in sleep upon her lap. 'I expect it's been delivered, but it may take time for him to make arrangements as Harrogate is far north. You'll hear from him one way or another within a week or two. Will you tell him of the marquess and his interest in you?'

'I've simply written that there are matters I can withhold no longer and wish for his help in approaching a dilemma.'

'Did the marquess say how long he was to be away?'

'No. I wonder how I shall hear from him again.'

'I am told the countess is curious as to his absence. She's been sending notes to Lydney almost daily,' said Biddy.

'Caroline must be under a blanket of blame.'

'How do matters stand between you and the countess, my dear? Is there still a coldness between you?'

'There's crisp formality. I feel she holds me in part responsible for Esmond's sudden withdrawal.'

There was a silence. The kitten stirred, flexed its paws and resumed slumber with a crackling purr. Biddy said, 'The countess was expecting him to offer for Caroline at the hunt supper. She's too ambitious for her daughter and drives suitors away.'

'Except Richard. She's met her match there. I don't think she'll ever drive *him* away.'

Prue rose and placed the book on the table. 'I'm in no humour for reading. Let me make some tea for us while you attend your little guest.' She suddenly stooped and placed a light kiss upon Biddy's cheek. 'You're a refuge for me, too. I'm so grateful for your friendship during these years.'

Biddy looked up, her brown eyes bright. 'I'll be happier when your vengeful feelings have passed their climax. A thousand blessings on you. Now put that kettle to boil, Prue.'

Prue was well advanced in her tea-making, when a tap on the door admitted Bessie, one of the serving maids. She curtsied briefly. 'Beg pardon, Missis Phipps, but her ladyship, the countess, asks Miss Smith to come soonest to her apartment.'

'Thank you,' answered Prue.

Bessie withdrew, closing the door behind her.

Biddy's eyes remained on the closed door. 'A direct summons. What's afoot, I wonder?'

'I wonder, too,' said Prue. She had little desire for a meeting with the countess. 'It could be one of a number of things. But first I'll pour your tea.'

'Do not,' said Biddy, arresting Prue's hand. 'Go to the mistress at once. The tea can draw until you return.'

Prue hastily left for her room, putting on her lace cap. Her heart was beating fast. Waves of apprehension washed over her, for she was seldom called at such a late hour. As she walked along the half-lit gallery leading to the countess's apartment, wild speculations rushed to her mind and just as quickly vanished. A footman rose from a settle and opened the double entrance doors.

The wax lights in the chandeliers dazzled her as a maid approached. 'Her ladyship is preparing for a card party,' whispered the maid, 'but she wanted you to be shown to her dressing-room as soon as you arrived.'

In an inner sanctum, the countess sat at a mirrored dressing-table where a maid was attending her. The countess wore a red powder-robe draped over her evening gown for the preparation of her hair. She was already rouged and bejewelled. She beckoned to Prue, who curtsied and came forward to stand behind her chair.

The countess engaged her with a cold stare in the mirror's reflection. 'Your patroness, Lady Wainflete, has written to the earl asking our permission to allow you a sojourn with her in Bath.'

'In Bath?' repeated Prue, incredulous.

The countess's expression did not change. 'I wasn't in favour but have been persuaded by his lordship and Caroline to allow you this privilege. You'll prepare to go the day after the morrow when the servants' coach will leave for its usual run to Whitchurch. Mrs Phipps may accompany you to settle you overnight at The White Hart, from where you'll take the early morning coach to Newbury and thence to Bath. I'm given to understand that Lady Wainflete has arranged suitable rooms for you in the posting inns *en route*.'

Prue was dumbstruck. She could but nod in acquiescence at

these surprising arrangements made by Lady Wainflete. Echoing her own thoughts, the countess continued, 'After her silence for three years, it's strange to me that she's extended such an invitation.'

'It's strange, indeed,' repeated Prue, worried that her precious hoard of guineas would be depleted in paying for fares and lodgings.

'It's also strange that rooms have been arranged and paid for in advance. I feel an anxiety that you're travelling alone but relieved that it appears Lady Wainflete has your welfare at heart.'

Prue felt her head swimming in shock. Her guineas were to be spared!

The maid was now arranging a purple silk turban on the countess's hair, spangled in crescents and stars. She appeared to Prue like an enchantress, conjuring word charms in the mirror's reflection.

Prue curtsied in gratitude. 'Thank you, ma'am, for permitting me leave for this visit. May I ask its duration?'

'That is up to Lady Wainflete, but I would urge no more than fourteen days,' came the stern reply.

'Yes, ma'am. Thank you. Shall that be all?'

The countess did not reply at once. She primped and poked the jewelled turban until it pleased her. 'There's one more thing: when you return there will be a change in your role as companion to Lady Caroline. I shall invite young ladies of the *haut ton* for extended stays with Caroline. They're more suited to her position.'

Prue gasped in dismay.

A frosted smile appeared on the face of the countess as she said, 'I'm not dispensing with your services. I think you'll fit in as one of my maids with quarters adjoining my room. That's all, Prudence.'

Prue turned and slowly withdrew. A true sorceress, the countess had countered all the charms with a final malison.

Chapter 8

PRUE'S heart galloped as she tried to walk back composedly to her quarters. Change, like an unleashed tyrant, was again poised to invade her life. Her mind raced. Why had Lady Wainflete lodged this unexpected invitation to Bath of all places?

She had met Lady Wainflete but once at Hybullen House eight years ago. Things were different then. She was sixteen, without a care in the world, preparing for a successful London season with Lady Wainflete as chaperon. Within a year, everything had collapsed around her and all Lady Wainflete could do was aid her in finding employment. She was grateful for that, but apprehensive of the present proposals of her patroness. Andursley suited her for it was a place where her brother could communicate with her. And Esmond? He would be unaware of this visit to Bath. Suppose he wrote to her again and the countess intercepted the letter in her absence! It did not bear thinking of. And how well would her meagre wardrobe serve her in Bath for two weeks? Sighing deeply and shaking her head in disbelief at her plight, she entered the apartment.

Biddy was nodding in sleep by a cup of tea growing cold at her elbow. She started as Prue quietly sat at the table, folding her arms upon it. Biddy turned and poured a cup of tea from the pot on the hob. 'It's well stewed by now, but warming,' she said, placing the tea before Prue.

Prue stared at it, mouthing her thanks.

'What did her ladyship want at this hour?'

There was a silence as Prue took a sip from the cup.

'Two matters, but both so baffling that nothing will ever be the same again, Biddy.'

'I thought something was amiss and couldn't retire until you came back. What are these matters?'

'The day after the morrow you are to accompany me to Whitchurch from where I'll take a stage to Newbury and then on to Marlborough and Bath.'

Biddy frowned. 'You're to travel alone?'

'Let me finish, Biddy. I'm invited to Bath by Lady Wainflete who is my mother's second cousin.'

Biddy's expression eased. 'That's not a calamity, Prue. It'll be a deserved excursion away from here.'

'Not entirely, but I'll come to that later. When I return from Bath I'm to serve the countess and move to a room in her apartment. . . .' Biddy took a deep breath but before she could respond, Prue continued, 'There's to be no resident companion for Caroline. Young ladies of the ton will be invited to Andursley for temporary periods.'

There was a silence as both stared at each other.

'Lord Lydney,' Biddy whispered. 'She wants to keep an eye on you, Prue.'

'It seems so. At least I'll have a roof over my head and be able to visit you, Biddy.'

'Ah, but it'll not be the same, my dear.' Biddy shook her head and gazed at the hob where the last of the coals glowed dully.

Prue rose and stood by the window. 'What troubles me is my absence from Andursley. I'm expecting James to arrive any day now. As for Esmond, he'd think to find me here when he returns, certainly not in Bath.'

'There's only one thing to do. Write letters to both and leave them with me. If either should call, I'll see that the letters are delivered into the right hands. Go to your bedroom and pen them immediately.'

Prue brightened. 'Of course! It's likely that James would join me in Bath. He knows Lady Wainflete and—'

A knock on the door stopped her flow. Both looked at each other with some alarm. It was well past eleven by the clock and most staff were abed. Prue motioned to Biddy to remain seated and moved to open the door.

Emerging from the shadows in the passage, a cloaked and hooded figure stepped across the threshold. 'I know it's late,' came a hushed voice, 'but I had to choose my time.' Tossing back the hood, Caroline faced them, flushed and breathless.

'Caro!'

Biddy opened her arms and Caroline fell into them. For some moments she remained there, until Biddy kissed the top of her head and beckoned to Prue to place a chair beside her. Prue did so after quietly closing the door, and returned to her seat at the table.

'I had to see you, Prue,' said Caroline, settling herself into the chair. 'Mama has told me of her plans for you and I'm devastated. The more I plead with her to change her mind, the more adamant she becomes. I know you've been invited to Bath but please, Prue, don't be tempted by another post. Come back to Andursley. I'll enlist Papa's help in changing Mama's mind.'

Prue could see that Caroline had been weeping. Her eyes were puffed. With a smile Prue said, 'It's not crossed my mind to find another post, Caro, and should your mama not be persuaded, it's no disaster as I'll be nearby, as will Biddy.'

Caroline shook her head. 'I know Mama, and she'll wish to know your whereabouts every minute of the day. She'll treat you like a prisoner. Not one of her maids has any freedom outside her apartment.'

'That's true,' said Biddy. 'Her ladyship's personal maids are kept apart from the general staff.'

'Then we'll have to think of another way. I'm sure we'll work out something,' said Prue softly.

Caroline shrugged. 'Perhaps.' With her shoulders hunched, she looked entirely unconvinced. Prue was swept with compassion and realized how deeply these changes could affect Caroline. She left her seat and stooped beside her, taking her hands. 'Caro, have faith. Your father will not see you unhappy. He'll take your part and reason with your mother and by the time I return there may be a compromise that will please everyone.'

With eyes brimming and lips trembling, Caroline whispered, 'Richard has been sent away.'

Prue exchanged a glance with Biddy. 'Where has he gone?' she asked.

Caroline gave a shuddering sigh. 'Mama arranged it all with the Harleys. Richard has left for the Exmoor estate of the Duke of Colyton to help with his hunters and staghounds. It's far from Hampshire and Richard is as unhappy as I.'

A cloud of helplessness descended upon them dousing the conversation. Then Prue said, 'How will you keep in touch with him?'

'By letter through Romany byways. Richard has taken a gypsy as his servant. I'm doubly unhappy. Richard has gone and you'll not be close by. But' – she straightened, pocketing a kerchief she had used to dry her eyes – 'I want something good to happen to someone, and I've brought this for you to take to Bath.'

Prue had been so startled by the appearance of Caroline that she barely noticed a portmanteau which Caroline had placed by Biddy's chair in the rush to greet her. Indicating it, Caroline added, 'Inside is a selection of robes, pelisses and trimmings suitable for the various functions you're bound to attend.' Prue started to protest but Caroline continued, 'They're dresses of your own design and making which have languished in my wardrobe since London days. Take them, Prue, and adapt them as you wish.' She smiled. 'I must have my lady companion give a good account of herself in Bath!'

Prue gasped. 'Thank you, Caro! I'd been wondering what to do about suitable apparel and now you've come to the rescue. I'll take good care of everything.'

'They're yours to keep.'

Prue looked from Biddy to Caroline, her eyes moist and face flushed in gratitude. Their unfailing support was a comfort, their kindnesses lessening her worries.

Suddenly the clock on the tower of the stable block struck midnight. Biddy said, 'It's late. You must return to your room at once. Your mama wouldn't approve of this visit and worse could happen should she find out. Remember, I'm here if you need me. Go with care, my dear.'

Caroline bent to kiss Biddy's cheek, then turned to hug Prue. 'The marquess has vanished from the face of the earth. No one knows where he is. But should he call, I'll tell him where you are, talented Miss Smith!' she teased.

'Not in your mother's hearing, or it'll certainly be my downfall and yours, too,' said Prue, kissing her.

Caroline returned her kiss. 'Goodnight, dear friend. Enjoy the delights of Bath.'

Caroline replaced her hood while Prue opened the door and advanced into the passage, listening for any sound. All was quiet. She beckoned to Caroline who glided past her, a pale hand gleaming in a final wave.

She remained in the dark, staring after the departing figure. Caroline's attitude toward her mother had hardened to the extent that Prue didn't dare speculate as to the state of affairs she would find when she returned from Bath.

After some moments, she crept back to the apartment. Biddy had retired and Prue removed the remaining candle to her bedroom. She opened her writing box to pen letters to James and Esmond for leaving with Biddy. To James she wrote with affection, inviting him to join her in Bath should time allow.

She pondered for some time her letter to Esmond. Should she tell him she would be in Bath? That would be forward of her, for he may read into it an implied invitation. No, simply a polite note regretting she had missed him by reason of an unexpected request to visit a relative.

Prue settled comfortably in a corner of the Andursley servants' coach, and reflected on the last occasion she had travelled by this means to Whitchurch. Everything was the same, yet not the same. The dankish air and grind of wheels on gravel were familiar accompaniments until Cap'n Pitch's unsuccessful bid had brought her face to face with Esmond.

In her hooped trunk she had packed a box containing everything he had written to her, including the brief plea still pressed inside the silver patch-box. The poem on absence had given her pleasure. But the bookplate raised questions in her mind. Until she could voice them, they were an impediment to her complete trust in him. But she smiled to herself as she recognized the bedraggled clumps of Michaelmas-daisies where Tom had landed on that memorable morning. It seemed so long ago.

Biddy and the two stewards nodded in sleep to the lurching of the coach. A fourgon lumbered behind them, loaded with Prue's trunk and boxes. She wore her grey cloak and hood, thinking to change into smarter travelling clothes and bonnet at Marlborough. Until then, she wished to present a respectable mien without drawing attention to herself, hoping the few neat darns in the grey cloak were not so obvious as to affect the quality of service and esteem from tavern staff along the way.

The yard of The White Hart was bustling with stage coaches leaving and arriving. The Andursley coach, followed by the fourgon, crawled through the throng until it reached its customary stand in the back lane. There the coachy and stewards left it, intent on offloading Prue's baggage from the fourgon when her room had been determined.

After booking in, Prue joined Biddy in the snug, a room behind the overflowing dining saloon, which was a retreat for overnight guests. Choosing a table by the window, they watched the passing parade on the street while refreshing themselves with tea and pound cake.

'There must be a good market today, judging by the crowds and drays,' Biddy remarked.

'That's so. The shopping coach chooses its visits to coincide.'

There was a silence as both sipped their tea.

'I'm pleased with my room,' said Prue. 'Mrs Figgis has arranged that my evening meal is served there so that I don't have to appear in the dining saloon. This suits my plans perfectly for I can devote time to the dresses that Caroline gave me.' She smiled. 'They'll require adaptation for a more mature wearer.'

'I know your skills, Prue, and I'm sure many heads will turn in Bath when you have tucked and stitched to your own taste.'

Prue looked out of the window. 'Biddy,' she said, hesitantly. 'Every moment that passes makes me feel I'm suffering a regression of some sort. For three years I've been sheltered in a great country house as Miss Smith, companion to Lady Caroline. As Miss Prudence Mulcaster Smith of Hybullen House, I was father's hostess from the age of thirteen after the death of mother, when decisions were mine to make. In Bath, Lady Wainflete will expect me to behave as that Prudence and the thought confuses me.'

Biddy reached for her hand. 'Be yourself, Prue. You are always the gentlewoman. It's evident in the way the Andursley staff regard you. D'you think the stewards and coachy would have volunteered their brawn in hauling a trunk and boxes to a room in the top gallery for anyone other than the countess? There were porters a-plenty, yet they brushed them away.' She paused. 'This brings me to another matter but perhaps I've gone too far and it's not my place to talk so.'

'Oh, broach it, Biddy!' cried Prue.

Biddy drew back. 'There'll be many a gentleman in Bath anxious to escort you and, no doubt, Lady Wainflete has planned social events. A London debut was denied you but I implore you to regard Bath as a similar initiation. Present yourself with all the charm that nature has bestowed upon you and receive with grace *all* those paying you court.'

'In truth I'll do so, Biddy. But when so elegantly pursued, one can't ignore the pursuer and you know well to whom I refer.'

'That's why I ventured to say what I did. The marquess's flirtation suffers from an imbalance in your social standing and, for that reason, it's possibly doomed.'

'I disagree, Biddy. Supposing' – she paused, her eyes dancing – 'he turns up in Bath! It's the season and, in reverting to my former self, such imbalance as exists might be repaired. Isn't that so?'

Biddy's voice held a plea as she replied, 'Reality is like broken glass. Harden your soles to tread upon it. The marquess could break your heart.'

Prue trembled within herself. Esmond's voice and countenance troubled her composure, inhabiting her thoughts and sending illusions hovering around her pillow. Biddy was airing fears that were similar to her own. She forced a smile. 'I shall take heed of your advice, Biddy.' She moved from the table and held out her hand. 'Come, take my hand – enough of this serious conjecture. Let's walk in the town.'

As they emerged from the porch of The White Hart, Prue took Biddy's arm and guided her away from the crowded thoroughfares to a road with treed lawns by the silk mill. Crossing a bridge, Prue spotted a seat. There they sat watching the gushing waters of the mill-race.

The road was busy. Cabriolets and gigs followed one another endlessly. A man wearing a faded military coat and mounted on a fine bay, rode along the verge. Prue judged him to be an outrider for the four-in-hand that was passing, full of ladies in feathered bonnets. She said, 'Have you marked the number of carriages travelling along this road? They must be going to Fittiwake's.'

'It's either a sale or viewing day,' said Biddy. 'Let's go there. Perhaps there's some porcelain on offer.'

Prue sighed. 'It could pass a pleasant hour. I've almost given up looking for the little courtier and I must husband the money I have, especially now.'

They passed several coaches in the yard, and the premises buzzed with gentlefolk inspecting the collections on display. Prue found her way to the porcelain room, where lights enriched the pieces arranged in serried rows upon green baize. Ladies crowded round, examining their catalogues. Overalled assistants bustled among them, fetching and carrying on demand.

Surveying the scene, Prue said, 'With this crowd it'll take too long to inspect everything, Biddy. I suggest you go to the right and I to the left. Should you see a lone bewigged figure, with slanting eyes like the damozel's, wearing a plum-coloured laced coat, it's bound to be Heberlein's work and—'

'Heberlein!' came a startled whisper from behind them, 'Nothing by him here, I assure you, madam.'

Prue turned to see a man in a drab warehouse coat. With a bow of the head, he smiled, 'I'm Mr Fittiwake's assistant, Mr Peploe, at your service, madam. I couldn't help overhearing, and trust you'll pardon my impertinence in commenting upon a remark not addressed to me. Your mention of Heberlein was a reminder that we have a commission to find a certain piece by him which will complete a rare ensemble.'

'A rare ensemble,' repeated Prue.

' "The Amorous Damozel",' said Mr Peploe.

'Oh,' said Prue, trying to hide a mounting excitement in her voice and manner. 'I've heard of this. It's the only ensemble made by Heberlein, is it not?'

'You're correct, madam. The gentleman client who owns a part has honoured us with the task of finding the companion piece. The complete ensemble was last known to be in the possession of the Mulcaster Smith family.'

Prue swallowed to relieve a constriction of her throat. She realized Mr Peploe was exceeding his discretion in these revelations but urging him further, she asked, 'Which part of the ensemble is it your hope to acquire for your client?'

'It's the damozel herself, madam. We'd so wish to please our distinguished client in finding her.'

'Your client is from Whitchurch?' she ventured.

Mr Peploe appeared unable to resist a final confidence to proclaim the high standing of Fittiwake's and looked over each shoulder before replying. Lowering his head and his voice, he said, 'We're entrusted with this commission by the Most Honourable Marquess of Lydney.'

Smiling broadly, he bowed a withdrawal leaving Prue and Biddy open-mouthed in astonishment.

Chapter 9

AFTER leaving Hampshire, Esmond had travelled to London, conferring with his financial mentors in the City and attending such sittings in the House of Lords as were expected of him. Apart from brief appearances at White's, he had cut the social round and within a week departed for Bath.

As he progressed westward, the weather worsened. Impatience heightened his weariness with the journey and it was with relief that he delivered the blue coach and bays to the grooms at Melodon, his mother's dower house in Sydney Place.

His mother greeted him with open arms which she clasped tightly around him. He laughed, endeavouring to release her hold only to find himself a prisoner of his two maiden aunts. He kissed them with affection, thinking how little they had changed over the years.

After a rest, Esmond joined the dowager on the terrace. She rose at his approach, placing a veil over her hair. 'The sky is clear,' she said. 'Let us take a turn in the garden.'

He smiled and offered his arm. He cherished such moments and looked for the initial coquetry in her manner, which never failed to amuse him. She was a treasured being, with the aura of the last century about her. They walked in contented silence as he led her to a seat in the gazebo. Sitting beside her, he wondered whether to broach the matter of Lady Wainflete, but his mother was first to speak.

'I wrote you, Esmond, that Captain Roper had heard rumours of

Cedric and Clancy in New England.'

'New England? As adventurers and gamblers I thought they would end up in the southern states.'

'You deride them,' she admonished lightly.

'What was the gist of the rumours?'

'He was vague on that, but I've no reason to suppose it was improper. They are still together and flourishing, no doubt.'

'No doubt,' he echoed, glancing at his mother. A salubrious expression marked her pleasure in the escapades of her son and nephew, escapades whose true nature he dare not reveal. How could he tell her that chicanery and fraud followed in their wake, and that Clancy Reedpath was barred from every club in London? Too many had been ruined by debts of honour to Reedpath, debts of honour which deny the name.

Esmond was once great friends with his younger brother, and suddenly he was not. 'I wonder why Cedric became Clancy's shadow?' he mused aloud.

'He must have discovered something admirable in him,' she answered.

His villainy, he thought.

He rose and shed his coat. 'Come, Mother,' he said, helping her to her feet and placing the coat over her shoulders, 'it's chill. The dew is rising and I think I hear activity in the carriage house.'

'Our card party guests.' She paused, and put a hand to his cheek. 'It's lovely to have you with us, Esmond.'

He smiled, placing his arm tenderly around her. Ruefully, he thought, Cedric and Clancy had stumped any hope of his raising the matter of Lady Wainflete that day.

It was on the second day after his arrival, while taking coffee with his mother in the salon ante-room, he felt the time appropriate to mention Lady Wainflete. He learned that Lady Wainflete was at present in Bath. She had recently returned after a long absence in Florence, where her husband kept a permanent apartment for his fine arts interests. She took a house in Daniel Street for her visits during the season.

'What is the purpose of your enquiries about Euphemia Wainflete, Esmond?'

'Euphemia? An unusual name.'

'She's from Edinburgh,' commented his mother, as if sufficiently enlightening.

He took a deep breath. 'Some years ago, Lady Wainflete found a post for a gentlewoman whose family had suffered a misfortune. I wish to know if she's related to that gentlewoman.'

'And the name of the gentlewoman?'

'Miss Prudence Smith.'

His mother gave him a measuring look. 'I know no one by that name but I don't presume to answer for Lady Wainflete.' She sniffed. 'Society is ever changing and these days I don't know everybody of note or notoriety. You must lodge your question with her, dear boy.'

Esmond rose and went to the window, thinking of Prue and relishing the pleasure it had given him to speak her name.

'Esmond.'

He made no reply.

'Esmond,' his mother persisted, 'are you suffering a love-fit?'

'That's a very common term, Mother.'

'It's a very common complaint.'

He turned to face her. 'I'm uncommonly afflicted.'

His mother replaced her cup upon the table with a clatter. 'I knew it,' she said, smilingly triumphant. 'There's a tendency for toying with food and a countenance indicating that you're dwelling with angels. The aunts tell me that last night you paced the room above them and slept hardly a wink. They were—'

'Mother! Have you nothing further to ask of me!'

There was a silence as they regarded each other seriously, searchingly.

'So it appears that the young lady, Miss Smith, who has engaged your interest, is possibly related to Euphemia Wainflete.'

'I wish to marry Miss Smith whether she's related or not.'

The dowager rose and joined him at the window. She took his

hand. 'Then we'll have to deal with this excess of tenderness and introduce you to Lady Wainflete to determine exactly what her connection is.'

'Whether she's related or not, Mother,' Esmond repeated.

There was a pause. In a softer tone, she asked, 'Is she very beautiful?'

'To simply answer "Yes" to your question demeans her sheer loveliness. I find it impossible to be moderate where she's concerned. Besides, she saved my life.'

'Brave as well as beautiful?'

'Mother, you're treating my very serious quest with a flippancy I can't share.' He withdrew his hand. 'Perhaps we should defer further talk about Miss Smith until you're ready to aid me in my courtship, which is proving excessively difficult.'

'Surely you don't find a courtship difficult, Esmond. That I can't believe. On other occasions—'

'This is different,' he interposed. 'I'm wholly committed and wish that were so in her case.'

His mother frowned. 'Most intriguing. Let's go back to the settle and I'll listen with sympathy, Esmond. Recount all from the beginning and we'll see what can be done.'

Esmond smiled. This was what he wanted to hear. He extended his arm to usher his mother's return to her seat.

Two days later, the dowager's levee at Melodon provided the occasion for a meeting between Esmond and Lady Wainflete. Diminutive, dressed in black, Lady Wainflete cut a dash with a large lime-green silk toque adorned with brilliants. She conversed animatedly about her sojourn in Florence, her hands flashing with jewelled rings. Her face had an enamelled look and rouge did not cheat the years, but Esmond warmed to her all-embracing smile.

Esmond escorted her to a window embrasure overlooking the terrace. 'This should make you feel at home,' he said, indicating the Italian statuary there displayed.

'Home?' she laughed. 'Where's that, pray?'

'I thought Italy.'

'No,' she said, 'that's my husband's home. It's not mine.'

'Bath perhaps?'

Her brown eyes twinkled as she said, 'Scotland is my home, though I left Edinburgh as a child. My family still occupy the manse there and I've visited it several times. I decided Scotland was my home after reading the poems of Robert Burns.'

'Ah, an excellent reason.'

'I'm gratified you think so, but I've met some from Scotland who think my claim erroneous since I'm always in Italy or England.'

'It matters only that you cherish it as home. Dash it all, it's a compliment to the place!'

'How kind you are.'

He paused, then turned to face her. 'Lady Wainflete, may I ask you about a young lady by name Miss Smith?'

She frowned. 'Miss Smith? What's her connection with me, My Lord?'

'I was hoping you could answer that. Take your mind back some three years. In Bath, you met the Countess of Andursley and put her in touch with a gentlewoman who had suffered a misfortune—'

Lady Wainflete nodded her head vigorously and placed her hand upon his arm. 'Yes, yes. Prudence. I'm her mother's second cousin. What relationship she is to me, I can't fathom. I was to have been chaperon for her London season, but then—'

'What's past, is past,' said Esmond briskly. 'It's the present that dominates my mind and possibly the future.'

'You're acquainted with Prudence, then?'

'I wish to marry her, Lady Wainflete.'

She gasped and placed her hands to her cheeks. 'Oh, she's to be your marchioness!'

He nodded. 'If I tell you that my courtship of her at Andursley has met with the grossest difficulties, you'll understand why I need your help.'

'But how can I help? My absence for three years has meant that

I've not seen or heard of her for all that time, although I did have it in mind to invite her to Florence—'

'Bath, Lady Wainflete. Invite her to Bath. Immediately.'

She pondered, her eyes fixed upon his face. 'Prudence, a marchioness,' she repeated softly.

Esmond turned, summoning a footman to bring champagne, then faced Lady Wainflete and took her hands in his. 'May I call upon you tomorrow morning to refine plans to that end?'

'I shall be honoured, My Lord.'

He suddenly felt a surging optimism and bestowed upon Lady Wainflete a conspiratorial smile. The footman approached with a tray upon which were glasses of champagne. Esmond presented one to Lady Wainflete. Raising his own glass, he said, 'Let's drink to our success, Lady Wainflete.'

She reciprocated shyly. 'To your future happiness, My Lord.'

'To my Prue,' he whispered to himself, taking a deep draught of the champagne.

He found Lady Wainflete charmingly eccentric. Although he had no wish to pry into Prue's family, she volunteered snippets about her antecedents that intrigued him in both the content and the telling. All was recounted as the epitome of a novel by Mrs Radcliffe, with characters identifiable but nameless. A beautiful titled heiress, courted by princes and dukes, spurned the high ranks of society to marry a handsome penniless baronet with whom she had fallen in love. He ached to learn more but they were joined by two matrons, friends of his mother, with marriageable daughters. Feeling he could achieve little by remaining in the company, he begged to be excused and withdrew.

The next morning Esmond made his way to the appointment with Lady Wainflete. The door of the gracious three-storey house was opened by a manservant who relieved him of his hat, top coat and cane. Then he was led upstairs to Lady Wainflete's withdrawing-room.

She rose as he entered, coming forward to greet him before gesturing to a sumptuous wing chair directly opposite to her own. A black cat snoozed in a basket by her feet and opened amber eyes as Esmond seated himself.

'This is Nero,' she said, arranging the pleats of her morning gown. 'He's not yet forgiven me for absenting myself for so long.' She smiled. 'I've arranged for a light refreshment to be served immediately so that we may use all of the time to concentrate on the matter in hand.'

'Excellent,' he said.

A maid entered with tea and cakes, followed by the manservant who opened the top of an escritoire.

'I think we'll need writing materials to record what each is required to do,' she said. 'No doubt there'll be correspondence.'

'That's highly likely and I commend you for your forethought.'

During the serving of tea she asked how he had met Prudence. He related all with gathering passion and Lady Wainflete responded keenly to his dilemma. Good fortune had indeed smiled upon him in finding a co-conspirator he could not fault.

'The situation begs careful thought,' said he, placing his empty tea cup upon a side table. 'I would like your invitation to be made through her employers, the earl and countess, as if a spontaneous thought of your own. My part mustn't be revealed. Any hint of collusion would besmirch us both, Lady Wainflete.'

'I agree, and that shan't happen.'

He smiled. 'It's not that I fear the judgement of society but Prudence has an independent nature and I'm anxious not to rouse her ire against my initiative.'

'Then we must allocate our tasks with that in mind. I'll write today to Andursley as you suggest. But I feel that I should arrange and pay for her accommodation *en route*. It would not be fitting for you to do so.'

He sat forward in his chair, clasping his hands together. 'It would cause me great dismay should any action on my part hint at impropriety. I'm ready to provide services, such as couriers of your letters to Andursley and the inns where she'll stay. My outrider Tom, who knows Prudence by sight, will shadow the coaches to ensure safety on the journey.'

'Ah, that's a matter I thought to raise with you. She'll be travelling alone. Is there anything we can do to correct that?' She smiled. 'A lady's companion for a lady's companion.'

He rose frowning, and leaned on the overmantel. It would be ideal if a young lady could be found not only for the journey, but also to accompany Prue in Bath.

'There must be someone,' she continued. 'Many young ladies find their way to Bath during the season and coaches bring them in droves.' There was a silence. Suddenly, she exclaimed, 'Bagby!'

'Lady Wainflete?'

'I've the solution, but we must hasten.'

'Are you referring to the brothers Bagby?'

'I am. Do you know them?'

'Not very well.'

'That's all the better. The Honourable Hubert and the Honourable Cuthbert Bagby of Bath are both courting Miss Agnes Shaw, daughter of Colonel Shaw of the Guards. She's due to arrive from London soon to stay with her aunt who is my neighbour here in Daniel Street. I'll call upon Lady Glenister and enquire how her niece is to travel.'

He smiled. 'As to Miss Shaw's affections, is it Hubert or Cuthbert in the ascendancy?'

Lady Wainflete shook her head. 'I don't know and have no intention of finding out.'

'It's just that I felt I might renew my acquaintance with the brothers.'

'That would be an advantage, My Lord, provided Miss Shaw's travelling plans coincide with those of Prudence.'

'It's for us to make sure that they do.'

They smiled at each other, pleased at the outcome of their first meeting. He moved to take her hand. 'I'll leave you to write your letters and send my courier to wait upon you tomorrow morning. May I call again to hear whether the Misses Smith and Shaw will journey together?'

'Of course, My Lord.' She rose to face him. 'I'll do all in my power to see that Prudence's visit to Bath will go as smoothly as if it were planned months ago. It's the least I can do to make up for my neglect of her.'

'But you had no choice.'

'I should never have introduced her to Countess Andursley. Instead, I should have insisted upon her coming with me to Florence.'

'I'm thankful it was otherwise, for how could I have met her?'

She sighed. 'Then I'll console myself that it was for the best.'

'Indubitably, Lady Wainflete,' he said, smiling and bowing to take his leave.

It had all gone so well, thought Esmond. He had visited Lady Wainflete several times to refine arrangements and was now so familiar a caller that the manservant smiled a greeting and left Esmond to bound up the stairs to her room. Even Nero roused himself and twirled against his boots in welcome. Tom had reported that Miss Smith had met Miss Agnes Shaw at Newbury and both young ladies appeared happy in each other's company, sharing meals and walks.

He was now on his way for a final visit to Lady Wainflete before Prue's arrival on the morrow. This morning he was to meet Miss Shaw's aunt, Lady Glenister, and tie up plans subsequent to Prue's arrival. After a brief introduction, Lady Glenister had left and later, over coffee with Lady Wainflete, their converse touched on the matter of the first encounter.

'It's best that it be a chance meeting in Sydney Gardens, where I'll walk with Mother every morning for the next sennight. Perhaps you and Miss Shaw might take the air with Prudence at a similar time.'

Lady Wainflete nodded absently. She appeared subdued.

With concern in his voice, he asked, 'Is all this too much for you?'

She didn't reply at once, then abruptly rose. 'I've something you should see. Come this way with me.'

He followed her through a wide passageway to the back of the house until she halted in front of a central doorway. 'This is the music salon,' she said, opening the two doors and preceding him into the room. Indicating a place in the centre of a large Turkish carpet, she added, 'I want you to stand here and look to your left.'

Doing as he was bid, he turned his head and stared in amazement. 'Incredible,' he breathed.

On the wall before him was a full-length oil painting of a girl in a garden. She wore a white gown gathered into a blue sash below a frilled fichu. The bright sun at her back was diffused by an open parasol, the silk lining of which was embroidered with peacocks' eyes of iridescent blues and greens. Her hair was piled high in the style of the 1780s, and single ringlets depended over elegant shoulders, the more bewitching as the locks were raven black. Moving closer he looked up to the heart-shaped face where dimpled cheeks hinted at the start of a smile and green eyes shone with a luminous light. It was an expression never to be forgotten.

'Prue,' he whispered, holding his gaze and stepping back.

Lady Wainflete sat facing him on the piano stool. 'The Lady Sarah Faulkoner, only daughter of the Marquess of Hybullen. It was painted by an associate of Joshua Reynolds when she was eighteen, before her marriage. The garden is that of Hybullen House in Buckinghamshire.'

Her voice reached him as if from a distance, the painting dominating all his senses. He couldn't take his eyes from it. Minutes passed and, with an effort, he broke the spell. 'She's the beautiful titled heiress you told me about.'

She nodded. 'Prudence's mother.'

He paused before asking, 'And the handsome penniless baronet?'

'Sir Edward Mulcaster Smith.' She broke off, and fidgeted with a tassel on the stool as if uncertain what next to say. Looking up, she continued, 'I'm unsure whether I should relate more, but think it fair that you know. Prudence abandoned the 'Mulcaster' in her name to lend credence to her employment as companion and to conceal her identity. She suffers from the poverty and disgrace of an ancient family dispossessed by a debt of honour.'

A tense silence hovered. His jaws locked and there was a constriction in his throat. Sir Edward Mulcaster Smith! A victim of Reedpath! What irony that his cousin had caused the ruination of Prue's family! Panic tore at his reason in combat with assurances that the circumstances were irrelevant to the power of his love. Anguish and fear swept through him. He felt his strength ebbing away. His breathing became hard and rapid. Damn Reedpath! With difficulty he suppressed mouthing vehement oaths that sprang to his mind. He was convinced that neither Prue nor Lady Wainflete were aware of this connection. How would Prue respond when she knew?

He started as Lady Wainflete approached. She said, 'Prudence has an older brother, James, heir to Sir Edward. I applaud your courtship of her with all my heart, but it's to James you should address your intentions.'

'Where may I find him?' His voice was strangled, unreal.

'He practises law in Harrogate.'

'Then I'll write, requesting a meeting.'

'Has Prudence never mentioned this matter?'

He turned to face her, struggling to compose himself. 'Believe me, Lady Wainflete, I'd no idea she was Sir Edward's daughter. Now it's clear why she insisted upon my deferring favours until a family matter is settled. She's mentioned her brother and his endeavours in that respect. I was eager to aid in it but she brushed my pleas aside, implying that all was proceeding. It seemed indelicate to press the matter.'

She gestured to the painting. 'I showed you this to help me explain that I'm not the principal person concerned in Prudence's life. I'm the only living relative of her mother, but James must be consulted.'

He nodded. 'There are some formalities remaining before I can logically do so. First of all, I presume you would approve our betrothal, Lady Wainflete?'

She smiled. 'Of course, My Lord. You have my unremitting support.'

'That said, I must next woo Prudence successfully. Where better but in Bath with all its charms? She's to be persuaded that her life must be shared with mine. Once she agrees, I'll apprise her brother.'

He stepped towards the large bay window, agonizing over Lady Wainflete's revelations, and hoped the shock he felt was not reflected in his countenance. What was done, was done, he reasoned. He lacked courage to amend his plans for Prue's visit and could not break the enchantment of his hopes. Reedpath was in America and there would remain. He dismissed it from his mind and returned to Lady Wainflete who was awaiting him by the door.

'If all goes as I've dreamed,' he said, looking once more at the portrait, 'Prue will sit for Lawrence in the regalia of my marchioness at the Dissolution of Parliament next June. It will dominate the gallery at Lydney Hall.'

She gasped. 'How wonderful! Perhaps Lady Sarah's portrait could join it there.'

He brightened. 'I was rather hoping you might offer that, Lady Wainflete. Apart from the obvious reasons, I have a sentimental attachment to that parasol.'

Chapter 10

A PALE moon hovered low in the dark morning sky. Prue sat huddled in a corner seat on the coach to Newbury. She had not slept well at The White Hart and was weary of speculating about Esmond and how he had come to possess the porcelain lover of the damozel and her grandfather's book.

Could it be possible that he had procured them at Hybullen? She felt ill at the thought that he might be connected in some way with Reedpath. She shivered and drew her cloak more tightly around her. Surely Esmond would shun anything dishonourable and never associate with cheats such as Reedpath. When next she saw Esmond, she would resolve these matters. She marvelled at the irony that she and Esmond were each in search of a complementary piece of 'The Amorous Damozel'.

During the overnight stay at Newbury, she met Miss Agnes Shaw who appeared to know the Bath Road and made short work of travelling alone. 'Have you visited Bath before?' Miss Shaw asked.

'No, though I feel I know it from books I've read, and am becoming increasingly receptive to its charms as the journey advances. I presume this is not your first visit, Miss Shaw.'

'I was there last season. Usually I stay with my aunt. May I ask where you are staying while there?'

'I've been invited to spend a fortnight with Lady Wainflete, a relative of my mother.'

Miss Shaw turned to face her. 'Lady Wainflete! She lives next to my aunt, Lady Glenister, in Daniel Street. We shall be neighbours!'

Prue responded warmly. 'Our meeting is a welcome coincidence.'

She wondered whether to broach the riddle of Lady Wainflete's invitation, a matter that grew in her mind as the journey progressed. But before she could form the question, Miss Shaw provided the answer. 'My aunt tells me that Lady Wainflete has been in Italy for over three years and has just returned.' Prue smiled, relieved at having discovered the reason for Lady Wainflete's silence.

They left Newbury early the next morning. It was still dark when they arrived in Marlborough, where they took breakfast. Converse dwindled as the coach continued to Chippenham. Miss Shaw, sitting opposite Prue, settled back, loosening the ties of her bonnet. Prue regarded her through half-closed eyes and decided that Miss Agnes Shaw was uncommonly pretty. That they were to be neighbours promoted intimacy and formal address was abandoned.

The coach slowed, wheeling under the arch and into the yard of The Plough, where it came to a stop. Agnes adjusted her bonnet. 'Refreshments are usually a scramble at Chippenham, Prudence. Let us take a plate to share and time will allow for a short walk.'

'Half an hour!' bawled the coachman, flinging down the reins to an ostler with the lordly manner of all good whips.

Prue and Agnes sipped barley-water and shared a plate of cold meats, pickles and bread. Then, gathering their cloaks about them, they walked under the arch in the vicinity of the coach.

'I must confess something to you, Prudence,' said Agnes. 'There are two brothers in Bath, each courting me, and I don't care for either of them.'

'Oh, shall you tell them or make it plain?'

She shook her head. 'I'm trying to find a way out but despair of it.' She sighed. 'I'm obliged to accept one of them in the course of this visit, otherwise I'll not be welcome at my aunt's house.'

'If you don't care for them, why should you accept?'

'Because theirs are the only offers I've had.'

'Perhaps you may meet someone else who's more to your liking.'

Agnes sighed. 'I fear I'm labelled 'Bagby – Do Not Approach'. Cuthbert and Hubert will be waiting at The Lamb, where we shall be put down, and they'll be with me the entire time as if I were draped in glue.'

'Marriage with either at the moment would seem out of the question. You're young and comely, not yet in love, and in Bath I should think the field is wide for such as you, Agnes.'

'And for such as you,' said Agnes. 'You will attract many beaux wishing to escort you.'

Prue, thinking of Biddy's advice, replied, 'Then I shall enjoy being so escorted.'

Agnes took her arm. 'We'll go out and about together and thereby I might break the Bagby precedence.'

Prue laughed. 'We'll be chaperon to each other, Agnes.'

With arms linked, they happily boarded the coach for the last stage. On entering verdant Somerset, Prue hoped the diversion of Bath might prove a respite from the ever-present matter of Esmond and Reedpath.

Lady Wainflete awaited her in the courtyard of The Lamb. Prue was caught up in an embrace, pressed close to a sable palatine, then Lady Wainflete held her at arm's length, smiling. 'At last, my dear girl! You must be weary. Was the journey tiresome?'

'Not really,' said Prue. 'But I'm happy to be here and it's lovely to see you again, Lady Wainflete.'

She really meant it, for here was someone of her own family with bright and caring eyes. Suddenly, she felt an overwhelming contentment as if she had come home.

Staff saw to her trunk and boxes, and the affectionate welcome continued during the carriage drive to Daniel Street. The house was a delight and she luxuriated in the comfort of her room which over-looked the garden.

'A nosegay has arrived for you, Prue,' called Lady Wainflete from below. 'It's beautiful, composed of the perpetual roses in bloom now. I'll ask Clara to bring it to your room.'

Prue frowned. A nosegay? Who would send her such a thing? She approached the landing as Clara, the maidservant, arrived at the top of the stairs and handed her several cream-coloured double roses enclosed in a starched and ribboned doily of white Brussels lace.

'How lovely!' breathed Prue, examining them with awe. Her eyes danced. 'Who could have sent them, or known I was in Bath?'

Ascending the stairs, Lady Wainflete said, 'I listed your arrival in all the usual places, so someone has responded.'

'But who could it be? I know no one in Bath who would have interest in such recordings.'

'Is there a label enclosed?'

Prue examined the nosegay further and noticed a small tab attached to one of the ribbons. 'Here's a printed florist's label. It says "Constancy".'

'That's the name of the rose,' said Lady Wainflete. 'The florist is the best in Bath. Clara will bring a vase and she'll place them in your room. Come and join me as soon as you are ready.'

Prue nodded dreamily and handed the roses back to Clara. A wonderful welcome, she thought, returning to her room to complete her toilette for dinner.

A short rest freshened her. She dressed in a low-cut gown of coppery silk and topped it with a velvet spencer of dark green. She coiled back her hair with dark green ribands and drew Biddy's pearls from their case. She regarded herself in a cheval-glass, and thought her costume would not be deemed high fashion in Bath society. This was the best she could do and it pleased her. But, oh, those pearls! They glowed lustrously against her skin and the long ear-rings tempted her to raise her chin to elegant effect.

Turning, she gently cupped in her hands one of the roses which Clara had placed in a vase upon the dressing table. She closed her eyes, enraptured by its perfume.

She found her way to Lady Wainflete's ante-room where she was to take wine with her hostess before dinner. After introducing the slumbering Nero, Lady Wainflete again expressed sorrow for her neglect. 'In retrospect, I'm horrified it was through me that you were obliged to spend those years in service to the Bucklands of Andursley.'

'Please don't blame yourself,' said Prue. 'You'll recall I wished to remove myself as far away as possible from Hybullen, and employment was the only answer.'

'I'm surprised that James agreed so readily.'

Prue shook her head sadly. 'It was more important that James regained a direction to his life. What little funds we mustered were applied to his law partnership. It was a wise move, and Andursley an ideal place to await improvement in our fortunes. My time there does no harm and teaches much.'

'You shall not return,' said Lady Wainflete, placing her glass upon a sidetable. 'I suggest you remain here in Bath for the season and return with me to Florence. That is unless—' At that point a shower of hailstones dashed violently against the windows. Startled, Lady Wainflete rose and looked out into the murk of a sudden storm. 'It's been raining incessantly for two days, and now this! Hardly the weather for promenading. Let's hope it will improve tomorrow.'

She moved to a chest, from which she withdrew lengths of Florentine silks and exquisite ornaments from Italy. She pressed these upon Prue as gifts, despite protests.

'Tomorrow a mantua-maker will call. She'll make up these silks quickly for you. Perhaps a visit from my Italian hairdresser may not go amiss, for I think he would agree with me that your style is too severe. Would you have any objection? Together we could set off those pearls to even greater perfection.'

Prue felt herself colouring. 'Is it necessary? After all, I'm here for such a short time.'

'Then we must make the most of it, my dear.'

It was like a fiction, thought Prue, a nursery tale with Lady

Wainflete a fairy godmother waving a wand of promise.

Any lingering exhaustion from the journey vanished in the music-room, to which they retired after dinner. For some moments Prue stood entranced by the famous portrait of her mother. How well she knew that garden at Hybullen, with the stone balustrade and cedars in the background! She turned to open the piano and entertained Lady Wainflete for the rest of the evening by playing her favourite melodies.

The next morning a fine rain fell, drenching the streets again after a dry night. Lady Wainflete hovered by the windows, searching the skies for a break in the clouds.

'Oh dear, not a day for walking,' she said. 'When is it going to clear? I always forget how inclement Bath weather can be.'

'I thought Miss Shaw was to call.'

'Yes, I hoped she might join us for breakfast and walk with us to Sydney Gardens.'

'Perhaps we could walk there before dinner if the rain has stopped by then.'

'Too late,' cried Lady Wainflete, turning to face Prue. With a heightening of colour, she added, 'That's to say, I feel the evening is a time for indoor pursuits.'

'Anything and everything,' Prue said reassuringly, feeling that her hostess's fluster was due to a desire to fill every moment with entertainment. 'I'll enjoy being with you and Miss Shaw whatever we do. Last night in the music-room was delightful and worthy of repetition.'

Lady Wainflete smiled, tempering her mood. 'Of course. That'll be a pleasure to come. Let's go downstairs as I think I hear sounds of Miss Shaw's arrival. We can start breakfast.'

Agnes greeted Prue warmly. Over breakfast she chatted happily, brushing aside Lady Wainflete's despair about the weather. 'We need only pattens and a good umbrella. We could walk to Sydney Gardens and retreat to the hotel. That's what everybody does.'

Lady Wainflete hesitated. 'Then perhaps we should venture.'

'Oh, do let us!' urged Agnes.

The manservant entered and stooped to Lady Wainflete's ear, presenting a card as he did so.

Lady Wainflete frowned, then read aloud, 'Vivian Mallory, Earl of Dartree, County Sligo.'

Prue gulped. 'Lord Dartree! Surely James is with him!'

The manservant shook his head. 'He's alone, ma'am, and awaits you in the salon ante-room.'

'Thank you,' said Lady Wainflete, as her manservant withdrew. 'A somewhat early call. I presume he's a friend of your brother, Prudence?'

Prue smiled. 'He is both friend and colleague. Thanks to Lord Dartree, evidence and witnesses are available to successfully pursue our claim. When James joined the law firm, he dealt with legal services to gentry. There he met Lord Dartree who nearly fell foul of Reedpath but, in his case, disaster was averted.'

'He must have seen your name in the lists,' said Lady Wainflete, still pondering the card.

'And recognized it immediately,' said Prue excitedly. 'Perhaps he has news of James.'

'Have you met him before?'

'No. I've not had the pleasure.'

'Then I shall go and greet him,' said Lady Wainflete, rising, 'and you will join me later.'

There was a silence. Then Prue said, 'Perhaps Lord Dartree is the sender of the nosegay.'

Lady Wainflete turned. 'I wouldn't think so, Prudence. How should the ideal of constancy apply to him?'

'His devotion to our family cause is surely a qualification.'

'Obscure and unlikely,' muttered Lady Wainflete as she left the room.

Chapter 11

ESMOND stood disconsolately by the windows of Melodon tapping a walking-cane against his boot. He frowned at the sodden garden and persistent drizzle. 'There's a demon in the weather,' he remarked, 'and it's having a diabolical effect on my plans.'

'Weather is an unreliable partner in any scheme,' replied the dowager, placing cards for a game of Patience. 'I'm surprised you relied upon such a fickle participant.'

'Would you have any objection to accompanying me this morning, inclement as the weather is?'

'I place more credence in the judgement of Lady Wainflete. She'll delay until it's sensible to promenade. Let us do likewise,' said she.

Nodding a reluctant agreement, he looked again from the window. Prue is here, he thought, over the wet roofs, a few streets away. By now she would have received a second delivery of roses. 'Constancy' was his message and his choice, despite the presence in Bath of several young ladies who would expect him to call. He wished only for Prue, to be with her, drive with her, dance with her and court her. His unbridled fancies were again constrained, this time by the weather.

He glanced at his mother, her face stern with concentration on the cards. Should he mention that Prue's father was the tragic Sir Edward Mulcaster Smith and that Reedpath, the black sheep of her family, had caused his downfall? How should he tell Prue? Could she be persuaded of his safe conscience, reinforced by a life-long rebuttal of all Reedpath represented?

Grasping the other end of the cane he flexed it, deciding he would volunteer nothing to his mother until she had met Prue. As for Prue, he longed to actively pursue his suit determined to avoid any matter that might threaten it.

He looked at the rain-streaked windows. Must he face another day like this, knowing she was so near? Perhaps he could find a book, any book, that he could take to Lady Wainflete on the pretext that he had borrowed it from her. This would banish weather from the situation and place him in control. The more he thought about such a ploy, the more it appealed to him and he knew Lady Wainflete would respond appropriately. The house was still, the aunts closeted in their separate rooms. The rustling of playing cards and ticking of the long-case clock pervaded the silence, wearing down his ability to endure more hours of inactivity.

The dowager ceased playing and regarded him. 'Don't be tempted to alter your plans at this late stage, Esmond. I can feel your impatience winning over good sense. Besides, you must consider Lady Wainflete.'

He whipped round to face her. 'Why couldn't I make a call upon Lady Wainflete, perhaps to return a book? Or some other matter. . . ?' His voice trailed as his mother shook her head. She was right. It was a ruse to assuage his disappointment.

The dowager rose and joined him at the window. 'Miss Smith's first sight of you escorting your old mother on a walk wouldn't offend the proprieties so much as a young man paying calls as if he's nothing better to do.'

'Nothing better to do!' he repeated with annoyance. 'How should I spend the time, Mother? Go off and invent a condiment or contemplate wet pebbles?'

'I'm simply pointing out how it might appear to a young lady, a special young lady.'

He paused before saying, 'So you feel the original plan is best?'

She nodded. 'Infinitely. I think both Miss Smith and Miss Shaw would welcome a day to recover from their journey and attend to such feminine pursuits of which you have no conception. Better that all is done on a rainy day rather than a fine one.'

He smiled, deferring to her suggestion.

That evening he was rescued from the onset of a depressing languor by a visit from the Honourable Hubert Bagby, with whom he took wine and chatted about Wykeham days. His aunts hinted at strange times when Esmond received a young bachelor rather than the usual bevy of young ladies.

He could not tell them that Hubert, escort of Miss Shaw, was most welcome because of a tenuous connection with Prue. Hubert had met the coach and remarked on Miss Shaw's travelling companion. 'A startling vision of natural grace and conquering charm,' he had said. That night on retiring Esmond dwelt on those words, hoping the coming day would make that vision a reality for him.

The morning sun blinded him as George, his valet, drew back the bed drapes. Elated, he rose and moved to the window. He saw a sky of unbroken blue and the crescents on the hill made gold in the sunlight.

He dressed without exaggeration of style, then left to join his mother below. He had the impression that his feet hardly touched the stairs, combined with a feeling that he weighed not an ounce. At last his courtship could proceed with all the proprieties observed.

The dowager was seated at her desk in consultation with a housekeeper. She smiled as Esmond approached. 'We have to decide when to hold our evening assembly, Esmond. I'll issue invitations for today week, if that's satisfactory to your plans.'

'That accords excellently with my plans. But when shall we leave for the Gardens, Mother?'

'About eleven of the clock. That'll give us time for a stroll and afterwards a light refreshment at the hotel. It's bright after the rain and I'm sure the entire population of Bath will be out today.'

It seemed to Esmond that an epoch passed before his mother was ready and dressed for their walk. She took his arm, and it was with difficulty he adjusted his eager pace to the stately stroll of his mother. If not the entire population, he thought, there was a goodly proportion taking the air in Sydney Gardens. Groups of ladies and gentlemen gathered alongside the walks, chatting and moving on in processions of amity. Esmond glanced at every approaching young face. In their slow progress, he and his mother exchanged greetings with many acquaintances but Esmond did not wish to dally. His mood became a checkerboard of fears and exultation. He felt he should recognize Prue's step among a thousand, or see her in a flash above all the bobbing heads, his ardour drawing her to him as a magnet attracts particles of iron even from a distance.

Suddenly his mother stopped and gestured. 'Here's Lady Wainflete, Esmond.'

He turned eagerly to see Lady Wainflete approaching and smilingly extending her hand. After greetings were exchanged, Lady Wainflete presented Miss Agnes Shaw. Esmond looked in vain for Prue.

'Prudence is following us. We left her on the bridge,' said Lady Wainflete.

'Then I'll go to her there at once,' he said, clapping his hat upon his head and striding off. He heard Lady Wainflete call to him but, intent upon his errand, continued on his way.

Dodging crowds and still scanning the faces approaching him, he came to the bridge where several groups were gazing at the waters of the canal flowing beneath. Suddenly, by a stone abutment he saw her and joy made for him a brighter brightness that morning.

There was a difference in her bearing, an air of confidence which delighted him, the more so since he felt responsible for promoting it. Here she was free of the restraints imposed by her service life and he relished the new course his courtship could take. A pert green velvet bonnet rested on the shining coils of her black hair, and a matching cape topped a coat of grey. Her finery could never erase other images a lovely face smudged with potting soil, delicate hands in gardening gloves, the plain frocks and sacking aprons. He had loved her then, and for that spark of defiance which had saved his life. Musing thus, it was with some shock he realized she was not alone. He frowned. Who was the gentleman beside her, bending his head in earnest conversation? From the fine cut of his coat he judged him to be a London swell of the first order. This must be her brother, he thought, and smilingly resumed his approach.

Within a few yards of her he stood quite still, willing her to glance his way. She turned to address her companion and in that moment looked at him. She stopped short, her eyes widening, and came towards him with a delicious sigh of pleasure. 'Esmond! What a surprise.'

Taking her hands, he slowly bore each to his lips, his eyes engaging hers throughout. Offering her hand again, she said, 'Please pinch me, Esmond, for I think I'm dreaming.'

'I'd like to break that conviction with a kiss, but all eyes are on us.'

She started at this oblique reference to her companion and turning, beckoned him forward. 'Esmond, the Right Honourable the Earl Dartree, a great friend of my brother. He arrived in Bath only yesterday with the infuriating news that James has journeyed to Andursley, not knowing I was here.' Then, facing Dartree, she said, 'Lord Dartree, I have pleasure in presenting the Most Honourable Marquess of Lydney.'

Esmond moved forward with a cordial greeting but Lord Dartree bowed stiffly and appeared uncommonly disturbed by the introduction. Esmond saw this was not lost upon Prue, who brought Lord Dartree forward, saying, 'Shall we continue our walk, My Lord?' He nodded and, ignoring Esmond, took her arm and guided her towards the main path. Esmond turned and strode alongside Prue, puzzled by the cold demeanour of her companion whose presence had shattered his dream. They walked together for some moments, tensely silent. Suddenly, Lord Dartree halted. Murmuring a formal regret for another engagement, he bent over Prue's hand. 'I hope you'll grant me a dance at one of the assemblies, but for now I'll leave you to continue your walk with the most honourable lord.'

'Of course,' she smiled. 'I'm sorry you have to leave.'

His grey eyes glinted. 'Needs must, I fear,' and touching his hat, he took his leave of them. They stood watching as he disappeared into the crowds on the path.

'I had no idea of this prior appointment,' said Prue. 'I hope in my ignorance I didn't detain him unnecessarily.'

'Then my arrival was timely in relieving him of a very tiresome young lady,' Esmond smiled, feeling a surge of relief at Dartree's abrupt departure.

'Esmond,' she scolded laughingly.

'Enough of Lord Dartree. Let's hasten and join Lady Wainflete and Miss Shaw who remained with my mother. She's anxious to meet you.'

Prue turned to him. 'You know Lady Wainflete?'

'My mother is well acquainted with her.' He took her hand and placed it upon his arm. 'Prue, I am here and you are here. Let's put all puzzlements aside and thank Providence for arranging it. Suffice to say I know your name is Mulcaster Smith. I saw your mother's portrait at Lady Wainflete's and thought it to be you!' She sought to interrupt, but he placed a finger upon her lips and smiled into her eyes. 'Come, I insist that you meet my mother. Afterwards there'll be time to talk. For the moment let me say that every aspect of your beauty, every gesture, and every pose of the head are graven with a diamond point upon my consciousness. I love you, Prue, and intend to court you relentlessly.'

'I am honoured by your esteem, Esmond, but I have some important questions to pose to you so it's as well we've met in Bath,' she answered.

'The idea of you is ever before me – nothing can affect that.' His free hand trembled as he placed it over hers that rested upon his arm. Leading her from the bridge he proceeded slowly in a silence of pure content. For the first time he could walk with her openly. There was every reason for him to be entirely happy but he felt a certain disquiet at the extraordinary behaviour of Lord Dartree. He had been less than polite and it was regrettable that he was a friend of Prue's brother. And had he imagined a degree of reserve on Prue's part? He admitted to a growing curiosity about the questions she wished to ask him. As for Lord Dartree, could he be a rival for Prue's affections? With that in mind he gently drew her closer, while his hand pressed upon hers in possessive reassurance.

Prue had been invited in company with Lady Wainflete, Miss Shaw and the Honourable Hubert Bagby, to an impromptu gathering for tea at Melodon that evening.

The dowager received her kindly and Prue warmed to her dancing blue eyes, so like her son's. As Prue curtsied, the dowager had taken her hands and aided her in rising. 'You're most welcome, Miss Smith. Esmond has told me you saved his life. He is your slave, and no wonder.' She had kissed both her cheeks and squeezed her hands before the next guest intruded.

The salon was but partially lit, wax tapers shining to infinity in giant mirrors placed on the walls and ceiling. Prue was grateful for the flattering light as it toned down a décolleté white dress of Caroline's which she had draped with dove-grey gauze. At her bosom she had placed one of Esmond's roses and another above her right ear. She wore her hair with soft curls about her face, coiled back within a pearl Italian ornament.

Esmond's sharp intake of breath when he saw her, and his proud smile as he escorted her into the salon made her glowingly confident. She felt a surge of gratitude to both Caroline and Lady Wainflete for her present finery.

They joined Lady Wainflete at a window table, leaving Hubert with Agnes in an adjoining embrasure. Esmond waited upon the ladies and brought tea, cakes and jellies. His lips brushed Prue's ear as he set these before her. 'Speak, and I'll satisfy your merest wish,' he whispered.

She smiled up at him. 'That this could go on for ever.'

'If it's in my power, it will,' came his fervent response. He was about to continue when his two aunts entered the salon and seated themselves with Dr Crouch, an old friend of the family. 'Before you take up your cup, Prue, there's one more formality. You must meet my aunts.'

At their approach the aunts immediately ceased their converse with Dr Crouch and stared at Prue in amazement.

'Sally Faulkoner,' they breathed in unison.

'Her daughter,' corrected Esmond. 'Miss Prudence Mulcaster Smith. My aunts, the Honourables Cicely and Louise Aumerle.'

Aunt Cis shook her head in disbelief. 'So like Sally who reigned supreme in all the salons of our day.'

'As sweet as she was fair,' commented Aunt Lou.

'Where have you been hiding her, Esmond?' demanded Aunt Cis.

'She had been hiding from me deep in the wilds of Hampshire,' he replied, 'until one day she decided to save my life.'

The aunts coo-ed with curiosity as Prue chided, 'Nonsense! He risked his life for us.'

Esmond recounted the incident for the edification of his aunts who, mindful of the risk to their beloved nephew, were full of praise for his rescuer.

Dr Crouch, who appeared incapable of removing his eyes from Prue, muttered, 'Indeed, she could be Sally. That's what Sally would do. She couldn't be trifled with.'

'You knew her, too, Dr Crouch?' asked Prue.

He nodded, took her hand and kissed it before saying, 'One of her many admirers, a long time ago.'

The dowager joined them and all reminisced about Lady Sarah Faulkoner and the enigma of her marriage to the handsome Sir Edward Mulcaster Smith, to whom she brought the immense wealth and possessions of the Marquess of Hybullen.

'She died tragically early,' said the dowager, 'which must have been a shock to Sir Edward.'

At this turn in the conversation Esmond placed Prue's hand upon his arm and begged leave to return to their table and Lady

Wainflete. As they left he whispered, 'Don't think I find the subject of your family tiresome by withdrawing so abruptly. It's of such importance to me that I'm reluctant to conduct it with those to whom it's merely gossip. The participants shall be limited to you and me alone. Say you understand and forgive me if, by clumsiness, I've offended.'

'Of course you've not offended, Esmond. I'll greatly look forward to our talk.'

In spite of her reassuring reply, Prue had been happy to talk about her family, welcoming it as acknowledgment of her status. She was puzzled by Esmond's insistence on their withdrawal but his explanation sufficed, and an irrepressible excitement possessed her at the thought of their talk to come. Soon she hoped to pose him those vital questions about the bookplate and the porcelain lover.

Lady Wainflete had been joined by Captain and Mrs Roper, who rose at their approach. After formal introductions, the Captain said, '*Prudence* is the name of the new vessel in our Lydney fleet, Miss Mulcaster Smith, to be launched later this year. She's very beautiful as, I observe, is her namesake.'

'Thank you,' said Prue, blushing. 'The name betokens caution which is well to observe when dealing with the elements. I've always lived inland, deprived of the sea, but I imagine a ship under sail a wonderful sight and one I should wish to see.'

Esmond laughed. 'You've voiced my own plan, Prue. You'll see ships under sail and be our guest at the launching ceremony!'

'That would indeed grace the occasion,' added Mrs Roper. 'It's a thrill to see the vessel slip into the water with a deep curtsy to the land as she takes leave of it.'

'That description does you credit, Mrs Roper. I envy you. I'm entirely ignorant of matters nautical,' said Prue.

Esmond reached for her hand. 'Then your education shall begin and I'll be your tutor. The first thing to arrange is a tour of the ship-yards and Captain Roper shall provide us dinner aboard our flagship, the *Lydney Amelia*, when she docks after her present Atlantic commission.'

She flushed with pleasure as her hand remained restfully in his, and drifted dreamily in a strong current which she fought to control. Doubts about Esmond surfaced, moderating her joy in the moment.

A footman advanced and whispered in the dowager's ear, whereupon she rose and stood by the door to welcome unexpected callers. Lady Nancy Summerson entered in a scarlet gown, accompanied by the two Verity sisters and four officers of Dragoons. Prue, introduced by the dowager, remembered these young ladies from Caroline's London Season when she was working in the shadows.

Lady Summerson smiled and murmured her pleasure, then moved to Esmond and tapped him on the shoulder with her fan. 'Esmond, why have you been so confined? We've hardly seen you. Please come to my rout tomorrow. I know you've declined but I'm here specially to change your mind.'

Prue saw that the flirtatious sweep of her eyes was to no avail, for Esmond coolly replied, 'What a pity you bothered, Nancy. You really should learn that when one replies in the negative, that is what they mean.'

Lady Summerson pouted. 'You really can't be persuaded?'

'I really can't.'

She turned to Prue. 'Won't you come, Miss Mulcaster Smith? There'll be other Dragoons and a naval officer or two. I'm really after making up the numbers.'

Prue replied with sincerity, 'Thank you, but I'm Lady Wainflete's guest and must decline.'

'Prudence has a prior commitment,' retorted Esmond, taking her hand and leading her away, 'and it's with me. Sorry, Nancy.'

Lady Summerson snapped open her fan, eyes bright with annoyance, and retreated to her friends who were still chatting to the dowager.

Prue knew that Esmond had once been closely associated with Lady Summerson and, affected by his peremptory response, felt bound to remark, 'That was a cavalier way to deal with Lady

Summerson's attempt to make you change your mind, Esmond.'

'You're a novice in the wiles of that woman, Prue. All was well until she invited you in that vulgar manner and I couldn't abide it, no more than I could the countess's treatment of you. You're not here to make up numbers in anyone's rout party. Your humility is a quality I revere and you're too much a lady to deal with the likes of Nancy Summerson.' He halted and faced her. 'You think me arrogant?'

'No,' she smiled. 'It's just that I'm unused to a champion in my affairs. Thank you, Esmond.'

He squeezed her hand. 'Look, the terrace is open and Lady Wainflete is seated there with Dr Crouch. Let's join them for a moment, and then I can whisk you away for our talk.'

After a light exchange with Lady Wainflete and Dr Crouch, she walked with Esmond to the end of the terrace. Steps descended to a paved courtyard set with planters from which towered gigantic ferns. Esmond led her to a seat.

Prue sighed with contentment. 'This is like balm, so peaceful.'

'It's as well,' said he, 'for there's a matter I raise with some trepidation. When I discovered, through the portrait of your mother, that you were the daughter of Lady Sarah and Sir Edward, I was shocked in the extreme. I thought it augured the end of our attachment, but reason persuaded me to tell you all the facts so that you can ponder them and pronounce judgement. Even as I say this, I'm fearful that your verdict may be pitiless. Without exaggeration, Prue, that would destroy me.'

Prue could hardly comprehend. She had sought to confide details of *her* family's downfall. How strange that *he* had something to impart. She turned to him. His pallor and the despair in his eyes startled her. She put out a hand to his face, which he clasped and held to his lips. Thus they remained for some moments until she straightened and gently withdrew her hand.

'Tell me,' she said softly.

Touched by her loving gesture, Esmond sought her hand again and held it within both of his. With head bowed, he said, 'I know of your father's gambling debt and the tragedy that followed. In the disposal of effects at Hybullen, I purchased the entire library as I heard it was to be broken up. It's safe at Lydney and is yours whenever and wherever you want it.'

She looked at him with astonishment and relief that the library had been saved. She drew breath. 'I have no right to it, Esmond.'

'You have every right,' he answered feelingly. 'From this moment it is yours to do with as you will. If you wish the library to go back to Hybullen, so be it.'

She turned away, her eyes suddenly moist. It was not only the fact of the library's survival but his generosity that stirred her and made it impossible to utter a word.

'Prue?' he enquired, touching her arm in concern at her silence.

Composing herself, she faced him again. 'Better that it's held at Lydney. Hybullen is a ruin.'

'If I can aid in the restoration, your brother has only to ask.'

She paused before saying, 'Why are you so willing to help us, Esmond? Our misfortunes derive from a debt of honour and nothing can alter that. We've suffered the consequences, but—'

'I've something more to say,' he interposed. A silence hung between them. 'Clancy Reedpath is my cousin.'

She stared at him, aghast. She could not believe what she was hearing, her worst fears a reality. She felt sick, bewildered. Words rode on her shuddering breath. 'Reedpath your cousin!'

'A ruthless reprobate, an outcast of this family. You must know he went to America and there remains.'

Disengaging her hand, she rose and stood stiffly, staring ahead.

He turned to her. 'My mother is unaware of Clancy's past and thinks he is in America for business reasons. It was a constant struggle to uphold our family honour while he was here. Many a duel I've fought and many a settlement made to stifle gossip due to his scandalous affairs.' He paused. 'Prue, this shouldn't affect us! Be assured of my clear conscience. Say, my dearest girl, that what's past is past and so long as he remains where he is, then all is well!'

She whipped round, eyes brimming with tears, her voice trembling with suppressed rage. 'He gained Hybullen by cheating my father while he was suffering grief at the death of my mother. Father lost his mind before death claimed him, our vigil lasting day and night over years.' She paused, her hands at her forehead. 'This is indeed a bitter pill. Reedpath strutted like a turkeycock – odious in the dismantling of our home – and – and. . . .' She shuddered at the thought of his leering face, hooded eyes and ugly hands always reaching for her.

In a moment, Esmond was beside her. Turning her towards him he placed his hands upon her shoulders. 'Prue,' he said softly. 'I know his ways. When and where did he accost you?'

'Frequently at Hybullen,' she said, disengaging herself. 'Let me remind you of Dr Crouch's remark about my mother – she couldn't be trifled with. Well, I'm in that mould. Reedpath offered to void the debt if I would wed him. James called him out, but he fled to America.' She looked up, unable to cease quivering.

'Oh, Prue,' he said helplessly. 'What can I say, what can I do?'

'He could be brought to justice if he returned to England. We've evidence of the cheating.'

She bowed her head. The resurgence of violent hatred for Reedpath was made worse in the recognition that nothing would ever be the same with Esmond. She had reached a turning point. The irony was that she had dreaded the revelation of her family's disgrace only to find that, should Reedpath return, Esmond's own affairs were potentially in greater danger. The strange behaviour of Lord Dartree on meeting Esmond was now made clear. He had discovered his family tie with Reedpath.

She shook visibly and stepped back as Esmond came closer. She had almost succumbed to his tender persuasion, but the memory of her father's ordeal thrust a wedge between them. She turned to regard him. How elegant and handsome he was! He had claimed a clear conscience. Yet how unblemished was his conscience when he had fought duels and made settlements to 'stifle gossip'? She recalled the innumerable young ladies that Biddy claimed had been associated with him. Were they the victims of Reedpath's iniquitous games, put to right by Esmond's expertise and resources? Could it be that she was next in line for such expiation? She bristled at the thought. How fortunate that Reedpath fled to America! While he was there Esmond's family honour remained unimpaired.

She had suspected a connection with Reedpath but never dreamed he was kin to Esmond. It was devastating to think of. She must leave. She could not remain another moment in his company. It was out of the question to return to the salon.

She turned away and made a step to depart. He caught her hand. 'I'll do anything to restore matters. I can't let you go from here without that promise.' His voice was quiet and strained.

With an imperceptible nod of her head, she withdrew her hand. 'Be so kind to ask Lady Wainflete to meet me at our carriage. Please convey my regrets to your mother. I – I simply wish to slip away. . . .'

'Has this been so dreadful a shock?'

'More than you realize.'

'Allow me to call upon you tomorrow – please!'

'No. I need time to think.'

He bowed his head, sighed heavily and raised his arms in a gesture of despair. 'I'll take you to your carriage.'

He placed her hand on his arm and led her through the garden to the carriage house. As he handed her in to Lady Wainflete's coach he looked at her sadly for some moments. 'I'll be back with Lady Wainflete,' he whispered before quietly closing the door.

His face was pale and downcast in the lamplight. She sat hunched with despair in the shadowed coach until the stamping of the horses and boarding of the coachman indicated imminent departure. Cruel destiny to allow a blissful reunion then tear it asunder on the same day! Tears of chagrin started to her eyes and, reaching for her reticule, she disturbed the rose at her breast; its petals tumbled about her like the dispersal of dreams.

Chapter 12

ESMOND lay slumped on the settle in his mother's room. Last night he had told her that Prue had suddenly become unwell and wished to leave. He had then escorted a bewildered Lady Wainflete to her coach, made his excuses and left the company.

He was still limp with the shock of seeing Prue inconsolably distressed. He knew its cause lay in reasons other than the material loss of Hybullen. Her hatred and revulsion of his cousin could not be ignored. His jaws were clenched even now, and his abdomen a hollow after an interminable sleepless night. Grief tinged with anger gnawed at him. He must see Prue again, and soon. But first he must talk with his mother.

She was playing an afternoon game of three-handed whist with the aunts. He looked toward the card table as she made a wry face. 'Cis! you're nid-nodding over your cards. Perhaps we should continue the game later.' The aunts did not demur and, murmuring apologies, left for their apartments.

Esmond quickly rose, plumped the cushion in his mother's chair and guided her to it. 'I must talk with you on a matter that affects our family.'

'Ah,' she said, seating herself and smilingly reaching for his hand, 'you're ready to offer for Prudence. Effie Wainflete is anxious to harbour her.'

'There's an elder brother, Sir Edward's heir.'

'You must invite him to Melodon!'

133

'He's on his way to Bath and will join a friend, Lord Dartree, at The White Hart.'

'We must receive them here, Esmond.'

He shook his head. 'In good time, Mother.'

'So you're not ready to talk of betrothal to Prudence. Judging by the looks that pass when you're together, delay would be unwise, to say the least.'

Withdrawing his hand, he stood by the mantel facing her. 'Mother, on the matter of Clancy. . . .'

She stiffened, raising her eyebrows. 'The matter of Clancy? I'd prefer to talk about you and Prudence.'

'As would I, but the unpleasant matter of Clancy is relevant.' She sought to interrupt but he suddenly directed her gaze to the heraldic plaster rose on the ceiling. 'The Aumerle arms,' he said, 'and the scroll bearing in gold our motto "Honour First".'

She frowned. 'What has that to do with—?'

Ignoring her question, he continued. 'Sir Edward Mulcaster Smith's debt of honour, which ruined his family, was due to Clancy. The debt was compounded over many weeks by systematic cheating with accomplices. Prue and her brother seek restitution and moves are afoot to prove fraud and lodge claims against Clancy. There's also the matter of Cedric. Heaven knows whether he's involved but he's been Clancy's companion for some time.'

She fidgeted uneasily. 'I knew Clancy gambled heavily, but a cheat, surely not!'

'If I'm to observe "Honour First" and effect Clancy's return to England, that motto will be held to ridicule. Even though Clancy isn't an Aumerle, his relationship to you will affect us should he be proven a cheat. If Cedric is implicated in the fraud, the tide of disgrace will engulf the Aumerles as well.'

She shook her head in disbelief. 'Is it really as serious as that. Can it be proved?'

'More than likely. I cannot ask Prue to join this family unless I can bring Clancy to book. Her early departure last evening was due to her distress upon learning he is kin to us.'

There was a strained silence. 'Prudence must know you had no part in the ruination of her father.'

'I've yet to convince her and also her brother,' he said, grimly.

'Isn't it better that Clancy remains in America to avert disclosure?'

'And have innuendoes and slanderous rumours of fraud go unchallenged? No. The onus rests on me for an honourable way out.' He strode to the window and stood silently, his hands clasped under the tails of his coat. Then, turning, he slowly paced before his mother. 'Until Prue's background was made known to me by Lady Wainflete, I was content for Clancy and Cedric to remain in America – a false security created by my own complacency. It's imperative that they return to answer charges.'

'Oh, what to do, Esmond?'

'I have the means to go to America myself to ascertain where their interests lie, and act accordingly. Captain Roper is on his way to Bristol to arrange immediate readying of the *Lydney Amelia* when she returns from Boston. She's expected about three weeks from now.'

'Esmond,' she breathed. 'Must that be?'

'It's the only way to convince Prue and her brother of my guiltlessness.' He ceased pacing and turned to look at her. 'Prue is . . . special to me. I wish to marry her. It's essential I make that plain to her before I leave for Bristol.'

'Oh, it's all so vague, unfulfilled. . . .' She drooped in her chair, her eyes moist with despair at the enormity of the disaster facing them. 'I can't believe Cedric is part of Clancy's conspiracies.'

'Nor I. But his association with him these past years would seem to confirm it.'

'Summon him back, Esmond. Tell him I'm ailing. It would be no untruth for I feel ill at this moment.'

He perched on the arm of her chair and took her hand. 'I'll not go down on hearsay. I know what I must do. And what *you* must do,' he said, taking a kerchief to her eyes, 'is to bear up as if there's nothing amiss.'

Daylight was fading. She stirred and sighed. 'How can I play cards tonight?'

Rising, he said, 'Because your guests will expect it.'

Composing herself, she came to stand beside him. 'You must do everything to preserve the family honour. I know your dear father would have done the same and I'll aid you in any way I can. Prudence is ideal for you and I pray for your happiness, Esmond.'

He kissed her lightly on the forehead before embracing her. 'I'll come later to wish you a good night, but for now I've arrangements to make and don't wish to be disturbed.'

He took up a lighted candle and assisted her through the unlit corridor to the stairwell. She looked at him as she prepared to descend. He saw the sadness in her face, and smiled his encouragement. Then he turned back along the passage to his room.

All the precious moments with Prue burned in his mind. He recalled the overpowering nearness of her and the delicious curl in the nape of her neck, so close to his lips as he helped her into the coach. He had wanted to pull her back, enfold her in his arms and kiss her until she was unreservedly convinced of his love and support. But he was faced with unyielding stiffness in the set of her shoulders and cold demeanour.

For the first time in his life he felt uncertainty in his power to direct affairs.

The morning after the tea party at Melodon, Prue joined Lady Wainflete in her ante-room. The mood was heavy. Prue felt a numbness of mind and spirit. Bright prospects had been dashed and all her imagined fears made real. She sighed heavily.

Lady Wainflete concentrated on her embroidery. Suddenly she said, 'It doesn't follow that Esmond has anything to do with Reedpath's malpractice. Esmond is unsullied by rumour, nothing odious attaches to his name.'

'In the main, I would agree,' replied Prue, taking an orange from the fruit dish. 'But there's gossip about certain affairs, financial settlements and duels on his part. I'm satisfied these were covert acts to hide the consequences of Reedpath's frauds. Esmond confessed this to be so last night.'

'That shows he's a worthy head of his family.'

'There are writs against Reedpath awaiting his return to the jurisdiction. Compensation for the ruined families can only proceed when that happens.'

'Then you can understand why Reedpath is in no hurry to come back and Esmond disinclined to persuade him.'

It is hopeless, thought Prue. After their return last night they had discussed the matter until her head swam. She so wanted to justify her behaviour, but Lady Wainflete remained unconvinced that their peremptory withdrawal had been necessary.

'Am I a terrible disappointment to you?' asked Prue.

There was a silence as Lady Wainflete parked the needle in her work before replying. Her expression softened. 'I understand your reaction because I know of your suffering. I'm simply concerned with retrieving the situation to mollify Bath society.'

'It's not my wish to make things difficult,' said Prue.

'Then you will receive Esmond, should he call?'

'I'll receive him,' said Prue, taking a knife and lightly scoring the orange, 'but that's all I'm prepared to do.'

Lady Wainflete sighed. 'It's enough.' She rose, lifted Nero from his basket and moved to the window, fondling the drowsy mass of fur. 'Are you expecting Agnes?' she asked.

'Yes – I presume so,' answered Prue hesitantly. 'That is, I hope she'll call as I'd like to explain our sudden departure last evening.'

'An apology will suffice without going into all the whys and wherefores.'

Prue peeled and divided the orange, placing the quarters on a plate. Her melancholy intensified. Lady Wainflete professed to understand her shock and dismay. But why did her responses possess that hint of accusation? It was obvious that Lady Wainflete favoured Esmond. She sighed deeply. If only there was no such person as Reedpath.

She was about to take a portion of orange when Lady Wainflete turned from the window and placed Nero in his basket. 'We have a caller,' she said.

Prue's heart jumped. Could it be Esmond? Voices were heard. Then the door was suddenly opened. The manservant entered, followed by a young gentleman wearing a bicorn hat, caped redingote and top boots. His long dark hair was worn *en queue*.

'James!' cried Prue, leaping to her feet. 'Oh, James, at last!' She flung herself into his ready arms.

They kissed and hugged in such joy that it was some moments before James turned to Lady Wainflete. He removed his hat, bowed and bent over her hand. 'My dear Lady Wainflete.'

'Sir James, you are most welcome,' she said smiling. Then, addressing the manservant hovering by the door, added, 'Mostyn, please relieve Sir James of his coat and hat and place them in his room.' The manservant nodded. James divested himself of his coat and handed both items to Mostyn who then withdrew, quietly closing the door behind him.

James flexed his arms and tidied his neckcloth. 'I apologize for my unkempt appearance and delay in arrival. Everything was well until Whitchurch when my mount went lame and made it impossible for me to continue to Andursley. The mistress of the inn secured another horse for me and it was in chance converse with her that she told me you had left Andursley for Bath. So I made haste to join you, knowing you would be with Lady Wainflete.'

Prue flushed with pleasure and relief that it was James standing before her and not Esmond.

'I hope my grooms are attending your horse,' said Lady Wainflete.

'I called on Vivian Dartree as soon as I arrived and he arranged for my horse to be stalled at The White Hart. His coach carried me here with my baggage. He's asked that we join him there for dinner tonight. I hope that's possible.'

'Oh yes,' smiled Prue. 'I've many questions to pose to both of you.'

'And we've much to impart,' said, he. 'But first, I must freshen myself.'

'Mostyn will attend you,' said Lady Wainflete. 'Then join us for some wine.'

James nodded and moved to Prue's side, placing an arm about her shoulder. 'You're looking well, dear sister, far better than I expected after being cooped up at Andursley. Vivian is already singing your praises.'

She blushed, whereupon James laughed aloud as he withdrew. There was a long silence. Prue seated herself again. Softly she asked, 'Shall you come to the hotel tonight, Lady Wainflete?'

'Of course. I couldn't permit you to take dinner alone with *two* gentlemen in a public place.'

'I'm relieved to hear it,' sighed Prue.

It was not long before James joined them again, refreshed and composed in manner. Prue regarded him. It was fully three years since she had seen him. He seemed to possess a faintly old-world air in comparison to the *beau monde* of Bath. His green coat was of a style seldom seen in these days, though he filled it well. He wore knee breeches and stockings, and his top boots shone with the high polish of time. The bicorn he had worn on arrival and his lightly powdered long hair gave the impression of a young man resistant to change, snapping his fingers in the face of fashionable society. He appeared to be a partial recluse, with a grudge against the gambling aristocrats who had cheated him of his inheritance.

Lady Wainflete produced champagne with which they toasted their combined reunion and exchanged pleasantries. After reiterating her welcome to both Prue and James, Lady Wainflete withdrew.

James refilled their glasses and sat facing Prue on the sofa. 'I expect you are anxious to know how our case is proceeding?'

'Not only that, but have you been to Hybullen of late? What's happening there?'

He laughed. 'One thing at a time, Prue. Of prime importance, I have been invited to meet three noble lords in Bath, my Lords Beddington, Owlsbury and Viscount Eades. These gentlemen

139

represent the governing committees of three major gambling clubs in London. Father's case precipitated concern for the reputation of their establishments. They're on Reedpath's trail and their lordships are adamant he will be committed to trial.'

Prue was open-mouthed. 'But how—?'

'By some mysterious means not divulged to me, their lordships have amassed evidence of the systems used, accomplices and witnesses. They've left nothing to chance. As soon as Reedpath returns, he's doomed.'

'Ah, but when shall he return?'

'According to their lordships, it may be imminent. I'm gaining in hope that we'll soon have satisfaction.'

'That's wonderful news, James.' She turned away. With a curious sense of pain, she thought of Esmond. It would mean disgrace for his family when Reedpath returned. This realization was tempered by her recollection of Esmond's magnanimous offer to return the Hybullen library – a spontaneous gesture, unbribed and uncorrupted. It saddened her to think she had uttered not one reassuring word to him that fateful night. Suddenly, she had no desire for the wine James had handed to her and wished she were a thousand miles from Bath.

'. . . so the garden and paddocks have passed to me, with full access as of old.' James had been speaking and was smiling, awaiting her reaction.

She stirred. 'I'm sorry, James. I missed what you were saying.'

'Hybullen, Prue. I've acquired several parcels of land which Reedpath conveyed to London personages in payment of gambling debts. Tenants are again in evidence, and gradually the wilderness of several summers is being cleared. I've left the main house locked and barred but have leased two of the lodge houses. Do you remember the Pickles family?'

'How could I forget them? They've served Hybullen for generations.'

'They're now in the East Lodge and I have retained them for stewardship over the house and grounds. The North Lodge escaped the damage wreaked by Reedpath. It could provide a habitation for us to oversee restoration of the main house – if it ever comes to that.'

'You've made real progress, James, far more than I expected. Is the carriage house intact?'

'Yes, but pitifully empty. I'll make that my next task. I intend to make frequent visits to Hybullen and for that I need equipage.'

Placing his empty glass upon a side table, he rose and crossed to the mantel. He rested his arm upon it and looked down at her. 'Vivian tells me that Lord Lydney has been paying court to you.' She felt the colour rise to her cheeks. He went on, 'I cannot permit it, Prue. There's a direct connection with our ruination in that family: Reedpath is his cousin.'

She nodded. 'Only last evening when we were being entertained by the dowager marchioness, Esmond disclosed it to me with anguish. I immediately left as the situation became grossly untenable.' She shivered as if cold, but her face burned. Lowering her head and her voice, she added, 'He will probably call when I shall tell him I've no wish to continue the friendship.'

James said, 'You sacrificed yourself to employment after our downfall, allowing me to use our funds for a new direction in my life. I shall never forget that and once our status is re-established, I'll see you make a good marriage.'

She fidgeted, admitting to discomfiture at his words and sought to change the subject. 'And you? Does marriage feature in your plans?'

'No,' he said without hesitation. 'I vowed to abstain from social activities until I could offer more than a disinherited, disgruntled and dissociable clerk.'

'Dissociable?'

'I've made myself so.'

'Now I understand why you appear as you do. While in Bath could you not indulge yourself a little? You have good looks, James, and could be a raging success.'

'I've neither the will nor the reason to indulge myself.' He paused, lowering his eyes. 'You think I need refurbishment as well as Hybullen?'

She smiled, but she was struck by the irony that she had been well placed for a marriage undreamed-of, had fickle coincidence deemed otherwise.

As if reading her thoughts, James said softly, 'Lydney's cousin is well acknowledged as the blot on the escutcheon. This I can swallow, with reservations. But, dammit, I can't abide the thought of his *brother*. A little nearer home, wouldn't you think? He's been Reedpath's companion for years and is in America with him. Father was their prisoner and they forced him to gamble until all was lost.'

She looked up, startled at this turn in the conversation. 'A brother?'

'The Lord Cedric Aumerle, younger brother of Lydney.'

'Oh, I didn't know. . . .'

She was shocked, taken aback. Esmond had not mentioned his brother. Why had he not told her last night that his brother was Reedpath's associate? Esmond had been less than honest with her. My withdrawal was well justified, she reasoned.

Conscious of her quickening breath she rose abruptly and moved to the window. She wondered what other truths were lurking in the obscurity of Esmond's connections. Perhaps he was not as guiltless as he claimed. In her rejection of him, she felt she had drawn back from a precipice.

That evening, Lord Dartree sent his carriage to bring them to The White Hart. He received them in the hall and led the way to a private supper chamber, quiet and intimate, isolated from the hubbub in the public rooms. A table was set, draped to the floor with a white cloth and dominated by a silver epergne laden with candied fruits.

The adornment of Dartree's coat, lawn stock and embroidered waistcoat verified his affluence. From James Prue had learned that Dartree had been early widowed and patronized English spa towns whenever he could leave his Irish estates.

Lady Wainflete, in striped silk and matching turban, was seated opposite to Prue. Throughout the meal she divided her attention with practised ease. Dear Lady Wainflete, thought Prue, how glad I am that you are here. She bestowed upon her an affectionate smile which was returned in good measure.

For the final dessert the cloth was removed, revealing the shining mahogany table upon which waiters placed sweetmeat glasses and dishes of comfits, nuts and fruit. Lord Dartree called for port, brandy and dessert wines to accompany these delicacies and, while James and Lady Wainflete chatted together, he moved his chair closer to Prue, leaning towards her as if to convey a secret. His wine-flavoured breath fanned her cheek.

'Bath is an excellent gathering place for those in a position to aid your brother.'

She turned to face him. 'I agree. James and I are very grateful for your support over all this time, My Lord.'

With an effulgent smile, he groped for her hand and placed it on the table, covering it with his own. 'Please, my name is Vivian. To me, in the years I have known James, you have always been Prudence.'

She nodded briefly to signify acceptance of his proposed informality, then asked, 'Do you know these noble lords who have asked to meet James?'

'They are friends I've consorted with for some time in order to bring this about.' Levelling his gaze to hers, he continued, 'I was almost a victim of Reedpath's cheating but I rumbled his game. Waiters were in his pay and made coded comments as they satisfied Reedpath's appetite for drinks and tidbits while in play. Cease the drinks and tidbits, I demanded of the club managers, then see how he fares!' With this triumphant close, Dartree's face shone like a rosy moon.

'And was your theory proven?'

'Entirely. I escaped ruination.'

'But others didn't.'

'He changes tactics, my dear. But I hounded him and kept in touch with the noble lords to bring about his downfall.'

'But then he fled to America.'

'Before I could complete my findings.'

Prue sighed. Her hand had become hot under his and she quietly withdrew it, saying, 'Now I see why you are so willing to help us. I assume you are the mysterious means by which their lordships are kept informed even now.'

'Do not doubt it, Prudence. All these arrangements are by my initiative,' he whispered urgently, demanding her approbation.

He turned and reached for a silver dish. 'A sweet for the sweet,' he murmured, selecting with a flourish a sugared almond which he endeavoured to place between her lips. She averted her face and diverted his hand with a deft movement of her own, taking the almond and putting it in her reticule. He smiled, impudently engaging her eyes. 'You will permit me to escort you for the remainder of your stay in Bath, Prudence? My carriage is at your disposal.'

'That is most kind,' she said.

There was a phrase he had used which caught at her heart: 'for the remainder of your stay in Bath'. Was it so soon to be over? Part of her felt relief, a desire to leave Bath and to be again with Biddy at Andursley. To await – what? James and Vivian had satisfied her questions about Hybullen. It was Reedpath's imminent return to look for now. She thought of Esmond. The high emotion she had felt upon his revelation had filtered down into her need to say things left unsaid that should have been said. Whether this was to be pursued on the basis of blame or reassurance rested upon the conduct of her next meeting with Esmond, an event she anticipated with a feeling of dread. But it had to be faced, there must be a conclusion, she thought sadly.

She started as Vivian's toe pressed upon hers under the table. He was flirtatious. She had marked his optative eyes and lingering glances at the swell of her bosom. But she was reluctant to fault him. His commitment had been central to James's success so far, and obviously he was still the principal informant to their lordships.

Lady Wainflete rose and beckoned to Prue. 'Permit us to withdraw for a short space, gentlemen,' she said. James and Vivian murmured assent.

She led Prue to a mirrored room set aside for ladies. Lady Wainflete snapped open her fan and offered Prue a vial of rosewater. 'It's too hot with all those wax lights in that small room. Dampen your temples with this, Prue.'

Prue thanked her. In removing a kerchief from her reticule, she saw the sugared almond she had placed there and popped it into her mouth. She dabbed rose-water on her kerchief and returned the vial to Lady Wainflete. 'I should tell you that Vivian has offered to escort me for the rest of my stay.'

'Oh.' There was a silence as Lady Wainflete furiously worked her fan. Closing it with quiet deliberation, she said, 'He tells me he has applied for tickets to a grand concert in the Upper Rooms. It's doubtful he'll be successful. It has been fully booked for some time. I bought tickets for us weeks ago, so I hope you'll join me and the Glenisters. It shouldn't be missed.'

'Yes, I'd love to,' said Prue. She was not disposed to decline such opportunities. Biddy's cautionary words came to her mind, '. . . *accept everything that's arranged with an open heart*'.

She linked arms with Lady Wainflete to return to the gentlemen. Suddenly, Prue broke away. 'Oh,' she spluttered, with a grimace. 'Excuse me, Lady Wainflete, this sugared almond is very bitter. . . .' Discreetly she discarded the offensive confection in her kerchief and added, 'Vivian gave me that sweetmeat and it's left a most unpleasant taste in my mouth.'

Chapter 13

IT WAS a morning of maddening winds. Prue watched the hurtling clouds and tossing trees from the bay window in the music-room. The house was quiet. Lady Wainflete was at the Pump Room taking the waters with Lady Glenister, and James had left to spend the day with the three noble lords of the gambling clubs. Prue welcomed the solitude. She opened the piano, gazing at a vase aglow with Esmond's roses. Few surfaces in the rooms of Daniel Street were free of their display. They were beautiful, and the message clear. But she wished they would cease.

As the days passed she had become nervous and jumped at every sound. When would Esmond come? Would he come at all? The thought that he might not, disturbed her. Yet she dreaded his appearance and possible confrontation with James. This very morning would be suitable, she thought, and this very instant a perfect time. Sighing, she made the piano keys chirrup by running her fingers across them. Suddenly her eyes were drawn to the opening door. Esmond stood on the threshold alone and unannounced. He had arrived at the perfect time.

Her eyes widened in surprise while her heart gave a bounce. He was hatless. A heavy grey, triple-caped coat draped as a cloak over his shoulders. He did not approach her, but slipped a smile as if unsure of his reception.

She swallowed. 'I'm glad you're here for we've matters to resolve.' There was an absence of formal greeting in her words and her voice sounded croaky and unsure. She was stupefied by his sudden appearance.

He spread his arms to indicate his apparel. 'Mostyn wished to relieve me of my coat, but as I persuaded him that my visit was to be brief, he allowed me upstairs to see you.' His smile broadened. 'I promised I would keep the door open.'

She started, 'Esmond—'

He held up a hand. 'Allow me to speak, Prue, as there's a certain urgency. To convince you and Sir James of my support in your cause, I shall go to America to find Reedpath and entice him back to the jurisdiction. I plan to sail on the *Lydney Amelia* in a few weeks from now.'

She gulped. 'And your brother? Shall you entice him back to the jurisdiction?'

He frowned. 'My brother?'

'Your brother who has been Reedpath's associate in his crimes and is also in America.'

His expression hardened. 'There is no evidence that my brother is a cheat. Reedpath ruined your father and it is he who shall answer.'

She traced a pattern on the carpet with her toe. 'You did not tell me of your brother, Esmond.'

'It had no relevance to the purpose of our talk.' He paused, regarding her closely. 'Then you are not impressed by my plan to go to America? Doesn't it give you hope that you may yet see Reedpath brought to justice?'

She nodded. 'There are others on his trail.'

He shrugged. 'That may be. But I have the competence and impulsion to do it. The competence rests in my ship. And the impelling force? Need you ask?'

She hung her head. She had rehearsed all she wished to say to him but her arguments lost strength and appeared merely petulant. Finally she said, 'But you cannot deny that you have fought duels and arranged settlements for the sole purpose of appeasing Reedpath's victims.'

At this he shook his head. 'Appeasement! Do you believe that is the reason for my pursuit of you? I am amazed.' He stepped closer and tipped his forefinger under her chin. His eyes coursed her raised face. 'How I wish your pretty mouth would say pretty words and dispense with your suspicions. It was a coincidence, Prue, that brought us together – and saved my life.'

Esmond took her hand and kissed it. She quickly withdrew and turned from him. He dogged her and sought to engage her eyes. 'Look!' he demanded. 'Look at me! Am I like Reedpath? Is there any resemblance at all? Isn't there a difference in his lust' – he dived to the floor on one knee and pressed the flounce of her dress to his lips – 'and my worship of you?' He rose slowly to face her, his face deadly pale. 'You blame me for his criminality!'

Startled by his action and the fury in his voice, she said with a sob, 'I blame you, as head of your family, for agreeing to his exile and covering up his crimes.'

He left her side and stood with arms akimbo at the window. There was a strained silence until he turned to her. 'I am ending his exile. I hope for his banishment when there will be no need to cover his crimes. By these actions I risk all.'

Tears stood in her eyes. 'I'm mindful of the effect on others in your family.'

'My mother has been made aware of everything and I have her support. I shall be away for many months.'

'Oh,' she sighed. 'I hope it meets with success.'

He approached her again. Softly he said, 'Let us not part like this. Please allow me the honour of escorting you to Lady Glenister's soirée?'

She turned away in an effort to compose herself before answering. 'That will not be possible. My brother is here and I'm committed to Lord Dartree for social occasions while in Bath.'

Esmond stiffened and drew back. Everyone except himself seemed set to enjoy Prue's company in Bath. Lord Dartree's participation roused frantic jealousy, a sensation new to him. He saw the pit yawning before him. It was as if a demon possessed him. 'Perhaps I think there are certain devoirs—'

'You mean, duties?'

He nodded.

'Duties owed to you by me?' she asked.

He detected a rising register in her voice which should have given him pause, but he pressed the point. 'How did you come to be here? Ask yourself that question.'

'I was invited to stay by Lady Wainflete.'

'At my behest, Prue. At my behest.'

She stared at him in astonishment.

'I wanted you to be free of Andursley and the humiliation you were subjected to.'

'Do you not think I am humiliated at this moment?'

Ignoring this, he blundered on, 'Lady Wainflete wanted to invite you to Florence, but I insisted she invite you to Bath. We arranged your journey so that you would be safe and come to no harm—'

'Agnes, too?'

He nodded. 'Agnes, too.'

Her face aflame, she said, 'How dare you order my life! It's enough that my father was manipulated by your family! I think you had better leave.'

He was shattered. He had gone too far and could not unsay what he had said. There could be no further argument. He bowed briefly and left her. He took his hat from the hall table, rammed it upon his head and let himself out to the street. Enraged, he walked he knew not where until with slackened pace and temper he blamed himself. He had been prepared to offer marriage, a secret betrothal while he was away. But everything had gone awry. Anger and mistrust stalked them both.

What had he done! He had betrayed not only himself but Lady Wainflete! The wind savaged his coat as it flowed behind him like a following dark cloud.

Prue stared at the piano for what seemed an eternity, her body rigid. She stirred at the slamming of the front door. Esmond had gone, leaving her with rage in her heart. She felt bruised and a little sick, dazed by the hurt that had surfaced between them.

Slowly she left the music-room and retreated to her own apartment. She lay on the *chaise-longue* regarding her luxurious surroundings with disfavour. It was a mockery – she had been beguiled, enticed to Bath ostensibly by Lady Wainflete. She trembled, weeping silently until sleep overcame her.

She awoke with a start to find Clara at the door. 'The mistress is back and asks if you would join her, Miss Prudence.'

Prue blinked, frowning. She had no idea how long she had slept. She nodded to Clara who then withdrew. Prue rose, changed her gown, bathed her face and tidied her hair. She would tell Lady Wainflete that she knew the truth about her invitation. She could not uphold the pretence.

Calmly she walked down the stairs and joined Lady Wainflete who was studying invitation cards that had been delivered. 'So many soirées! We shall have to be selective.'

Clara entered and served cups of chocolate. To Prue she said, 'I've put out your twilled sarsenet dress for the theatre tonight.'

Prue nodded absently. She had forgotten about the theatre and, after the morning's drama, had no desire for more.

'Vivian will call for us,' said Lady Wainflete. 'I hope James will be back in time.'

As soon as Clara closed the door behind her, Prue said, 'Esmond called here earlier.'

Lady Wainflete looked surprised. 'Indeed? What passed between you?'

Prue sipped her chocolate. 'A very unpleasant scene.'

'I'm grieved to hear it.'

'Among other things, I learned of Esmond's part in my invitation to Bath. He revealed this in justification for what he called "devoirs" and I regarded as "obligations".'

There was a silence. Lady Wainflete said, 'He must have been under some strain to do so, for he knew the consequences should our plan become known.'

'I think I know what prompted it. He asked to escort me to Lady Glenister's soirée, but I told him I was committed to Lord

Dartree's attendance while in Bath.'

Lady Wainflete's cheeks burned scarlet. She shook her head sadly. 'Esmond was jealous and no wonder.'

'I have little sympathy for him,' said Prue coldly.

Lady Wainflete put her cup down with a clatter and came to sit on the arm of Prue's chair. 'There's more you should know, Prue. Esmond was honourable throughout. He was propelled by an attachment which he wished to pursue with a view to marriage. I know how you have suffered and it seemed to me that here was a way where you could regain your place in society through a love that might banish the bitterness in your commitment to retribution. His attention to the minutiae of your journey was evidence of a desire to protect you, even to the point of finding a travelling companion and his personal outrider accompanying you all the way.'

Prue fell silent. Lady Wainflete gently stroked her hair for some moments, then rose. 'I hope you're persuaded that I acted in your best interests. I'm sorry that other factors intruded which neither Esmond nor I could have foreseen.'

'Thank you, Lady Wainflete. I've one question to ask of you: was Agnes aware of her part in it?'

'No, she was not.'

'She's too good a friend to lose. She shall remain in ignorance.'

Remorseful, Prue recalled the ease and comfort she had enjoyed on her journey to Bath, the best rooms and service, and the company of Agnes. She now understood the reason for Esmond's anger and her attitude softened. Sadly she could do nothing to reassure him, knowing James would strongly object to any moves she might make to that end. She rose and held out her arms to Lady Wainflete. Embracing her, she whispered, 'I'm sorry for all my uncharitable thoughts, dear Lady Wainflete, ungrateful creature that I am. I've been unfair to him.'

Lady Wainflete returned her embrace and kissed her upon the forehead. Nero intruded between them with raised head and a plaintive mew. Prue took him up and cradled him. 'Nero, you're displaying signs of jealousy. It's been a common fault today.'

Later, Vivian arrived and was surprised at the absence of James. 'I thought he'd be coming to the theatre with us.'

'James is not very sociable, Vivian, and he'd employ the merest excuse to escape the theatre. But he has good reason, as you probably know,' said Prue.

'I do not know. Hence my comment.'

'He is with their lordships of the gambling clubs and has been so engaged all day.'

A frown passed over Vivian's brow which was immediately replaced by a lambent smile. 'Then it's to my advantage.' He stepped closer and clasped her hand. 'I shall have you to myself.'

'Not entirely,' said Prue, withdrawing her hand and turning as a swish of silk heralded the entrance of Lady Wainflete.

'I'll bide my time,' he said.

The carriages were jammed in Beaufort Place, a sign that the theatre was full. Vivian's box was well placed and though her companions leaned forward eagerly to catch every word of the dramatic presentations, Prue sank back in the shadows. Vivian was over-attentive to the point of annoyance, and she felt out of sorts. The morning's meeting with Esmond set the *coup de grâce* on her peace of mind. She fidgeted, anxious to return to the house to hear how James had fared.

Wine and cakes were served in the box during the interval. Before the raising of the curtain, Vivian remarked, 'I haven't seen Lord Lydney about the town since I met him at Sydney Gardens. I assume by his withdrawal from the scene that he failed in his mission, Prue.'

She frowned. 'His mission?'

'It's my view that you were sought out by Lydney as a means of persuading us to abandon our claims against his kinsmen.'

Lady Wainflete turned to face him. 'Then you are mistaken in that view. It was in my home, before Prue had arrived in Bath as my guest, that Lord Lydney discovered she was Prudence Mulcaster Smith. Her mother's portrait in the music-room was the key. Up to that time he had thought her to be plain Miss Smith, companion to the Lady Caroline Buckland at Andursley.'

Vivian's forehead shone in the meagre light. 'It could have been contrived on his part, Lady Wainflete.'

'Fudge!' exclaimed Lady Wainflete, 'And the manner of their meeting? Could that have been contrived, too? I don't think Lord Lydney is in league with highwaymen or has importuned my staff to provide details of the paintings in Daniel Street!'

Vivian was silenced by her outburst.

'Nothing on earth would persuade James to drop his claim, Vivian,' said Prue, softening Lady Wainflete's rebuke.

The curtains opened as Vivian groped for Prue's hand. It rested inert in his. She thought him a victim of hopes too high and fancies too prodigious.

After the theatre they returned to the ante-room at Daniel Street where Vivian joined them for a gin posset in the hope of seeing James when he returned. But as the hour advanced, he took his leave after arranging to escort them to Lady Glenister's soirée at the Guildhall on the morrow.

So soon as Vivian left, Prue and Lady Wainflete were startled by James's sudden appearance from within the house.

'I have been here for a while,' he said, pouring wine from the cooler. 'I heard your return but had matters to ponder and remained in my apartment to do so. Did you enjoy the theatre?'

'It was excellent,' enthused Lady Wainflete, but Prue declined to comment. Regarding him closely, she remarked, 'You appear more at ease after meeting their lordships. Are they near to effecting Reedpath's return?'

James smiled. 'A good day's work. I'm to meet with them again.' He stood by the mantel and took a sip from his wine. 'I've heard some surprising things which I'm not at liberty to divulge.'

The door opened and Mostyn entered with a salver on which was a sealed letter. 'This has just arrived, ma'am, with instructions to pass it immediately to Sir James.'

'Thank you, Mostyn,' said Lady Wainflete.

James took the letter and seated himself, carefully examining the seal as the manservant withdrew. 'A shield charged with three birds. Ravens, perhaps? Ah, I see the connection. *Le merle*, the blackbird. Lord Lydney is aware I'm here.'

James read the letter. Minutes ticked by. Having read the letter once, James read it again. Prue could contain her curiosity no longer. 'Does it please you?'

'Indeed it does. Let me summarize it for you. He writes that all his energy will be devoted to enticing his brother and Reedpath back to England to face charges, knowing this will bring disgrace upon his family. He believes his family already tainted by whispers and innuendo, which he begs me to quash until proven. He intends to take immediate and direct action by preparing to sail for New England on a Lydney ship once he has settled affairs in his marquessate.'

'Is there more?' asked Prue, her breath quickening.

'Yes,' he said, taking up the second sheet of the letter. 'He assures me of his sympathy at the turn in our fortunes and is ready not only to serve the cause of justice but also to aid in the restoration of Hybullen.'

There was a prolonged silence. James folded the letter and thrust it into an inner pocket of his coat. 'Dammit, he *is* honourable,' said he. 'I have a duty to show this to their lordships.'

'I applaud the action he contemplates,' said Lady Wainflete.

James nodded. 'One could speculate that there's proof of his own guiltlessness in the fact that he's willing to take such risks.'

'What do you mean by risks,' asked Prue.

'He will himself voyage to America on one of his ships being readied for the purpose. To my mind, at this time of year, that's a risk.'

Prue stared at him, her eyes wide with shock. Esmond had told her of his sailing plans only that morning. Blinded by anger she had not visualized the danger in this undertaking. She quailed at visions of mastless ships in mountainous seas. 'It's terrifying to contemplate,' she murmured. Surely Esmond must have expected her to voice such sentiments but, to her shame, the moment had passed in bitter accusation. Her apparent indifference was at variance with her innate compassion. The deeper meaning had escaped her, that he was prepared to risk the life she had saved.

James's voice suddenly interrupted her maudlin preoccuption. '. . . difficult to fathom his intentions.'

She stirred herself. 'I'm sorry, James, I lost what you were saying. Fathom whose intentions?'

'If you should see him, be circumspect in your dealings. Live up to your name, Prudence,' said James, finishing his wine and moving to withdraw.

'You mean, if I should see Esmond?'

'No,' came the surprising retort from the doorway, 'Vivian!'

Chapter 14

PRUE failed to gain enlightenment on James's obscure comment about Vivian. She argued that her questioning was justified since she was constantly in Vivian's company and thought him vital to their case. James sought to reassure her that nothing was amiss. But she harboured doubts.

That evening Vivian called to escort Prue and Lady Wainflete to the Glenister's soirée. Their coach joined a line of carriages waiting to set down guests at the Guildhall, and despite ushers holding flambeaux to give light and assistance, progress was irritatingly slow.

As they inched forward, Lady Wainflete said, 'I've heard that Esmond's mother has unexpectedly returned to her home at Clifton. She's cancelled sponsorship of her usual assembly and that's most unusual for Dora.'

'What can be the reason?' asked Prue. 'I hope it's not a matter of health.' She felt a stab of disquiet at the news.

'Apparently, the Aumerle aunts remain and if they are at the soirée, I shall enquire of them.'

'Perhaps she's sniffing family scandal and has gone to ground,' said Vivian.

'That's an indelicate supposition, Vivian,' said Prue. 'If anything, I should think her withdrawal is at Esmond's insistence rather than her own.'

Vivian said, 'For the same reason, no doubt.'

Prue did not comment and joined Lady Wainflete in staring from the window until the coach door was wrenched open and ushers stood ready to aid them.

After formal greetings from Lord and Lady Glenister, they entered the splendid banqueting room. How lovely it is, Prue thought, a privileged invitation. Yet, she felt ill-at-ease, silently critical of Vivian's extravagance in dress. She thought his purple stock and pantaloons ostentatious. He postured, angling for her praise, but she stepped ahead of him and linked arms with Lady Wainflete. She was happy when Agnes and Hubert joined them.

The room was thronged and the sound of music floated down from the gallery. Feathers tossed in the hair of the ladies, while gentlemen flaunted richly embroidered waistcoats. The musicians suddenly ceased the light music they were playing and performed a fanfare to herald the arrival of honoured guests. There was a buzz of expectation as the entrance was cleared to admit the Duke and Duchess of Landemere, the Marquess of Lydney with the Honourables Louise and Cicely Aumerle, and other *haute noblesse*.

Prue stared as Esmond entered, his tall figure in full dress of black, a solitary diamond in his white stock. In that flamboyant procession he was an outstanding example of the grace of understatement. How handsome he is, she thought, quite the most elegant gentleman present. Her heart beat wildly as she recalled his request to escort her to this function, but circumstances had made it impossible for her to accept. She felt a growing discomfiture and was glad of the crowd in front of her. She took refuge behind her fan. The procession passed. Before turning away, she saw Esmond surrounded by a dazzling company of young ladies. Her eyes sought Lady Wainflete, who shook her head despairingly.

'No roses came today, Prue.'

'Good,' said Prue, but the word belied her true feelings. Esmond troubled her heart's ease.

Barely an hour had passed when refreshments were served. Agnes and Hubert vanished in the crowds pressing about the tables and Lady Wainflete left Prue's side to seek the Aumerle aunts.

'What's your pleasure, Prue,' Vivian asked, propelling her to the refreshments.

She felt faint. 'Is there an ante-room, away from the crush?'

'I'll look for a place. But don't you wish for something, some wine, perhaps?'

She shook her head. 'It's too hot and crowded. But don't let me prevent you from taking some refreshment.'

'I will find somewhere where we may sit. Then we'll sip champagne.'

She nodded, and turned towards a niche in the wall. 'I'll await you here.'

She leaned back, fanning herself furiously. Her eyes searched for Lady Wairflete or Agnes, but she stilled her fan and held it to her face when some gentlemen concentrated their quizzing glasses upon her.. Turning away she almost confronted Esmond. He was approaching the refreshment tables with a beauty on each arm. She gasped as her heart twisted. Thankfully, he had not seen her. She could not face him. Not here. Not now.

She ventured back along the wall, looking vainly for a familiar face. Suddenly Vivian hailed her and she made her way to him. He led her to a small porters' hall lit only by a single candle. She seated herself on a shabby settle, relieved to be out of the banqueting room.

Vivian sat beside her, whereupon a footman appeared with a tray upon which was a flask of champagne. She did not demur as Vivian offered her a glass and, taking another for himself, dismissed the footman with a wave of his hand.

They sipped the champagne in silence. Then his lips brushed her ear and he whispered, 'Your response to my desire for intimacy is as unexpected as it is miraculous.'

Prue stiffened as he kissed her shoulder, and his arm that had been placed along the back of the settle dropped to encircle her waist. 'Vivian,' she said sternly, 'I do not welcome advances of this kind. I ask that you desist and allow me to finish my champagne. Please take your hand from me.'

He relaxed his grip on her waist, but raised his hand to her shoulder. She shrugged in an effort to shift it.

'Why are you resisting when you made it plain you wished to be alone with me?' he asked.

'I was overcome by the heat and pressure of people in the banqueting room. That should have been obvious to you.'

He sighed and withdrew his hand. There was a strained silence. To relieve the tension, she said, 'I think James is encouraged by their lordships' belief that Reedpath's return is imminent. By this time next year, we could be back at Hybullen.'

'That's very important to you, isn't it?'

'Of course,' she smiled. 'The restoration of stone and mortar will accompany a renaissance in our fortunes.'

'Provided that such restoration occurs.'

She looked at him. 'Have you any doubt, Vivian?'

He smiled. His eyes gleamed in the candlelight as he finished his champagne and placed the glass by the settle. He rose, adjusting his stock and smoothing his coat. He paced in front of her. 'Have you ever been to Almack's, Prue?'

She hesitated, puzzled by this turn in the conversation. She had been to Almack's but attending Caroline as her companion. 'No,' she said boldly. 'I have never been to Almack's.'

He nodded. 'When your social status is established, shall you be seeking a husband in such places? I think not,' he said, answering his own question.

She frowned. 'Why are you talking about my seeking a husband? It has nothing to do with Hybullen.'

'It has everything to do with Hybullen. Time has moved on, Prue. You are no longer a nubile candidate for the marital stakes in places such as Almack's. There's no fortune to tempt. The longer Hybullen remains unrestored, your chances become less.' She was stunned to silence. He ceased his pacing and stood in front of her. 'I may decide to delay presentation of certain facts that might prevent a successful conclusion to your case.'

'What are you saying, Vivian?' she breathed.

'Waiting for Hybullen is a waste of time. There is another way to ensure your status.' He suddenly raised her, dashed her glass to the floor and pulled her to him, his voice low and purring. 'You must marry me, Prue, and you'll immediately enjoy the social status to which you aspire. It's quicker than waiting for Hybullen.' His mouth crushed upon hers as she fought his wandering hands.

'Vivian!' she sputtered, pushing him from her.

He stood facing her, breathing heavily. 'Well, Prue. That's an offer to wed. What do you say to it?'

She bowed her head. Her mind raced. She recoiled at the thought of marriage with him but there had been a threat, that he could withhold information of value to them. Only James could assess the validity of such a threat. He had warned her, '. . . be circumspect.' Vivian was contemptible, posing options like a lesser Reedpath.

She calmed herself, smiled. 'I must speak with James before I answer you, Vivian. That's reasonable, isn't it?' Escape was in her mind as she added softly, 'He has probably returned to Daniel Street by now.'

His eyes glowed as he took her in his arms. 'Are you willing to leave immediately and seek his approval on our betrothal?'

She nodded, releasing herself. 'I'm ready for my cloak, Vivian.' She longed to be back in Daniel Street, away from Vivian, away from the Guildhall.

On the short coach journey to Daniel Street, she suffered his advances. Mostyn answered the door and said Sir James was out of town and not expected until the morrow. Relieved, Prue pleaded a headache and insisted upon retiring. He moved to embrace her but Mostyn hovered nearby. Instead, he kissed her hand, murmuring, 'My beautiful charmer, tomorrow we shall celebrate.' He left reluctantly without entering the house.

Prue asked Mostyn to bring a cup of chocolate to the ante-room where she would await Lady Wainflete. But the hour grew late. She wondered whether Vivian had returned to the Guildhall to bring Lady Wainflete home. Prue knew she should have mentioned this but her desire to depart from him had driven all else from her mind.

It was imperative that she see James before Vivian called the next morning. How could she avoid this man who had framed his proposal with such insolence? She trembled with pent-up anger at the thought of it, coupled with anxiety at Lady Wainflete's tardiness.

She heard the jingling of harness outside but dared not approach the window, supposing it was Vivian's carriage. She waited by the door. As Lady Wainflete entered, she fell into her arms. 'I've had such a terrible time at the soirée,' she whispered. 'I'm quite discomposed.'

'As am I,' snapped Lady Wainflete, disengaging herself. 'I'm not accustomed to being taken to a soirée with no means to leave it. Is there to be any function, Prue, where you will stay to the end? I could not find you anywhere. What happened?'

By the time Prue had concluded her account, Lady Wainflete's ill temper had been replaced by sympathetic concern. 'James must be told of Vivian's atrocious behaviour,' she said.

She rang for Mostyn. 'Please bring us two gin possets, Mostyn, and make them as strong as you dare.' She turned to Prue. 'A posset will calm you and aid sleep.'

'Did you talk with the Aumerle aunts?' asked Prue.

Lady Wainflete nodded. 'It appears that Melodon is to be closed next week for the rest of the season. It coincides with Esmond's departure for Bristol.'

So soon! Prue's heart died a little death as the image of Esmond flashed before her. She lapsed into dreamy speculation as to how different the soirée could have been in his company.

Mostyn entered and served the possets.

Taking up her glass, Prue asked, 'Who was kind enough to bring you from the Guildhall, Lady Wainflete?'

'Esmond,' was the short reply.

Prue ached to know what had passed during Lady Wainflete's journey home with Esmond but, observing her weariness, bade her an affectionate good night.

Vivian's barbs about her age caused Prue to devote an unusually long time to her toilette the next morning. Lady Wainflete and Clara were in attendance, full of reassurances about her exquisite features, *belle tournure* and unimpaired complexion.

'You outshine all those silly young gels in grace and intelligence,' said Lady Wainflete. 'Vivian is incapable of recognizing those qualities, let alone pay court to them.' She paused, cupping Prue's face in her hands. 'From the first, I didn't approve of him, Prue. There's something about him. . . .'

Prue smiled. 'It's clear where your preferences lie.'

She hoped that Lady Wainflete might reveal more about her ride home with Esmond last night, but Clara approached with a pale-green muslin dress. 'For this morning, Miss Prudence?'

'An excellent choice, Clara.'

Going downstairs, Prue realized James had not yet returned. She was unwilling to receive Vivian until she had spoken with James and the ensuing hours were spent peeping from the ante-room windows to watch for arrivals. A lone rider came into view and entered Lady Wainflete's carriage house. The black bicorn identified James. With relief, Prue took a shawl and rushed outside to meet him.

He had dismounted and she waited while a groom took his horse to a stall. Then she walked with James through the back entrance to the house and accompanied him upstairs to his apartment. There he kissed her lightly, dumped a satchel he had been carrying, and flung himself into a chair. He drew breath then puffed out his cheeks.

'Phew! It wasn't pistols at dawn, but I was prepared for it. Vivian Mallory, Earl of Dartree, is leaving Bath immediately under whip and spur. He'll not be calling here again!'

Prue, ready to condemn Vivian in the strongest terms, was struck dumb. She sank onto the bed facing James.

His eyes were bright with anger. He continued, 'Last night I was the guest of Lord Beddington at Charlcombe, where we were joined by Lord Owlsbury and Viscount Eades. Since meeting these gentlemen and learning of their moves against Reedpath, it became clear that Vivian's evidence and witnesses were fakes. Their lordships denied all knowledge of him. I made enquiries, and this morning challenged Vivian at The White Hart. He is not a belted earl, there are no castles in Ireland. He is an out-of-work actor who seeks aggrandisement by applying theatrical fantasies to reality. Not only this, but his source of wealth is highly suspect and worthy of investigation. *Ergo* I shall expose him if he has not left Bath within the hour.'

'He – he offered for me . . .' she said in a daze.

'What audacity! I hope you rejected him with all vehemence, Prue.'

'I withheld before seeing you, as he threatened impairment to our case—'

He leapt up, grabbing his satchel, his face aflame. 'Then it *shall* be pistols!'

'No!' she cried. 'I do not desire vindication against a man of straw such as he. Let him be.'

She shuddered, and he took her hands. 'No man shall have my precious sister as an ornament to his vanity.'

She smiled, sighing deeply. 'I feel a weight has lifted from my mind.'

He kissed her forehead. 'Prue, this meticulous investigation against Reedpath is proceeding apace. Their lordships assure me the net is closing.'

'You have done well, James.' She moved to the door. 'And thank you for vanquishing Vivian.'

'I should mention that their lordships are full of praise for Lydney. I showed them his letter. More than that I cannot reveal.'

She heard this with pleasure, having already decided to approach Esmond should she see him or, if not, to write him a note.

Every moment since his quarrel with Prue had been misery for Esmond. Moody and melancholy, he had attended a few functions and taken in a conversazione with Mr Wilberforce. Despite impatience to start his search for Reedpath, he cursed his foolishness in undertaking such a commitment! It had seemed so simple. As prime owner and ship broker, the choicest ships were at his disposal. He had been drawn by honour into a journey full of ambiguities.

Often he awoke in the night, thinking of Prue, marvelling at their meeting on the road to Whitchurch. That was barely two months ago, two months since he had felt a restless need at the thought of her. She had charmed him utterly. He must speak with her before he left and make matters right between them.

His approach required careful planning as to timing and occasion. From the hint dropped by Lady Wainflete when he brought her from the Glenisters' soirée, he judged the Assembly Rooms to be the perfect venue. She mentioned she would be there for the grand concert in company with Prue.

Bella Verity invited Esmond to join her party for the concert, which he was pleased to accept since it imposed no strict obligation upon him. Dancing was to follow. He was determined to make plain his intentions to Prue and all present by partnering her for the first two dances of the evening.

He dressed carefully for the event, wearing his full black evening suit. His coach was waiting and he left immediately, thinking it advantageous to be early.

A large company had gathered in the elegant ante-chamber. As Esmond entered, the doors to the Concert Hall opened and all filed through. A hand sought his. It was Bella, leading him to the block of seats she had reserved. He was directed to a chair at the end of the first row of the auditorium. He stood for a moment, looking back hopefully for a glimpse of Prue and Lady Wainflete but failed to see them in the confusion of those seeking their places. He sighed and took up a programme that Bella had placed on his chair. He was indifferent to the musical offerings being discussed by all around him. Primarily, he was here to speak with Prue. But studying the programme, he identified the most exciting item as Ludwig van Beethoven's Piano Sonata *Quasi una Fantasia*,[1] to be performed by Beidermann, a pupil of the Master.

[1] Known in mid-century as the 'Moonlight' Sonata.

164

The concert started with a string quartet playing Mozart and it was not until the sonata began that he saw Prue. He had raised his eyes beyond the hunched figure of the pianist. She was in full view at the end of the row in which he was seated, which curved in an arc so that she was directly opposite him.

She appeared to him in a roseate glow, her black hair studded with brilliants. He held his breath in a conscious look at her. He had never seen her so captivating. His eyes took possession of her with unrelenting intensity. The *adagio* promoted the most potent messages, whispered phrases, a question and gentle chord in answer. She was staring at him, leaning her head upon her hand, lips parted in a half-smile of private rapture. God! she felt it, too, the echo of avowals fiercely sweet. Anguish was expressed in a run of notes, a sort of dialogue tenderly delivered. There were silences alive with emotion as he locked her eyes to his with a deep penetrating look to banish all doubt. The delicious snatched moments with her he saw again in a melodic parade. With the *allegretto* came a racing demand and response, a galloping affirmation.

Prue had been anticipating the Bath debut of Beidermann with excitement. Confidence bloomed with her release from the cloying presence of Dartree. She felt light-hearted, determined to enjoy the concert and dancing to the full.

The first notes of the sonata took command of her. Her eyes were drawn to other eyes that held her with a strange magnetism so that she was unable to glance away. She savoured Esmond's concentration and felt a radiance coursing through her. The music evoked a subtle, sweet unfolding of love for him. The sonata had nearly run its course. It had touched the extremes.

Suddenly there was an intrusion. A white-haired gentleman entered from a side-door and tiptoed to Esmond's chair. A message was whispered, whereupon Esmond rose and quietly accompanied the gentleman in leaving the Concert Hall. Prue's eyes followed Esmond to the main door. It was a jarring note, so brutal a departure. She played a game upon herself. If he should look back with one more love-warmed glance before he vanished through the portals, she would throw propriety to the winds and follow him to Bristol. But he did not look back.

The sonata came to an end. The audience rose in an uproar of adulation for the piece and the pianist. Prue felt she had awoken from a dream as a pleasurable numbness suffused her. She sensed a common feeling of devastation with Esmond, that the whispered message was of such profound importance that he was forced to break the spell. She trembled and felt herself handfasted, her fate sealed and rendered to him. He had assumed domination of her heart.

Lady Wainflete gasped, 'What an experience, Prue!'

Prue nodded, but that which had passed between her and Esmond would lose in the telling. She nurtured it within herself.

Esmond, with Viscount Eades in the deserted ante-chamber, despatched a footman for his cloak. He stood listening closely to the viscount until the footman returned. Fastening his cloak about him, he stepped quickly back to the Concert Hall in the hope of seeing Prue once more. But she was hidden from him. All present were on their feet, the auditorium reverberating with sustained thunderous applause.

He would write to her with urgency. He left with the utmost regret but a feeling of exultation remained strong within him. There was no denying the romantic interlude which had blossomed between them in the playing of the sonata. Wild horses could not have driven him from it. Only a summons so irresistible, so vital to them both, caused his peremptory withdrawal: 'Come, Reedpath is back!'

Chapter 15

Esmond parted with Viscount Eades outside the Assembly Rooms, found his coach, and returned to Melodon. There he changed and ordered the readying of Tom's bay for his own use. After some errands in the town he swung into the saddle, clapped spurs to his horse, and was gone – a flying shadow on the road to Charlcombe.

'Reedpath is back!' He was bemused by that whispered summons from Viscount Eades. Esmond had left the Concert Hall like an automaton, aware that something had happened in the aching notes of the sonata. He only knew he directed his eyes to Prue's and she had held them, sharing the sweet fever that fills with longing.

As the bay's hooves scudded the road, his mind reeled with relief that he had been spared his undertaking in the nick of time. The *Lydney Amelia*, now lying ready in his wet dock, was destined to sail without him.

Viscount Eades's instructions were to leave immediately for Lord Beddington's house at Charlcombe, where his associates from the London gambling clubs were refining plans for Reedpath's arrest. More than this Esmond did not know. As he neared Charlcombe his anxieties increased. Was he to be party to the arrest of his brother as well?

He kept up the strong pace until he slowed in response to a swinging lantern. A gatekeeper beckoned him up a drive to a lighted porch. A groom took charge of his horse as Viscount Eades came from the house to meet him. He was escorted to a book-lined study.

The saturnine Lord Beddington rose from behind a desk. 'My Lord Marquess, you are most welcome. Sir James Mulcaster Smith has acquainted us with the content of the letter you wrote to him. You may think that is the reason for this meeting, but you would be in error.'

Esmond inclined his head. 'Indeed, My Lord. Then I am burning with curiosity as to why I have been called here.'

Lord Beddington smiled. 'Come to the billiard-room. There is a gentleman there you must meet without delay.'

Viscount Eades and Lord Beddington led the way to a room downstairs. Esmond was momentarily blinded by Argand lamps suspended above the green baize of a billiard table. Two shadowy figures moved at play. One executed a long shot, scoring a double winning hazard. His opponent groaned in part-envy and part-dismay. 'A fluke!' he claimed, indicating the wall marker. 'I think this game is yours, My Lord!'

There was a familiar timbre to the voice. The young gentleman replaced his cue. Esmond stared in astonishment. Then he quickly strode towards him, grasping the lapels of his waistcoat and looking into his face. ' 'Pon my soul! It's really you, Cedric! I'd recognize that straw-coloured mop of yours anywhere.'

They hugged each other, laughing with delight.

Their lordships shared their joy. Champagne was brought in, and a toast proposed by Lord Beddington. 'To you, Cedric, welcome back, and our gratitude for all you've done!'

They sipped the champagne. Lord Beddington lowered his glass. 'By way of explanation, My Lord, your brother has been our appointee for some years. It is thanks to him that we have sufficient proof of Reedpath's systems to satisfy any proceedings in a Court of Law. We three shall withdraw. You will have much to relate to each other. It is an honour and a pleasure to welcome you both to my house.' He indicated a bell pull. 'Ring for anything you need.'

Esmond regarded his brother. 'Cedric, you are a key to many things. I wholeheartedly welcome you to these shores because you have come to me instead of I to you.'

Cedric smiled, took his coat from a hook and put it on. 'I reached here only this morning, and must confer with you on a highly important matter. It will mean leaving for Bristol with all speed.'

'Bristol?'

Cedric nodded. 'But first, tell me about Mother. Is she well? And where can she be found at this moment?'

'She's in good health and at Clifton. She'll be relieved you're here.'

'I'll call on her at the earliest opportunity.'

'Now tell me about Clancy,' said Esmond, seating himself in a leather chair by the fire.

Cedric lifted his coat tails and sat on an upright chair beside him. 'Where to start? As you heard from Lord Beddington, I have been their lordships' agent all this time. This knowledge is given you as my trusted brother and secrecy must be observed.'

Esmond held up a hand. 'Cedric, I must ask you a question that is vital to our future. You've been Clancy's companion for some years. Have you ever participated in his fraudulent gambling schemes, or aided in their perpetration?'

Cedric rose and stood by the fireplace, looking down at the rising flames. His eyes were hard in the reflected firelight. 'No,' he said firmly. He turned and looked directly at Esmond. 'I repeat, no. The noble lords are my proof.'

Esmond nodded. 'By chance of fate, I'm committed to obtaining satisfaction from Clancy on behalf of a very special party.'

Cedric shook his head. 'There are so many,' he said quietly, 'and I'm aware of them all.'

'How did you arrive here, and where is Clancy?'

'I sailed home with him on a big American square-rigger, the *Providence* out of New Orleans. She's loaded with Louisiana cotton, probably worth three or four thousand guineas. I left

Clancy on board sick with terror from the storms we encountered. He's a bad sailor and remained below decks for the entire voyage.'

'Where's the *Providence* now?'

'She was too deeply laden to pass up the Avon so she's at a place called Hungroads for lightening.'

Esmond frowned. 'Why the Avon? Why Bristol? Surely Liverpool would have been more appropriate for such a cargo.'

Cedric smiled. 'A logical question, but there's more to tell.' He paused. 'Clancy is the sole owner of the vessel.'

'Clancy the owner! How did he acquire it!'

'By dubious means, of course. He met a planter in New Orleans, his equal as a gambling braggart. A huge debt accrued to Clancy. He was offered the plantation or the ship and cargo. He chose the ship to escape from other pressing matters. It was the opportunity I'd been waiting for. Here was a moveable asset. Contracts were cancelled as soon as the ship changed hands so he was blocked in converting the cotton to cash. He wants to sell the ship and its cargo. Most American cotton goes to Lancashire but I persuaded him to use Bristol. That's why we must make sure this asset is held in your wet dock in Bristol.'

Esmond rose from his chair, recognizing the opportunity presented. 'We've got him, Cedric! We should lose no time in securing the *Providence*.'

'Their lordships are leaving immediately to alert the constable there.'

Esmond paced before the fireplace. 'Captain Roper will engage a pilot and crew to confine the *Providence* to an inner berth in our wet dock. He must see that one of our ships is tied up alongside so that she cannot leave. Mr Bennet will handle the formalities. Well done, Cedric.'

'I have the ship's papers with me. I'll bring them for your inspection.'

'We must ensure there are no irregularities as regards ownership,' said Esmond, as Cedric quickly left the room.

Esmond ceased pacing and stood with his back to the fire, elated at the turn of events. The *Providence* was well-named. Everything had radically, changed. He was again in control.

Cedric returned and handed a leatherbound box to Esmond. 'All the ship's papers are there. Clancy agreed I should take them as he thought I had a purchaser in mind. I could not disclose the nature of the disposal we contemplate.'

Esmond took the box and settled again in the chair. 'This isn't a direct change of subject, Cedric, but I have fallen in love with a young lady and wish to marry her.'

Cedric stared. Then a smile lightened his face. 'Not you, dear brother! The notorious "twice-only" man!'

Esmond ignored the bantering. 'I was not seriously concerned with Clancy's activities until I met her. She, with her brother, has suffered ruination through Clancy's cheating of their father.'

'Her name?'

'Prudence Mulcaster Smith.'

'The Mulcaster Smith case is often cited by their lordships. It precipitated concern for the reputation of their establishments.'

'Prue and her brother would have legitimate claims upon any funds recovered from Clancy. Their lordships must be acquainted with that possibility.'

There was a pause. 'The young lady is obviously not rich. Is she handsome, Esmond?'

'You shall judge for yourself. I hope a formal announcement will be made at our annual ball.'

Cedric reached for his hand and shook it warmly. 'I'm happy for you and will have the greatest pleasure in meeting your Prudence. It's strange, but Clancy also has a secret love. I think it was why he risked everything to come back. He spoke of her on occasion, but I didn't gain the impression his amours were reciprocated.'

Esmond laughed. 'That's no surprise.'

He opened the box of ship's papers. As he examined a large wad something small and shining fell to the floor.

Cedric picked it up. 'No wonder Clancy couldn't forget the love of his life. This must be a miniature of her. A girl, so very beautiful,' he said, handing it to Esmond.

Esmond stared at the young face of Prue. His jaw tensed in shock, his eyes darkened. 'This is *my* Prudence, Cedric. The miniature is obviously loot from Hybullen House.'

There was a silence. 'Is it possible that Clancy knows her whereabouts?' asked Cedric.

'Heaven forbid!' Esmond exclaimed, thinking of Prue safe in Bath with Lady Wainflete. But was she safe? He rose quickly to his feet. His heart raced as he thought of her. When the *Providence* was secure and the business in Bristol done, he would return to her in Daniel Street to make good his offer of marriage.

'I'll take charge of this,' he said. He took the miniature, placing it in an inner pocket on the left-hand side of his coat and held it close to his heart.

After Esmond withdrew from the Concert Hall, a brightness dimmed for Prue but left a glow within her. The sonata had expressed something felt, longing and exultation, a heady reconcilement.

Prue stayed for the dancing to please Lady Wainflete. She looked constantly for the reappearance of Esmond, but resigned herself to thinking he had been called to Bristol. Her spirit plummeted in contemplating the many months he would be away and the risks to which he was exposed.

In the following days she could raise no enjoyment in walks and shopping excursions with Agnes, and viewed with dread the assemblies so dear to Lady Wainflete. The grey void of Esmond's absence imposed itself strongly upon her in Bath. Her instinct told her to remove herself in order to escape it and she suddenly felt a desire to return to Andursley. She wondered about Caroline and longed to see Biddy again. Best to await developments at Andursley, she thought, where duties would engage her mind.

The music-room, dominated by the portrait of her mother, became a retreat. Although it reminded her of the bitter scene with

Esmond, the image that persisted was of him at her feet, kissing the flounce of her dress. This had become a cherished moment which she relived again and again.

James joined her there for coffee while she completed ruching velvet over a bonnet form. 'Bath is indeed a pleasant place,' he said, 'but I feel all spa towns and watering places share that gentility, one being the same as another. That is why I hope you won't mind too much in changing your abode to Harrogate, Prue.'

'I have no plans to go to Harrogate, James.'

'Then shall you remain with Lady Wainflete and go to Florence with her?'

'I intend to return to Andursley.'

'But there is no need for you to pursue employment there or anywhere else, Prue.'

'The countess will expect me and—'

'There's no need. Developments at Hybullen have some bearing upon my insistence.'

'How so?'

'The cottages were made ready and tenants installed. I have funds for you, being your allowance retrospective to the date of the new tenancies. I repeat, there's no need for you to continue your employment at Andursley. Come back with me to Harrogate.'

She shook her head. 'I must return to Andursley. I gave an undertaking to the countess. There are friends I must see, and some possessions which I should retrieve.'

He sighed and seated himself beside her. 'What do you wish me to do about your funds?'

'Hold them for me. I'll not need money at Andursley, but the reinstatement of my allowance grants me a welcome independence.'

'I wish it were otherwise, for then you would be obliged to come to Harrogate with me.'

She smiled. 'I'm not so imbued with independence that I cannot ask to accompany you on the stage to London. When do you propose to leave?'

'Our London attorneys wish to see me so I shall be boarding the stage the day after the morrow. Do you intend to leave that soon?'

Having made the decision, she did not wish to delay her departure. She held the unfinished bonnet at arm's length, balancing it upon her index finger. Gently spinning it, she said, 'I shall be ready when the ties are stitched to this.'

'So soon?'

'Yes. We'll travel together to Newbury, where I must leave you. The coach to Whitchurch leaves from there and the shopping coach will deliver me to Andursley.'

'I don't like to think of you travelling alone for part of the journey. Allow me to go with you the whole distance to Andursley.'

'And have you incur delay in your London meetings! No, James.'

'Then I shall see you aboard the Whitchurch coach even if it means a stay at Newbury for me. At least grant me that.'

She nodded in agreement. Now to confront Lady Wainflete. She must decline her offer to bestow her in Bath and Florence, and stress her desire to return to Andursley.

She sewed the last riband to the bonnet. Satisfied, she snipped the thread.

Prue sat with Lady Wainflete by a window in The Lamb. They were watching James and the porters in the yard dealing with their baggage.

Lady Wainflete linked arms with Prue, drawing her close. 'Suppose Esmond comes to call. Shall I tell him you are at Andursley?'

'It's most unlikely he'll call. Agnes and I walked by Melodon the other day. The house is firmly closed. I fear he must have embarked on his voyage to America.'

Lady Wainflete sighed. 'If I hear to the contrary, Prue, I'll let you know. But be assured you'll be welcome whenever you wish to return. There will always be a place for you with me, be it in Bath or Florence.'

Prue kissed her cheek. 'Dear Lady Wainflete, you are a refuge for James and me. Words fail in expressing my gratitude. You are much loved by us both.'

There was a silence. Then Lady Wainflete whispered, 'I'm aware that the sonata lived up to its name – *Quasi una Fantasia*.'

Prue faced her. 'You mean, you saw. . . .'

Lady Wainflete nodded. 'It shall remain our secret.'

Prue kissed her again. 'It will help me endure his absence.'

'Esmond spoke long with me on the night of the Glenisters' soirée. Everything will happen for the best, Prue.'

Prue took comfort from the platitude. They rose on seeing the coach enter the yard and walked quickly outside in response to James's furious beckoning. 'Come, I've secured a corner seat for you,' he called.

Farewells were purposely brief. Crammed full, the coach clattered from the yard, and jingled and jolted its way eastward. But James grew impatient at the slow pace.

The overnight stay at The Castle in Marlborough passed pleasantly enough. Passengers from several coaches crowded the taproom. James assisted Prue to a settle and ordered a quartern of rum for himself and a posset for Prue.

'Would that we had our own equipage,' James grumbled. 'I'm losing my taste for public conveyances. As things improve at Hybullen, I should make more visits and shall seek a diligence of sorts.'

'Patience, James. You've achieved wonders.'

The racket stumped converse and for a time they sat silently sipping their drinks. Then James bent to her ear. 'God grant your marquess success in his endeavours,' he whispered. 'We have all to gain and he to lose. I admit to a grudging admiration for his action.' He took another sip of rum. 'Reedpath is a lost cause, and this I can stomach. My objection to Lydney's wooing of you rests on the behaviour of his brother. But we'll soon know the truth of it.'

She sat back, surprised at his words, and admitted to a feeling of warmth that James might be moderating his opinion of Esmond. 'I have reason to believe he has started his journey, James,' she said.

'That makes my visit to London the more timely.' He sat still, then added. 'These events were set in train by acts of weakness in both our families.'

She frowned. Was it possible that James felt responsible for all the attendant dangers in forcing Esmond to act? She placed a hand on his arm. 'That is true, and it follows that neither you nor he is to blame.'

He nodded and was silent. Then he rose, assisting her to her feet. 'But there was criminality,' he said.

Alone in her room she sat by a solitary candle, wondering where Esmond was at this moment. Her memory touched upon the music of the sonata. It was like a gift of mind, mysterious and overwhelming. A sadness came at the thought of bidding farewell to James on the morrow. All was in flux, nothing resolved. She wondered, would there ever be settled and happier times for her?

The journey to Newbury was direct and uneventful. All in the coach were silent, absorbed in thought, and Prue was glad of the diversion as they drove through the thronged thoroughfares of the town. At The Pelican, where she thought fondly of Agnes, the coach to Whitchurch had arrived from Oxford. Passengers were already seated and they were obliged to hasten the unloading of Prue's boxes and portmanteau.

James took her hands in his. 'You'll be first to know of any developments even if I have to bring the news to Andursley myself.' He drew her towards him. 'Dearest girl, have faith.'

She freed her hands to embrace him. 'Dear James. I shall long to see you again, whatever happens.'

He smiled, then indicated the appearance of the coachman. 'Come, you should take your seat.'

The doors slammed shut, the coachman cracked his whip and they rattled under the archway of the tavern. She looked back and glimpsed James's tall figure standing motionless in the hubbub of the yard as the coach turned south on the road to Whitchurch.

Prue was glad she had changed into her lace cap and grey cloak on leaving Marlborough as Mrs Figgis of The White Hart recognized her immediately. 'Miss Smith! What a pleasure to see you again. Did you have a pleasant stay in Bath?'

'Indeed I did, Mrs Figgis. Have you a room for me? And if so, could you serve me a meal there this evening?'

'Of course, my dear,' said Mrs Figgis, checking the key board. 'Would you like the room you had before?'

Prue nodded. 'Do you know when the Andursley shopping coach is expected?'

Mrs Figgis frowned. 'It hardly comes at all lately, but if it's Andursley you're wanting, there's a wagon leaving for Squire Harley's in the morning. I'm sure the carter could take you to the big house.'

Prue accepted eagerly.

'Then I'll arrange it,' said Mrs Figgis. 'Wait in the residents' room while I send for a porter.'

Prue thanked her and entered the snug behind the main dining-room. She sat in the same seat where Biddy had spoken warnings about the marquess's courtship of her. She shivered with pleasure at the outcome she could relate to Biddy.

The day was almost spent. Prue rose as Mrs Figgis opened the door and beckoned, handing her a key. 'Everything's in your room, Miss Smith. I'll see that you're called in good time for your journey and served with something before you go. Josh is the carter and he has a willing heart.'

Prue nodded as she took the key. 'Thank you again.' Hasten the morrow, she thought, as she mounted the stairs.

A morning mist swirled in the yard as Prue made her way to the wagon. Her baggage had been loaded. Josh brushed straw from the wooden seat beside him and offered a gnarled hand to haul her up.

'Sorry about them, miss,' he said, indicating live pigeons in a slatted box at her feet. 'It'll be a footrest for 'ee.'

The town was soon behind them. Prue posed a question. 'What news of Squire Harley and his lady?'

'They'm well, miss.'

'And Mr Richard?'

'He's well, miss.'

'Is he still in Devon?'

'He's well, miss.'

Prue settled to silence for the rest of the journey, reluctant to press further questions upon him. She looked back fleetingly at The Roebuck Inn and later recognized the glade where they had encountered Cap'n Pitch. Musing thus, she passed the time during the wagon's slow progress.

The grey mass of Andursley appeared through a screen of trees and soon she saw the little-used track to the back entrance of the apartment wing. The wagon halted and Josh unloaded her luggage into the small entrance lobby. 'Would you want 'em up the stairs, miss?'

She jumped down from the seat. 'No, please leave them here. For your help, Josh,' she said, opening her reticule and giving him some coins.

She entered immediately and ran up the stairs. Breathlessly, she walked down the passage and knocked on the apartment door before opening it. 'Biddy!' she called at the threshold.

Biddy was not there. Her chair was occupied by Bessie, the young kitchen maid.

'Bessie! Where's Biddy?'

Bessie, whose mouth was still open in surprise, gulped. 'She's in Scotland, miss.'

'In Scotland?'

'With Lady Caroline, miss.'

A woman, unknown to Prue, joined them from the bedroom. 'I'm Ellen,' she said, 'a new housemaid. You've been away and don't know Lady Caroline eloped with Mr Richard Harley. It caused terrible ructions. The countess dismissed everyone having anything to do with Lady Caroline.'

Prue felt giddy and put a hand to her forehead. Bessie rose and guided her to Biddy's chair. Ellen continued, 'They're wed, and with the earl at his Scottish estate.'

'The countess is still here,' added Bessie. 'Most of the house is closed up and she won't see anyone, miss.'

'I must see her,' whispered Prue.

Bessie said, 'Talk in the kitchen is that she blames you. She says you knew it was to happen as soon as you left for Bath.'

Prue shook her head in disbelief. 'Nevertheless, I must see her, Bessie.'

Ellen said, 'You should report to the house steward who may be able to persuade the countess to see you. You could stay tonight in your room. Bessie could use the truckle-bed.'

'Thank you. There are some things I left in my room that are precious to me.' There was a silence. Prue roused herself. 'Ellen, could you ask the house steward to visit me here as soon as possible. I think I should keep out of sight until I have seen the countess.'

Ellen nodded. 'I'll go now, miss.' She took a shawl from behind the door and quietly left.

'I'll make some tea,' said Bessie, busying herself. 'It's been a terrible time. The countess won't even speak to the earl. She says Lady Caroline could have married Lord Lydney, says as he offered for her. . . .'

Prue's mind was numbed with shock. She sipped the tea Bessie handed to her, unaware of the passing of time. She stared dully at the grate, deaf to the torrent of gossip from Bessie.

The door opened and Ellen entered, closely followed by the house steward. He bowed. 'I'm sorry, Miss Smith, but the countess refuses to see you. She has asked me to say you are dismissed from service and that you have two days to remove yourself.'

Prue nodded. 'I expected that. Are you in touch with Mrs Phipps?'

He shifted uneasily. 'The countess destroys all letters delivered here that are not addressed to her. Only by the good will of the squire are we in touch with Mrs Phipps. He delivers and receives our letters.'

'Then by that means tell her I am well and will write to her when I can.'

'I'm sorry, Miss Smith,' he said again as he withdrew.

Ellen and Bessie helped Prue to bring her boxes and portmanteau from the lower hall. She remained in her bedroom. There was only one item she wished to take with her. She unlocked the drawer in the chest, drew back the linen layers to reveal the porcelain damozel. The beautiful yellow dress gleamed brightly, and the amorous little face glowed in readiness to taunt the absent lover. Taking her up, she hugged her. Then gently she replaced the linen wrappings and hid the damozel in her portmanteau.

She lay on the bed to collect her thoughts. The countess, brooding in her apartment, had failed to mark the desperation wrought by her manipulative separation of Caroline and Richard. At least they were together and, it appeared, had the support of the earl. She sighed. The house was so changed. Loyal staff had been dismissed and Biddy was far away in Scotland. There was not one person there with whom she could leave a message.

Where should she go? Where could she rest her head in the nights to come? She had thought Andursley offered a refuge among friends, with food and shelter provided, but it was closed to her ever more. She cursed her stupidity in refusing money from James. Lady Wainflete was in Bath and James, after his visit to London, would be in Harrogate. She had limited means, none to reach Harrogate and hardly enough to return to Bath.

A frenzy seized her. What *was* she to do? Tear-blinded, she left the bed and looked from the window. The afternoon was closing in. A lone magpie, endowed with a fleeting share in sorrow, explored the bare branches of the ash tree.

Chapter 16

A STORM set in over Bristol. The sky darkened and gales marshalled the rain in fearful torrents. Esmond leaned into the wind, clutching his oilskins around him and held fast to his hat as he looked over his shoulder to see how Cedric was faring. He saw Cedric lurch into a doorway to escape a strong gust. Esmond turned back and joined him. They were in the entrance porch of a tavern, Ye Llandoger Trow. He pushed open the door and entered, ushering Cedric before him.

A servant of the inn took their sodden outer garments and gestured to a room where a low grate held piles of glowing coals. They went immediately to the fire, spreading their hands over its warmth.

'A good refuge,' Cedric remarked.

'None better,' Esmond smiled, moving a table and chairs nearer the fire. 'It's well after five of the clock and we might do worse than sup here. We've marched the cobbled streets of Bristol enough for the day.'

Cedric nodded agreement and took a chair beside him as a waiter placed a branch of waxlights upon the table. 'We'll have a remedy for the weather,' Esmond said to the waiter. 'First, two quarterns of rum with a jug of hot water and, to follow, two bowls of your Flemish soup.'

Esmond watched the rain outside cascading down the casements. Captain Roper had carried out his instructions. The

Providence was secure in the Lydney wet dock, and Mr Bennet pursuing buyers for the cargo. His brother had lured Reedpath into a trap – a trap yet to be sprung. This, with Cedric's assurance that he was never involved in fraudulent dealings, must surely nullify any objection harboured by Prue and James.

The waiter brought the rum and hot water.

'You appear preoccupied since receiving Lady Wainflete's note. Is all well?' asked Cedric, dispensing the drinks.

'I sent a letter to Prue at Daniel Street. But Lady Wainflete writes that Prue has returned to Andursley and she will forward my letter to her there. That was unexpected. I had thought her safe with Lady Wainflete.'

'Is she not safe at Andursley?'

'Perhaps even safer, and preferable to her remaining in Bath where she might be exposed to overtures from others.' He paused with Dartree in mind. 'Isolated in the confines of her employment was a factor that blocked my own pursuit of her.'

'My dear fellow, how did you pursue your courtship?'

Sipping his rum, Esmond related the Cap'n Pitch incident and all the subsequent difficulties that had blighted his suit. Cedric was spellbound. 'It's incredible that she happened to be the daughter of Sir Edward Mulcaster Smith.'

'Were you present to witness his downfall?'

'Sadly, yes. Reedpath had a hound's nose for sniffing out victims with inherited fortunes. The games took place in the annexe of a club. Sir Edward was physically prevented from leaving until he was squeezed dry. But there was a final card to play. Reedpath saw himself as Lord of the Manor of Hybullen, thinking that Sir Edward was a rich widower with an only daughter. But then he learned that the title and house were entailed to Sir Edward's heir. This was a bitter discovery and possibly contributed to the relentless stripping of the house and estate.' Cedric paused and bowed his head. 'It was a tragic thing to behold.'

In his mind's eye, Esmond saw Prue on the terrace at Melodon. Helplessly, he had watched the tears tip from her eyes. Never could he forget that Reedpath offered to void the debt if she would wed him. Her rejection and contempt of him must have added impetus to his malicious wrecking of Hybullen. Esmond mustered his mind to the present.

'What was the amount of Sir Edward's debt of honour?'

'I think it to be nearly twenty-five thousand guineas.'

The waiter returned, placing wheaten bread and bowls of hot thick soup before them. They ate in silence.

Suddenly, Esmond struck the table with the flat of his hand. 'Demme! That ship, the *Providence*. She's Baltimore built and fine enough to grace our fleet. I'll buy her for thirty thousand guineas! That's ample to cover the Mulcaster Smith claim!'

Cedric stared open-mouthed, then smiled broadly. 'There's summary justice here, Esmond. Proceeds from the cotton could be allocated to minor claimants.'

'You are certain Reedpath has no other assets?'

'Money rushes through his hands like water. He possesses nothing else of value.'

'Then he'll go to a debtors' prison.'

'Their lordships will press more serious charges. Perhaps they have a card up their communal sleeve. They're very powerful men with connections in the highest and lowest of circles.'

'We shall soon learn their intentions. Come, Cedric, I think the wind has abated. Let's get back to the wharf.'

Esmond felt light-headed, bewildered by his impulsive proposal to purchase the *Providence*. The price was excessive but he cared not a whit. It promised the essential retribution he sought.

Striding through drenched streets, they entered a tall stone building abutting the Lydney wharf, where lighted candles burned in the windows of Esmond's apartment. His footman relieved them of their coats before saying, 'There's a visitor, My Lord. He wishes to see you urgently and awaits you in the withdrawing-room.'

Esmond frowned as he opened the door. Viscount Eades leapt out of a chair. He was flushed and breathless. 'At last you're here, gentlemen! There's bad news—'

'What's amiss?' gasped Cedric.

'Reedpath has gone ashore and left the city!'

It was still dark when Prue rose the next morning. She bound up her hair, sponged herself and dressed for travelling. Irresolution had been left on her pillow. The rank despair vanished as she prepared plans for the coming day. Thinking it wise to be unencumbered with boxes, she packed everything in her portmanteau. She could not stay another minute and resolved never again to set foot in Andursley. She must return to Whitchurch and from there determine her best course. She entered the kitchen, where Ellen and Bessie were tending the fire.

Bessie regarded her with genuine concern. 'Oh, what will you do, miss?' she wailed.

'I'll join my brother in the north,' answered Prue calmly, 'and to do that, I must go back to Whitchurch. Is there a chance the shopping coach will be going there today?'

'No, miss,' said Ellen. 'That's another thing the countess stopped.'

Prue's heart plunged, but she maintained her composure. 'The carter who brought me here yesterday – is it possible he's still at the squire's house?'

'We could find out,' said Ellen helpfully. 'Bessie, go you 'cross the meadow to squire's stables and see if the carter's still there and going back to Whitchurch. And if he is, tell him to be sure to call here for Miss Smith.'

Bessie was out of the door before Ellen could draw breath and Prue express her thanks. She joined Ellen in sipping tea by the fire and tried to control her sadness in recalling similar occasions with Biddy. 'This was such a happy house and I hope it survives these troubled times. I'm grateful for your help, Ellen, and I'll not forget it.'

Ellen shrugged. 'Let's hope the carter's there, miss.' She finished her tea and left for her duties in the house.

Time passed. Prue drummed her fingers on the table to release her anxiety. If no carter, what then?

Loud shouts echoing up the stairwell announced Bessie's return with Josh. In an instant, Prue had fastened her grey cloak, grabbed her portmanteau, and thanked Bessie as Josh helped her to the seat beside him.

Josh's whip tickled the leading horse, and the wagon surged forward. 'Where are you bound now, miss?' he asked.

Dazed, she replied, 'I'm not sure, Josh. I'll go to Whitchurch and think on it.' It was the truth.

'A gel should be at her father's house 'til she be taken by her husband to his house,' declared he.

'My father's house is at Hybullen in Buckinghamshire.'

'Where should you be then, but at your father's house,' he intoned as if from a religious text.

Her father's house. James had said the North Lodge was habitable and that he occasionally called at Hybullen. It was possible he might visit the house on the way back to Harrogate after his business in London. The more she thought of it, the more likely it became. Her funds would extend to a journey from Whitchurch to Bicester and thence to Hybullen where she could await James.

She decided. 'I shall go to my father's house, Josh.'

He nodded and smiled but uttered not one word more until he bade her farewell at Whitchurch.

Mrs Figgis of The White Hart proved as helpful as before. She gave Prue a note to the proprietors of the inn at Oxford for the overnight stay, and told her to change at Bicester for the stagecoach to Buckingham.

The next day, in the late afternoon, the coach stopped in the village of Hybullen. She stepped down, glad that she had limited her baggage to a portmanteau. She turned towards the churchyard. Climbing a stile, she found herself in a field where a solitary worker was tending the hedgerow. She hailed him. 'Is Ben Pickles about?'

He shouldered his hedging-bill and approached. 'I can take you to him, ma'am, in the East Lodge.'

'Then do so, please,' she said, breathless.

He took her portmanteau and led the way over another stile

through gates to the East Lodge. She was in her father's domain at last.

Through the trees she caught sight of the main house. She halted, numbed with shock at the desolation. Weeds were rampant in the garden, once so lovingly tended. Gaping windows had been boarded up, and it pained her to see the crumbling steps leading to the Palladian entrance. She turned away, remembering the grand balls hosted by her parents. So long ago. No replenishment of plaster and stone could bring back those times. It seemed a lost cause.

Despite help from Ben and Hetty Pickles, kin of Hybullen retainers, the North Lodge proved a less than desirable abode. It was sparsely furnished and intensely cold. Ben filled the woodshed and lit the fire for her, but smoke curled everywhere as the chimney was full of birds' nests.

' 'Ow will you manage, ma'am?' Ben asked.

'I'll manage very well, Ben,' she replied confidently, hoping to impart that she was no helpless gentlewoman.

But Hetty intervened. 'No lady of this house shall fend for herself. I'll come in daily, and until there are some proper crocks in the lodge you're welcome to sup with us.'

'That's kind of you, Hetty, but you have a lot on your hands with the poultry, and there's the children.'

'My sister will look after Darrow and Lucy, and the hens mostly looks after theirselves, so it'll be no trouble. The longer you stay, the more comfy we can make it.'

For three days, Hetty and Prue worked in the lodge. Later, Prue shared their meal in the cosy East Lodge, walking back along the lane accompanied by Ben and little Darrow, each carrying a lantern to light the way.

The next afternoon Prue looked from the window in the gable bedroom. From end to end the sky was grey, and deepened the melancholy she had felt since Andursley. Sighing, she took a shawl, unlatched the door and stepped outside. It was time for her to join the family.

The track was overgrown and scattered with fallen boughs. She walked slowly, looking where she trod. Preoccupation with her plight and discomforts had kept her low spirits within bounds, but as simple routines of life were restored she thought wistfully of Esmond. The days in Bath seemed to her a golden time, and she tenderly recalled the sulkily handsome cast of his face after their quarrel in Daniel Street. When they had looked long at each other during the playing of the sonata, she felt a spiritual ecstasy. She held it in her heart. She shivered. Where was he now on the wide, wide sea?

A break in the hedgerow revealed the main house. Again she felt the deep despair which had struck her on first beholding it. James was still lord of the manor, dedicated to its restoration, but the task appeared insuperable. She surprised herself at her indifference. For the last six years she had thought of Hybullen as part of herself, an intrinsic habit. Now she wanted to discard it like a garment that neither pleased nor fitted her. With all her being, she desired the presence of Esmond, to be at the threshold of his house.

'Miss Prudence!'

The piping call heralded little Darrow running towards her. Laughing, he took her hand and led her through the garden to the open kitchen door. Hetty and her sister Dorcas greeted her. Prue entered unceremoniously, removed her shawl and began to assist by ladling soup into the several plates.

'We're but five to sup, ma'am. Lucy's abed with the beginnings of the branks, or as some call it, the mumps.'

'It's in all the villages,' added Dorcas.

'Darrow'll be the next so he's to be kept in. We've had it as children. Have you had the mumps, ma'am?'

Prue nodded. 'Long ago. There was a time when Sir James and I were confined to the nursery for weeks, with one thing following another.'

'That's as well, then,' said Hetty. 'For the coming weeks we'll be a sick house, so Dorcas'll come to you instead.'

Prue smiled at the fresh-faced girl. Anything, she thought, to break the monotony of each day and divert her woeful imaginings.

187

Ben entered and said he had found a crate full of unused crockery in the cellars of the main house. 'Tomorrow we could collect what's necessary for your use, ma'am. All the pieces bear the Hybullen crest of your grandfather. I think they were put aside when Sir Edward took over the house.'

'I'll be happy to come with you, Ben.'

'It's a wonder the Black Dog missed them.'

'The Black Dog?' asked Prue.

'That's what we all called him,' said Ben. 'The man who cheated your father and plundered the house and estate. A black dog is a counterfeit coin, ma'am, and he's a counterfeit gentleman.'

'Reedpath,' whispered Prue. 'An apt name for him.' It was comforting to know she was not alone in her hatred.

'We've not seen him for many a day and don't wish to.'

After the meal, Prue did not dally. Ben lit the lantern and walked with her to the North Lodge. 'Thank you, Ben. I'll go to the main house tomorrow morning and together we'll inspect the cellars and select some crockery.'

'Very good, ma'am. I'll wait for you by the service entrance.'

The morning was dull with the chill of late autumn. She wore her grey cloak and began to walk towards the main house. She had not progressed far when she was startled by a crashing sound coming from the copse. It was a man running towards her, leaping over and bursting through the underbrush. She stood rigid with fear until she recognized the pale face of Ben, staring at her with frantic eyes.

'Ben! What's wrong?'

He stopped to regain his breath. 'Talk of the devil and you'll see his horns. I spoke of him last night and he's come back this morn to punish us!'

'Who has come back, Ben?'

'The Black Dog, ma'am.'

'It couldn't be. He's in America. You're mistaken.'

' 'Pon honour! I stand here a fool if I didn't see him in the house as I waited for you this morning. He's back. The Lord save us!

He'll undo all the good Sir James has done. We'll not have a roof over our heads, and the children ailing an' all—'

'Nonsense, Ben,' Prue said firmly. 'Even if it were him he owns nothing here, nothing. Your tenure is safe. It's a trespasser you saw and one you have the authority to remove.'

Ben shook his head. 'It's the Black Dog, ma'am.'

'How can you be so sure?'

'I'll never forget him from those old days, the way he walked, holding his head low, like.'

She shuddered, sharing the vision. Her heart beat violently and sudden quiverings raced over her limbs. Could Ben be right?

'How did he arrive here?' she asked weakly. 'Show me a carriage and I'll believe you.'

Ben hesitated. 'I didn't see a carriage at the back of the house but there may be one standing at the front. Let's approach through the shrubbery and see for ourselves. I know a way where we'll not be seen.'

She gathered her cloak around her and set the hood. Ben pushed aside the bushes and she followed him through overgrown trails until they could see the full aspect of the house. Parting the branches, Ben said, 'See, ma'am, there is indeed a coach.'

It was a black coach with a pair of unmatched horses. A hired coach. She regarded it for a moment then said, 'It could be my brother, Ben.'

He shook his head. 'Sir James always comes to the East Lodge before he enters the house, as I hold the keys. The Black Dog's broken in. He's inside now.'

This was a hatchet-stroke. Her throat constricted and became dry. Gripped with a desire to hide, she retreated deeper into the shrubbery, followed by Ben. He looked to her for some instructions, some action. She must think, think. By a stand of firs, she came to a stop. Stooping, she picked up a small branch and her trembling fingers peeled its bark. If only James would appear at this minute!

If Reedpath was here, did it mean that Esmond had left on a wild goose chase? That terrible voyage to no avail? And what of his brother? Had he returned, too?

She must put aside her fears of Reedpath and engage him to extract answers to these questions. Don't look back, she told herself, make him *your* victim. How could she do it?

She ran her fingers along the new-peeled branch, smooth to the touch as the cane handle of her parasol. She had acted with spontaneous courage against Cap'n Pitch. Could she muster it again to outwit Reedpath? She tossed the branch aside.

'Ben, I want you to enter the main house and seek out Sir Clancy Reedpath. Greet him and mention that you thought it was Sir James come to visit. Then go on to say that I'm staying at the North Lodge. My instinct tells me he'll make his way there, and I'll be ready for him. Let an hour pass, then come to the North Lodge with Dorcas as usual. Is that clear?'

'Yes, ma'am,' he replied eagerly. 'Shall I go now?'

'Allow me time to reach the lodge, then you may go.' She turned. 'Ben, don't think the Black Dog is back for ever.'

'No ma'am. You're here to take care of that.'

She hurried back to the North Lodge, terrified that the maze of shrubberied paths would cause her to lose her way and forfeit time. Soon she spotted the gables among the trees, and moments later was unlatching the door. She hung up her cloak and rushed upstairs to her bedroom. Her heart galloped as she stood tense by the dressing-table, her clenched hands pressed into her cheeks. This man, whom she loathed with such intensity, would soon be aware that she was here alone. She shivered with repulsion, remembering fleshy hands groping for her bosom and his thick lips seeking hers. But she needed answers to those questions. Somehow she must control the interview, keep him at a distance and restrain him from touching her.

Suddenly, she knew what she must do. Opening the drawer containing the porcelain damozel, she carefully removed one of the protective linen wrappers and tore it into wide strips. From one she formed two small pads and, going to the dressing-table mirror, affixed them behind and below her ears, binding all in place with another scarf-like piece around her neck and head. On top of this she placed one of her white caps. She dashed blanching powder over her face until her eyes sank into dark circles. Regarding herself, she was satisfied. She looked as if she was suffering from mumps at its most contagious stage.

Downstairs, huddled in her shawl, she sat in a wooden armchair by the fireplace to await Reedpath. She felt certain she would repel him – not only because of her sickly appearance, but also by natural caution when he was made aware of her supposed affliction. It was a ploy to stop him physically engaging her.

Time passed slowly. She watched the single hand of the mantel timepiece and listened to the wood shifting in the grate. She shivered, and placed another log on the fire. If only she could stop trembling. She heard the door quietly open and close. Reedpath had entered and was watching her from the shadows. She cringed at the sound of his laboured breathing in the tension of those first moments.

'By the devil's luck, Miss Mulcaster Smith, I wouldn't have taken odds that you'd be here.'

His voice was as she recalled it, sneering and insidious. Her stomach churned as she turned her head awkwardly as if in pain. He came out of the shadows to confront her. Adopting a husky voice, she said. 'You find me at a disadvantage. Mumps is all over the estate.'

'Mumps,' he said. 'Is there a physician attending you?'

She shook her head. 'I thought you were in America.'

He moved to lean against the small casement, his hooded eyes expressionless. He was hatless, his dark hair sparse and groomed to cover approaching baldness. A black coat revealed corpulence, his face was fuller and more blotched. His tongue coursed the inside of his thick lower lip, causing a gathering of slaver which he wiped with a large kerchief drawn from a pocket in his coat. An obnoxious foible, she thought with a shudder.

Ignoring her comment, he said, 'I had another wager with

myself. I thought you to be wed by now. Is it not so, then?' She did not answer. 'You'll be buzzing in my brain again if there's the merest chance—'

'Tell me about America,' she interposed, to quickly change the subject.

'Why are you here alone in this ruined place?'

'It wasn't always a ruined place,' she said pointedly.

His dull eyes suddenly flashed in anger. 'The ruination rests upon your shoulders. One word from you and all could have been avoided. Even now there are assets I could dispose of to restore Hybullen to its former glory. Say that one word now. Don't reject me again!'

Tremors gripped her. She shook her head and fingered the wrappings about her ears. 'There is someone—'

'Confound him, whoever he is!' He turned and paced, dabbing at his mouth.

'Why have you come to Hybullen? My brother has bought back most of the land and the house still stands to him.'

'A shell, a useless shell. It gives me joy to see it, an example of immense weakness and immense power.'

'You've come to gloat.'

He gave a rasping laugh. 'Every man has a need to inspect the site of past victories.'

'Obviously you've returned because America was a disaster for you,' she said evenly.

'On the contrary,' he said, taking up his stance at the casement. 'I've had great success in America and am here to sell a cargo of cotton. I own cotton plantations with many slaves, three houses with more rooms than Hybullen. I'm the sole owner of several ships. One, the *Providence*, I sailed personally to Bristol.'

With purposeful naïvety she asked, 'How did you acquire such wealth in three years?'

'By skill in gaming. Americans are targets. It's a pleasure to take my gains and run I can make paupers of them all.'

She quashed the angry retorts that sprang to her mind. There were questions still to be answered. 'When did you return?'

'Some two weeks since.'

'So you have a ship loaded with cotton actually in Bristol?'

'In the Lydney wet dock.'

Her heart leapt at the name. 'Is that owned by the Marquess of Lydney?'

He strutted in front of her. 'I am related to the marquess. My long-deceased mother was sister to the old marchioness. The marquess is in Bristol with his brother, Lord Cedric Aumerle. I hope to play a few games with them while I'm there.' He laughed. 'I've never had the opportunity to fleece the most honourable marquess. There's rich pickings there.'

'Are you staying in Bristol?'

'When there, on board my ship; in Bicester, at a tavern in Sheep Street, where I'll remain until you're recovered.'

'I wouldn't wish to keep you from your sport.'

He flushed and dabbed his lips again. There was a long silence as he regarded her. 'While I still breathe, I want you for my wife. What luck to discover you alone like this! I can't let the opportunity pass – to find you and not embrace you! Come, a kiss,' he pleaded, falling upon his knees and reaching out to her.

She shrank back. He was like a black dog at her feet. 'But my sickness – are you not afraid?'

'Of mumps?' He laughed loudly. 'I had it as a child.'

She froze in horror as his hands moved over her ankles, then higher to her calves. He started to pant and saliva gathered on his slack lips. Desperation gave her brute strength. She forced her feet to his chest and pushed violently. He fell back on to the floor. She quickly stepped around him, went to the door and opened it. In her normal voice, she said, 'There's nothing for you here. You're a trespasser. Please leave – I can summon help.'

He slowly rose to his feet and came towards her. Suddenly, he grabbed and unwound the linen bands around her head. She struggled as he unfurled them and bound her tightly against his chest, his one hand holding them taut. 'Not so sick now, my heart, my diamond,' he whispered. His eyes moved over her face greedily. Then he dived his head and his mouth coursed moistly over her throat. She shuddered in a convulsion of hate and turned her head aside.

'You're like a new pack of playing cards,' he murmured into her ear, 'shining and virginal. I find pleasure in breaking the seal and making the cards perform for me. Be my wife, my heart, my only diamond—'

'Oh-hh-hh!' Mustering all her physical power she pushed him from her. Retching from his foul breath, she untangled the linen bands and ran outside, almost colliding with Ben and Dorcas on the path. 'Ben! the Black Dog is in there. Get some help and take him to the constable! Hurry!' she shrilled.

Ben ran off. Prue clung to Dorcas in near collapse.

'Let's sit you down, ma'am.' said Dorcas, making a step towards the lodge.

'No, no!' cried Prue.

'There's no one in there now, ma'am.'

Reedpath had fled through the back door.

Ben returned with others from the estate. They searched the gardens and adjacent forest until, satisfied that all was well, they left.

Prue, now calm, settled again in her chair. Esmond was in Bristol. The impossible had happened. Reedpath and Cedric had returned before he took to sea. She thought of Reedpath's boastful utterances, then a cold chill gripped her. Suppose he were to come back! Tonight! He was brazen enough to do so. She shivered and almost cried aloud at a tap on the door.

It was Ben with fresh victuals. 'The Black Dog's gone, ma'am. He was seen leaving in that coach.'

Relief surged through her. There was another task yet to do. 'Is there someone here who can take a message to the constable at Bicester, Ben? Reedpath must be apprehended immediately. There are warrants for his arrest.'

'There's a stable lad could ride a nag there,' he said.

She drew out her writing box and penned a note, which she handed to Ben. 'That should keep the Black Dog from Hybullen. Pray it will be in time.'

'I'll see to it,' said Ben, quickly withdrawing.

She then wrote a long letter to James in Harrogate, relating every detail of her interlude with Reedpath and urging James to come south to pursue their claim.

She decided to leave on the morrow. Those late experiences demonstrated the pitfalls of a young lady travelling alone with limited means. Why had she voluntarily left Lady Wainflete and the comforts enjoyed under her patronage? But she had learned something about herself – her bitterness had gone and Hybullen no longer dominated her existence.

Carefully, she packed her clothes and reckoned up her remaining funds. Her resources were slender indeed. She would be obliged to ride outside on the stages and travel to Bicester on the Hybullen market wagon. She could well tolerate sitting among turnips and mangel-wurzels *en route* to that refuge in Daniel Street. A breath away from Esmond.

Chapter 17

'WHERE do you suppose Clancy is at this moment?' asked Cedric, seated beside his mother in her Clifton house.

Esmond, studying marine designs at the table, looked up. 'I can't speculate. He'll not remove himself for long since all his worldly assets rest in our wet dock. He's bound to return and then we can leave everything to their lordships.'

'They've asked us to attend a meeting in Bristol at the Bank Chambers in the Dutch House. All claimants will be there, too.'

'When is it to be?'

'Tomorrow, after banking hours in the forenoon.'

'Good. I'd like to leave for Lydney this week.' Esmond rose from the table. 'I'm puzzled by the lack of communication with Prue and her brother. I've written letters to Sir James but all is silence, and Prue should have received my letter that Lady Wainflete directed to Andursley. I shall call upon the earl and make my own inquiries.'

'Then let's travel together in the blue carriage,' said the dowager. 'I can achieve more at Lydney in planning our grand ball than by remaining here at Clifton.'

'I'd like to return to New England as soon as we've settled the Clancy affair,' said Cedric.

'You may return to New England, Cedric, but not until after the Lydney Ball,' said the dowager. 'You've not been present for three years, and the tenants and gentry are owed a sight of you.'

Cedric made a grimace. 'May I forgo a domino?'

'No,' said the dowager. 'Everyone must wear one or be costumed and masked.'

'You're fortunate to have a choice,' said Esmond. 'I'm doomed to wear the suit of great-grandfather, the first marquess, wig an' all!'

'It's been the tradition since the 1730s,' said the dowager. 'The first marquess was comely and had exquisite taste.'

'Who would believe such a peacock to be the intrepid seafarer who built our first vessels,' laughed Cedric.

'There's something finer in him than his sartorial splendour,' said Esmond quietly.

The dowager left her seat and crossed to the door where she turned to face her sons. 'We shall *all* leave for Lydney as soon as your business is done. I realize it's concerned with Clancy. I don't wish to know the details, but he'll never be received by me again.'

Esmond nodded approval in the brief silence that followed. Then he said, 'The grand ball is the ideal occasion for me formally to offer for Prue. I'd like Sir James and Prue to be our honoured guests.'

The dowager smiled. 'Then you must make sure that Prue and her brother receive notice of your intentions. It will be our pleasure to bestow them at Lydney for as long as they require.'

'That's my earnest wish, Mother,' said Esmond.

'It will be perfect if there's a full moon, essential for a successful ball,' she said.

Esmond smiled to himself as she left the room. Her happiness was complete. She was pursuing her favourite pastime, preparing a grand ball, but this alone was not the reason for her lightsome mood. Her younger son had returned from America with an unblemished reputation bordering, in the opinion of diverse gentlemen, upon the heroic.

That night Esmond sat with Cedric after dinner in the salon of his wharf apartment. He inspected the records of fraudulent card-play that Cedric had collected over the years. No gaming club had escaped the cunning of Reedpath.

'I forgot to say I have presented Clancy's coat to their lordships,' said Cedric.

'For what reason?'

'To show them the innovations of an arch cheat: hidden pockets and false linings, hiding places for marked cards and cogged dice. He wore shirts with ruffled cuffs, full of linen caverns to aid sleight of hand in concealing and replacing dice.'

'I'm astonished,' said Esmond. 'I wonder what tomorrow's meeting will bring.'

On retiring that night Esmond yielded to an inescapable despondency. He could not suppress the thought that all was not well with Prue, and he despaired of the recurring minutiae that delayed his long-desired call upon her at Andursley.

The next morning they walked to the timbered Dutch House which stood in the medieval heart of the city. A uniformed bank messenger ushered them into a large room on the first floor. A score of chairs surrounded a massive central table. In an ante-room their lordships were gathered with a group of soberly dressed gentlemen. There was a drone of conversation and wafting tobacco smoke indicated a conference of long duration.

Viscount Eades and Lord Beddington detached themselves and came towards them. The old viscount could not conceal his excitement. 'There's been a development!' he whispered in a fluster. 'Reedpath is in the hands of the constable here in Cumberland Street. He was apprehended in Bicester.'

'Bicester? 'Pon my soul, he's been snared in someone else's net,' said Esmond. 'What was he doing in Oxfordshire?'

Lord Beddington shook his head. 'Who knows?' He paused. 'By rights he should be removed to London where all charges have been laid. What do you think, Lydney?'

'My Lord, you are the prime plaintiffs. It would seem he should be charged there and bail set in the normal way.'

'I oppose bail,' said Lord Beddington. 'He's the owner of a seaworthy ship and could sail away out of all jurisdictions. He's vanished once from under our noses.'

'Then he must be prevented,' said the viscount. 'Lydney, can you hold the ship by some means?'

Esmond said, 'No arrangements have been made for payment of keelage charges. It's within my right to place an attachment on the ship and cargo. But I'd like to purchase the *Providence* for thirty thousand guineas.' Their lordships stiffened, staring at Esmond. He smiled and continued, 'This money should be set aside for the Mulcaster Smith settlement. The cotton cargo will raise enough to satisfy other claimants. Can you effect these arrangements, My Lord?'

Lord Beddington raised a cautionary hand. 'I must consult further and suggest we adjourn for an hour.'

'That sounds somewhat circumspect, My Lord,' said Cedric. 'Surely the constable is able to deliver Reedpath to London.'

'Perhaps that won't be necessary,' said Lord Beddington inscrutably.

Esmond was furious at the adjournment. Why were their lordships delaying? He withdrew to a chop-house with Cedric. They ate in silence until Cedric said, 'Their lordships are thinking on a different tack.'

'Whatever it is, they should not postpone. Reedpath is too slippery a fish,' Esmond replied. Against his will, he was becoming inextricably associated with the matter. His enforced separation from Prue kindled a deep tenderness, with anxiety an additional ingredient. Sir James was not among the claimants present, of that he was certain. When would he appear and make good his claim?

The time passed slowly. He was impatient to leave, and well before the hour had elapsed they were on their way back to the Dutch House. More claimants had arrived, chatting in parties crowding the hall. Esmond took a step towards the boardroom when he was approached by a portly gentleman in a well-cut black coat. With a slight bow, he said, 'Am I addressing the Most Honourable Marquess of Lydney?'

Esmond smiled. 'You are, my good sir. May I be of some service to you?'

The gentleman nodded, extending his hand. 'My name is Jonah Arkwright. I have the honour to be a solicitor associate of Sir James Mulcaster Smith.'

'You are here about his claim?'

'Indeed. But I am also the bearer of a letter which Sir James urged me to personally place in your hands at the earliest opportunity. My Lord Owlsbury indicated your presence to me.' So saying, Mr Arkwright handed Esmond a sealed letter which he had removed from an inner pocket of his coat.

'I'm relieved to have this from Sir James, Mr Arkwright. As it's relevant to this meeting, would you excuse me while I scan its content?'

Mr Arkwright beamed. 'I'm available to clarify any aspect, being aware of Sir James's intent, My Lord.' He then withdrew to a discreet distance.

Esmond eagerly broke the seal and took out a single sheet of paper. He read quickly and saw that James had received his letters, was grateful for the timely advices and would travel south so soon as Reedpath was charged in London.

The second paragraph of the letter dealt with a matter close to Esmond's heart: . . . *It would seem that events dictate the pursuance of your own claim and I am happy to cease my opposition. I leave it to you to take whatever steps you deem necessary.*

With a sharp intake of breath, Esmond recognized he now had James's blessing on his courtship of Prue. Flushed with delight, he thanked Mr Arkwright profusely.

They made their way into the boardroom. Esmond sought Cedric and, after introducing Mr Arkwright, left them to chat while he lingered by one of the casements, staring at the bustling street below. He longed to desert that sober company, leap into the saddle of his bay and ride, ride, ride to Prue. She was his beloved betrothed. There was no doubt about it now that he had the approval of her brother. His fancies took flight. Nothing could dim his ascending star. He realized he had felt hardly alive for weeks and wanted to shout his joy to those around him.

He drew out the letter to read again that part which had reassured him. In doing so, he noticed he had missed a postscript written on the back of the single sheet: *I know well that Reedpath has returned to this country. I am told he has again imposed his beastly presence upon my sister.*

He felt a surge of alarm. Where had this occurred? At Andursley? How had Reedpath found Prue at Andursley where Esmond had thought her safe in the service of the earl? His ascending star had dimmed. Rage stalked his helplessness. There was some consolation in knowing Reedpath was now in custody. He wondered, was this due to any action on Prue's part? Such speculation brought him a measure of comfort. The 'beastly presence' of Reedpath had given her a motive and she was possessed of ample spirit to thwart him. Thinking thus, restored his composure.

The sharp crack of the viscount's gavel upon the table brought him back to reality. He took his seat alongside Cedric and Mr Arkwright as the meeting came to order.

There was a hush as Viscount Eades rose. Esmond's attention lapsed as the venerable gentleman welcomed all present. He felt leaden and distant from the proceedings. He wondered why he was there at all when a sudden hubbub erupted from the table.

'What is it? What did he say?' he asked Cedric.

Cedric sat stonily staring ahead. 'They're withdrawing all charges. No trial in London,' he whispered.

Claimants were on their feet angrily gesticulating. The viscount held up his hand. 'Gentlemen,' he said in conciliatory tones, 'Please hear our alternatives!'

Protests gradually subsided. The gentlemen seated themselves again and all eyes turned to the viscount.

'We are united in our view that resort to the courts would be unwise. Think, my lords and gentlemen, of the exposure. I address those representing gambling clubs. Do you wish systematic cheating at your premises to become public knowledge spread over months, perhaps years? And claimants – are you willing to see your claims shrink in payment of legal fees after a long trial? We are proposing swift justice but support must be unanimous.'

Esmond rose. 'Your arguments are valid, My Lord, but do they mean that Reedpath will walk free to continue his crooked play?'

The viscount smiled. 'My Lord Marquess, you and your brother, above all present, must approve our recommendation. Your family name shall not be sullied in a public airing.'

'But what is to happen in the case of moneys proved lost through cheating?'

A buzz of assent came from those present. The viscount called upon the taciturn Lord Beddington to answer. Slowly, he rose to his feet. 'My lords and gentlemen, let me summarize our intentions. Reedpath shall not escape justice. He will be given a choice. Steps have been taken to appropriate his assets and payment of all claims will proceed through the Central Bank.'

'I thought their lordships had another card to play,' mused Cedric.

Lord Beddington continued, 'Sir Clancy Reedpath is below and will be brought to hear our options. Are there any dissenting?'

All were silent.

So we are to see Reedpath in his disgrace, thought Esmond. The sight of him would bring to mind every obstacle that had dogged his courtship, the near calamity of his loss and that dread phantom, the molester of Prue. He felt no remorse that he and Cedric had aided in his downfall. Looking around at the claimants, present not because of cardplay but dishonest cardplay, he knew he could not have faced them had he not taken this stand.

The door opened. Reedpath entered with guards in train. He stood hunched, his head thrust forward and eyes downcast. At his appearance there was a loud outcry until Lord Beddington brought the gathering to order. Reedpath was led to the vacant chair at the far end of the table.

'Your cheating systems in cardplay and dice are a matter of record, as are the names and addresses of your accomplices,' Lord Beddington began.

Reedpath interposed, 'I hope they include Lord Cedric

Aumerle. He's been sustained by fraudulent successes ever since I've known him.'

'That is a falsehood and irrelevant,' replied Lord Beddington. 'You alone are brought to answer here.'

Reedpath mopped his lips, glancing maliciously towards Esmond and Cedric.

Lord Beddington continued. 'There are two options: we have sufficient evidence for a trial for fraud in London. You will be convicted with harsh sentences for the harm you have done.'

Reedpath looked around the room at the many claimants staring at him. 'And what other choice have I?' he growled.

'That you be taken to the Pool of London where you will be put aboard a ship and banished to Australia for life. Should you ever return to these shores you will be arrested,' declared Lord Beddington.

'A court hearing will vindicate me!' Reedpath shouted. 'I have the means to pay for the whole panoply of law to prove my innocence!'

A scornful murmur rose from those round the table.

'If that is your choice,' answered Lord Beddington calmly, 'you will be detained in custody in London until the case is set. You will be held on a Thames hulk as London's prisons are overflowing. Thus you'll be well placed for transportation when judgment is given.'

Reedpath sat glowering.

Lord Beddington cleared his throat and continued, 'As to your means, the ship *Providence* and her cargo have been impounded for payment of claims against you. I ask you again: is it still your choice to recourse to a court of law?'

Esmond listened as Reedpath's responses ranged from defiance to threats and then to wheedling attempts to extract pity. He thought of Prue and James, their years of distress, their home laid to waste. Finally Reedpath muttered, 'No courts, then. Banishment it shall be, and the devil take you all!'

Reedpath rose. As he was being led away, he suddenly turned to

Esmond and Cedric. 'How can you, as my kinsmen, watch my ruination?'

'As easily as you watched the ruination of others,' Esmond rejoined. 'Sir Edward Mulcaster Smith, for instance.'

'I can make amends,' Reedpath blurted out. 'His daughter feels no bitterness. Prudence has entertained me, she loves me – she – she—'

He stopped short as Esmond flung himself over the table and grabbed Reedpath by the collar of his coat. 'You're not fit to speak her name,' Esmond fumed.

Reedpath flinched at his fury. 'I – I have been with her – she has promised—'

Esmond could bear no more. He thrust Reedpath from him and delivered a resounding crack to his jaw. Reedpath stumbled, only to receive another blow from Esmond's fist. 'That one is for Sir James.'

Esmond rubbed his knuckles then adjusted his coat and stock. Reedpath lay across the landing barely conscious.

'Get him out of my sight,' said Esmond, stepping over the prostrate Reedpath to descend the stairs. 'Come, Cedric. All is done that had to be done.'

Oh, the tedium of settlements, apportionments, deals and dispensations, thought Esmond. Would he never be free to leave Bristol without being called upon to adjudicate in such matters? His despatch of Reedpath had brought no clear-cut end to his involvement, rather the contrary. He had unintentionally become the claimants' champion, especially when it was divulged that he had supervised the transition of ship and cargo to hard cash. Delegations and individual claimants heaped praise upon him, and their lordships extolled the honour of his house.

Forty-eight hours had passed since the resolution and he could brook no further postponement in leaving for Andursley. He sped endlessly between the wharf offices and Clifton, where finally he implored his mother and Cedric to hasten as he was bound to leave that day be it morning, noon or night.

'You're like a vacillating compass-needle seeking its pole,' complained Cedric.

The dowager, having at last closed her trunk, called for footmen to load it onto the big blue coach being readied in the carriage house. 'I had wondered,' said she, drawing on her gloves, 'whether we might stay awhile at Melodon. There's some shopping I'd prefer to do in Bath. Or is that out of the question, Esmond?'

'For now, out of the question. But there's no reason why you should not go to Bath for a day or so prior to the ball,' said Esmond.

She sighed. 'I'll have to be content. How can I reason with a worshipper separated from his goddess?'

'Have patience with me, Mother. I've a feeling of disquiet which will only be allayed at Andursley.'

' 'Twas ever thus for those in love,' shrugged the dowager, slipping some necessaries into her reticule.

Esmond had sent Tom forward to arrange fresh horses and livery along the route. The dowager, spurning taverns, preferred to stay with friends whose grand houses and amenities were always at her disposal. After a stay in the Vale of Pewsey and at Friars Hill on the Hampshire Downs, they were soon approaching Whitchurch. This busy coach interchange lightened Esmond's mood by warm feelings of association with Prue. He had been bound for Whitchurch when he first set eyes on her.

They left the town bustle behind as the road narrowed into the treed lane Esmond recalled. After passing The Roebuck, he looked eagerly from the window hoping to locate the glade where Prue had attended the semi-conscious Tom. The toll of late autumn had so transformed the scenery that his heart leapt at several possible places. Eventually, he leaned back surrendering his thoughts as to how he would greet Prue at Andursley. She must remove to Lydney and remain as the dowager's guest.

He sat up alert as grass swards by the entrance to Andursley came into view. The coach turned left and came to a halt. Suddenly, the relief coachman's face appeared at the window. 'The gates are closed fast, My Lord. Shall I enter by the side-gate and find some-one to open them?'

Esmond frowned. Looking to the right and left he noted that the grass was overgrown, and it seemed that few coaches had travelled the drive of late. He nodded. 'Yes, go and bring someone to the gates. The carriage house and stables are on the right of the large shrubbery. Hasten.'

The waiting seemed interminable until he saw his coachman returning with a man holding a key-ring. The man wrestled with the lock and soon the gates were opened sufficiently to allow the coach to pass through.

Esmond thought that the entire house had an air of neglect. Most of the windows to the front were shuttered. The coach slowed by the porch. Esmond hardly waited for it to stop before he was out and bounding up the steps. He hammered on the tightly closed double doors. There was no response. He stood back, looking up at the windows, but no shutter opened. They could be away, he thought, but somehow he knew this was not so. He turned and ran to the stable block. Only one of the boxes was occupied. The rest stood empty. The earl's coach was absent. The black shopping coach was outside, neglected and shabby. A groom approached.

'Is there someone who can take me to the earl or the countess?'

'The steward has access to the countess but he is not here. The earl is in Scotland, My Lord.'

'Is Lady Caroline about?'

'She is in Scotland, My Lord.'

'Is her companion, Miss Smith, also in Scotland?'

'No, My Lord.'

'Then she is here?'

'No, My Lord.'

In mounting desperation, Esmond kicked a pebble from his path. 'Is Mrs Biddy Phipps here?'

'No, My Lord. She, too, is in Scotland.'

'Then let me into the house. I must see the countess.'

'She sees no one these days, My Lord.'

Esmond stood, arms akimbo, staring at the ground. Then the groom added, 'Here's someone who may be able to help you.'

He turned at the approach of a maidservant. She bobbed a curtsy. 'I'm Ellen, personal maid to Countess Andursley, My Lord. She saw your coach and sent me down to see you. She cannot entertain you and sends regrets.'

'I do not wish to be entertained. I must know the whereabouts of Miss Prudence Smith, erstwhile companion to the Lady Caroline.'

'The Lady Caroline eloped some weeks ago with Mr Richard Harley. They were wed in Scotland and the earl followed them, along with Mrs Phipps. They are living on his Scottish estate. The countess dismissed most of the old staff as she thought they helped in the elopement. Miss Smith was blamed. When she came back from Bath she was given two days before she was forced to leave, My Lord.'

Esmond's face was ashen at this news. His jaw clenched as he asked, 'Where did Miss Smith go when she left?'

'It's thought she joined her brother in the north.'

'Did she leave no note, no letter?'

'No, My Lord. But the countess asked me to give you this.'

Ellen produced a small wooden box. Esmond opened it and saw within the letter he had addressed to Prue. Unopened, it had been torn into little pieces. Prue had never received it. He stared into the box. 'The countess must be mad.'

'Her bitterness has made her so.'

'Thank you, Ellen. Give my compliments to the countess and express my sorrow for her.'

Ellen curtsied and withdrew.

Esmond thanked the groom and slowly walked away. He opened the box again and took out the remains of his love letter. At the base of the box, there were light green fragments of another letter. He could see it was addressed to Prue and had suffered the same fate as his own. He sorted the fragments to determine the sender so that he could inform him or her of the position. To his consternation he saw that the writer was Vivian Dartree.

He walked he knew not where until he realized that he was near the lake. He sat on a stone seat by the shoreline. Where was Prue? Had she joined James in Harrogate? He cursed his stupidity in not asking Mr Arkwright if Prue was there. But he had no reason then to suppose she was not at Andursley. His heart was leaden and his dreams dashed.

He took the letter fragments into his hands and allowed a breeze to carry them over the lake. They danced for a moment on the surface of the water, the green paper mingling with the white, until all had vanished.

Chapter 18

SHE was fleeing shadows in the echoing halls of Hybullen. Ghostly shades approached and melted into nothingness. But one pursued her at every turn. Glancing over her shoulder, she saw it was Reedpath. She screamed, but no sound came forth. 'Don't look back!' came a command. The voice and vision was of Esmond, standing ahead, his arms ready to receive her. She could not reach him. Panting and struggling, she saw a light and followed it.

Indistinct faces hovered in an atmosphere of kindly comfort. The calm countenance of Dr Crouch was poised above her. 'The fever has left her,' he said.

'What a blessing!' A voice so welcome, so loved. Lady Wainflete brushed Prue's brow with a kerchief soft as a butterfly's wing. 'Prue, my dear, you have been very ill. But you've come through.'

Prue gave a shuddering sigh of pure content. 'Thank you both,' she whispered.

'Her convalescence can begin,' said the doctor.

It was many days since she had left Hybullen in the market cart. At Bicester she had boarded the wrong coach. When fellow passengers told her the coach was bound for Coventry, she pulled the check-string and had been set down at a remote crossroads. What followed was a succession of disasters. Fearful of leering faces in the public rooms of taverns, she had remained outside, sheltering in doorways from driving drizzle. One night she slept in a hay-loft, but eventually secured an outside seat on a coach at Speenhamland on the road to Bath. Every day it rained. At Chippenham she collapsed. But there her misfortunes ended. Lord and Lady Glenister, returning from London in their own coach, happened to call at The Plough where their help was sought to take a sick young lady to Bath. They found Prue, barely conscious, in the care of an ostler's wife, and immediately continued their journey and took Prue in haste to Lady Wainflete.

Prue's recovery from pneumonia proceeded well. Dr Crouch soon ceased his daily visits and every day Clara helped Prue down the long staircase to a *chaise-longue* in Lady Wainflete's room.

One afternoon, Lady Wainflete said, 'I think it's time for you to pen a letter to Esmond, Prue. I'll gladly bring your writing box if you wish.'

Prue shook her head. 'Not yet. Perhaps tomorrow.'

'You should let Esmond know you're here. He'll want to be by your side immediately he's aware of your illness.'

'I'll write to Esmond when I feel better. He has many matters deserving of his attention now that his brother and Reedpath are back.'

'He'll think you still at Andursley.'

'I want to be *well* when I write to him, Lady Wainflete.'

Lady Wainflete sighed as she rose. 'As you will. Shall you join us for dinner? Dr Crouch and the Glenisters are my guests. Agnes may come later.'

'Yes, I'd love to join you.'

'Good.' Lady Wainflete smiled as she withdrew.

Prue longed to see Esmond, to be with him. She had dreamed of an idyllic meeting, running joyfully to him on first sight. Weakness and convalescence had no part in that fantasy and she wanted to be fully recovered before she wrote to him. Was she right to delay? There had been no news from him, no direct contact between them. Did Lady Wainflete have a reason for pressing her to write? Perhaps Esmond was tiring of his undertaking to bring his cousin to justice.

Clara popped her head round the door. 'Are you ready to go down, Miss Prudence?'

'Yes, Clara. But I'll manage the stairs myself.'

'Are you sure, ma'am?'

'Yes, Clara. Don't wait. I'll be down forthwith.'

Fired with determination she rose from the *chaise-longue*, stood for a while, then proceeded slowly downstairs. Cries of delight greeted her as she entered the dining-room. She brushed away a tiny tear of triumph, and accepted the arm of Dr Crouch who had rushed to her side.

The meal was a turning-point in her recovery. She partook of every course, happy to spurn the invalid dishes in cook's compendium. The converse was light-hearted and she joined in with alacrity.

Thus stimulated, Prue looked forward to Agnes's presence. But she was late in arriving. 'I'm sorry, Prue. I had thought to read to you but haven't chosen a piece.'

Prue reached for a poetry anthology and smilingly handed it to Agnes. 'Then let the book choose. Open it randomly and read me the poem that appears on, say, the left-hand page. Then we'll discuss it.'

Agnes did so and silently read the poem, hunched over the book. There was an unusually long pause and Prue was surprised to see Agnes's eyes brimming with tears.

'Agnes, what's amiss!'

'The poem is Fletcher's *Melancholy*. I can't read it sensibly. Oh, Prue, Hubert offered for me again and I can delay no longer. I cannot love him and nothing can make me.'

Prue was silent. The alternatives for Agnes were few. A young lady was vulnerable without protection. Prue had been made more than aware of that during her disastrous journey from Hybullen. She knew that Lady Glenister would favour the marriage, dismissing the loveless state as something to be endured for the benefits endowed. Prue drew Agnes close and both sat pondering in the candlelight.

Prue turned as she heard the door open. A tall young man in a tan coat and shining top boots stood at the threshold, hands on hips and feet astride, looking quizzically at them. His hair was full, black and fashionably quiffed. Dark eyes flashed. 'Why so sullen? I'll not allow it!'

'James!' she cried, attempting to rise, 'How wonderful to see you – and so changed!'

'A shift in one's fortunes warrants changes in mood and appearance.' He stepped forward and helped Prue to her feet, embracing her. 'Your marquess has achieved the impossible,' he whispered. 'Full recompense and no court appearances. Reedpath is banished to Australia. Lord Cedric Aumerle is guiltless, a principal player in the game of justice.'

Prue was radiant. Hugging him, she said, 'Oh, James. Such good news.' She drew Agnes forward. 'You didn't meet my friend, Miss Agnes Shaw, when last you were here.'

He smiled, bent to Agnes's hand and bore it to his lips. 'Miss Shaw, a pleasure. But how can I forgive you?'

Agnes, blushing, bobbed a curtsy. 'Forgive me for what, Sir James?'

'For not permitting us to meet before now.'

Agnes's eyes danced. 'You must forgive me. I insist.'

He pursed his lips, retaining her hand. 'Upon a condition.'

'What is it, pray?'

'That you personally escort me in my exploration of this charming city.'

'Oh, willingly,' laughed Agnes, her melancholy fled.

He smiled. 'I have a new equipage for the purpose. Standing in the carriage-house is a four-wheeled Clarence and pair, ready to convey you wherever you choose.'

'James, how lovely! Why not take Agnes for a drive tomorrow,' suggested Prue. 'I'll remain here as I've important things to do, but I'm sure Lady Glenister will be delighted to accompany you.'

He turned to Agnes. 'Pray for good weather. I'm inclined for a long excursion.'

She nodded eagerly, her eyes shining.

The manservant entered with glasses and champagne in a cooler, followed by a joyous Lady Wainflete bearing a dish of fresh oysters. 'Let's celebrate this excellent outcome!'

Prue trembled with happiness. It was a moment to savour. She could not take her eyes from James in his newfound elegance, favouring Agnes with courtly grace. His praise of Esmond set her pulses racing. Hybullen's restoration was assured and release from old resentments a welcome feeling. She approached Lady Wainflete.

'The time has come. Quills and writing paper tomorrow!'

Late autumn sunshine flooded into Prue's room the next morning. Seated at the escritoire, she had attempted several letters to Esmond. She sat in a daydream, brushing her lips with the feathered tip of the goosequill. '*My love*', she had started on a fresh page, but her pen faltered. A letter could not keep pace with her desire for an immediate sight of him. She would ask James to drive her to Bristol on the morrow in the new carriage.

Suddenly, she was aware of sounds from downstairs disrupting the morning peace of the house.

'Effie!' came a voice, loud and demanding. 'Where in this world is Prudence Mulcaster Smith?'

It was impossible to ignore such a question. Prue left her room and looked over the landing banisters to the hallway below. The street door was open. Filling the aperture was the dominating figure of the Dowager Marchioness of Lydney.

In a flutter of silks, Lady Wainflete rushed to greet her. 'Dora, my dear. When did you return to Bath?'

'I haven't returned. Melodon is still closed up. I'm staying at the hotel for a night or two.'

'Oh, can't you stay here?'

'Well—'

Lady Wainflete marshalled her manservant, Clara and the dowager's maid. 'You'll be my guest. Mostyn and Clara will arrange everything. Come to my withdrawing-room and I'll answer all your questions. Are you here to do some shopping?'

Prue returned quickly to her room as they started to ascend the stairs. Breathless, she stood behind the door. Was Esmond in Bath, too? Excitement drove away all thoughts of writing. Instead she attended to her appearance, expecting soon to be summoned to join the ladies.

Lady Wainflete settled the dowager on a sofa and sat beside her.

'He is *impossible*!' hissed the dowager. Her vehemence awoke Nero who regarded her with wide amber eyes. 'Ever since we left Andursley, he's like one possessed.'

'Esmond?'

'Esmond.' There was a silence. 'Andursley is not the place it was, Effie. The countess has lost her mind. She dismissed Prue and destroyed Esmond's letter to her. No one knows where Prue is. Esmond is preparing to leave for Harrogate as he's convinced she is there with her brother.'

'Oh . . .' breathed Lady Wainflete, clasping and unclasping her hands. 'Dora—'

'Worse!' interposed the dowager. 'The Lydney ball starts in five days with over five hundred guests. Esmond says he'll stay only for the initial formalities and within an hour will depart. He shows no interest in anything and is often seen staring at nothing. I've asked him to delay until after the event, but he's adamant. He's inconsolable—'

'Dora! Prue is here recovering from a serious illness!'

The dowager turned to her with a wide-eyed glare. 'In this house?'

'In this house. Last night we were joined by Sir James, so you must stop Esmond going to Harrogate.'

'Only one person can do that. May I see her, Effie?'

Prue was not surprised at the urgent tapping on her door. She opened it to admit Lady Wainflete, flushed and breathless. 'Esmond's mother is below, Prue. He thinks you're in Harrogate and is preparing to go there, seemingly wrecking the Lydney ball. She wishes to see you.'

Prue smiled. 'That will give me the greatest pleasure.'

She sat long with the dowager and Lady Wainflete. They

adjourned for a light refreshment and returned again to the with-drawing-room. Many questions had been posed and answered when talk turned to the Lydney ball. To Prue's joy, the dowager agreed to aid in her meeting with Esmond at the ball. Prue wished it to be delicately planned, involving only Esmond and herself. It was a happy connivance.

'I'll have to employ stealth in the arrangements, but Esmond is beyond noticing anything at the moment,' said the dowager. Then, taking Prue's hands into her own, she added, 'My dearest girl, we'll celebrate your betrothal to my son at the ball on the stroke of midnight!' She gathered Prue to her in a gentle embrace.

Lady Wainflete, her eyes moist with tears of joy, helped Prue to rise, and kissed her. 'All happiness, Prue,' she said, her voice break-ing with emotion.

Prue smiled. 'Dear Lady Wainflete, I have immediate need of your mantua-maker.'

'I'll see she's here first thing tomorrow.'

In her bedroom later that night, Prue opened her portmanteau and carefully withdrew "The Amorous Damozel". She held her at arm's length. 'Your partner awaits you,' she whispered, 'as does mine.'

The November sun was setting as they left The White Hart at Whitchurch. Perfect timing, thought Prue.

The long journey from Bath to Lydney was almost done. At the inn, Lady Wainflete's groom saw to the change of horses. Prue, James and Agnes, dressed for the masquerade, were heavily cloaked. They looked with wonder at Lady Wainflete whose concession to disguise was an enormous red Venetian tricorne and mask, adorned with brilliants and feathers, which she had with-drawn from a massive hat-box set upon a roof rack of the coach.

The mood was light, despite lurching on the rough road. Prue leaned back, lulled by the noisy accompaniment of the hastening coach. Every inch they travelled brought her closer to Esmond. She thirsted for the sight of him, to feel again the rapture of his nearness. Esmond's sacrifice and his brother's heroism made her heart beat with revived dreams, as joy rippled through her like a mill-race, washing away the dark distrust she had harboured. She was set astir with senses so sharpened that she thought herself weight-less, as if part of the golden light that flooded through the coach windows. Her mind galloped, outrunning reality so that she visibly jumped when James spoke.

'So Esmond is not aware you'll be at the masquerade, Prue.'

She paused before replying, needing time to collect her thoughts. 'He is not expecting me to be there. I have a special birthday gift for him which requires staging in the giving of it. His mother and brother Cedric are helping me to set it up, so they know I'll be present.'

'I begin to pity Esmond,' said James, 'with such an array of collusion around him.'

'Esmond is not beyond a little collusion on his own account,' said Lady Wainflete with feathers a-nodding.

'I didn't know this ball is to celebrate Esmond's birthday as well as the annual feast for the county,' said James, stretching out his legs. 'I suppose there are events on the estate the entire day. I'm glad we're just taking in the masquerade.'

'The dowager told me it's always linked to the birthday of the marquess,' said Prue. 'Festivities begin early with both sons joining tenants and villagers in feats of strength. The masquerade starts when it's dark and is always opened by the present marquess costumed as the first marquess, Godwin Aumerle, who started the shipping in the 1700s.'

'They're sumptuously dressed,' added Lady Wainflete. 'It's the custom for the marchioness, or in this case, the dowager, to wear the style of gown favoured by Godwin's wife, Lady Amelia. Lilac, always lilac.'

'So that's how we'll recognize them,' said Agnes.

'They're unmasked to receive,' said Lady Wainflete, 'and play a guessing game with their guests who disguise their voices to avoid recognition.'

There was a silence as the coach rocked violently. James stood to look from the window. 'There's the entrance to Andursley,' he said suddenly. 'The gatehouse appears unmanned.'

Prue glimpsed a flickering lantern hoisted on locked gates. 'It's unlikely the countess will be at Lydney,' she said, 'but perhaps Caroline and Richard are back from Scotland and able to go. If they have returned, I might even see Biddy again.'

Thinking of Biddy prompted the memory of her excursion to Fittiwake's that foggy day. She mused on the mystery of coincidence. The mists had parted and nothing was ever the same again.

Lydney was ablaze with light as they entered the crowded drive. One by one the coaches moved up to allow guests to descend by the porch steps, aided by ushers with flambeaux.

As James assisted the ladies to step down from the coach, a plumed cavalier approached. He swept off his wide-brimmed hat and bowed over a beribboned shoe.

'Lady Euphemia Wainflete?' he enquired.

Lady Wainflete nodded.

'Cedric Aumerle, at your service.' He turned to James. 'Sir James Mulcaster Smith and Miss Agnes Shaw,' he said, with another bow. Then, turning to Prue, he smiled. 'Prudence, you are most welcome, and a sovereign remedy for our glum fellow.' He kissed the ladies' hands and said, 'Put on your masks and dominoes, and follow me.'

He led them through a maze of rooms and corridors. By way of an ante-room he admitted Lady Wainflete, James and Agnes to the thronged salon. He beckoned Prue to a stairway leading up to a long gallery. *Torchères* stood at intervals decked with wax-lights which shone on the paintings lining the walls. By a full-length portrait of a lady in a hooped gown of lilac silk, he paused.

'This is Lady Amelia, and the door directly opposite leads to Esmond's study.' He smiled. 'Everything is in place according to your wishes.'

'Thank you,' she breathed, dropping her mask.

He fell on one knee, reached for her hand and kissed it gently.

'Prudence, you live up to and beyond all that Esmond claims for you.'

She smiled. 'You and Esmond should feel pride in having acted rightly. James and I are very grateful and cannot thank you enough for your vigilance.'

'It's reward enough that you're here,' he said, rising. 'Esmond wants to be on his way to Harrogate as he thinks you are there with your brother.'

'Then we must stop him, Cedric.'

He offered his arm. 'Come, replace your mask and let's to the salon. All should be in full flow.'

Cedric led her by the same route to the rear of the salon. With a conspiratorial wink, he withdrew, leaving her standing dazzled by the light from a myriad crystal lustres. More impressive was the show of colour and movement in the fabulous costumes of the guests, against which the silver and blue livery of the attendants appeared austere.

She mingled in that illustrious company and held her breath as Esmond, with his mother, slowly progressed down the long double line of guests. Amid all the bowing and simpering, there were savoyards, corsairs, centurions, princesses from Araby and fair Quakers. But she saw only Esmond.

His full-skirted coat of maroon velvet, resplendent with gold lace and large button-back cuffs, swung as he turned from one party to another. A white tie-wig, romantically waved back from his forehead with two tight curls at each side, enhanced his handsome features, the brilliant gaze, the same sweet and proud mien. Her heart gave a bounce. She was moved with heady delight. There was a detachment in his manner and a slight impatient look towards his mother when she dallied too long. She loved him for it, longing to cry out that she was near. Removing her cape and hood, she left them on a chair and turned to face the company. It was time to present herself.

Esmond, after his slow procession, gave a signal and the music started. As the floor cleared for dancing, matrons pressed forward to present their daughters. Impeccably polite in every greeting, he made for the door to the terrace and garden.

The illuminated lake bore scale models of the Lydney fleet, outlined with pinpricks of lights. Fireworks started and the lawns were lively with parties feasting and making their way to the entertainments, dancing and card salons.

He leaned against the balustrade, arms folded and fingers clutched under his elbows. Everything is going well, he thought, and none would miss me if I left now. His mother had asked that he remain until midnight, but he did not wish to do so. He looked at the moon, high in the sky, bright as a shilling. A torch to light his ride to the north. What awaited him in Harrogate? Prue, convinced of his probity and ready to receive him? His jaw tensed. God grant that Dartree was no longer on the scene.

The terrace was attracting assignations, with couples locked together in the shadows and arbors. Abruptly, he turned away. He must leave to seek his own partner.

He was about to re-enter the salon when he was stopped in his tracks by the sight of a masked girl. She was standing quite still in a whirl of dancers, smiling at him. Was she a phantom? Her demeanour suggested something familiar and extremely dear to him. He stared and, in his mind, was reading again at Fittiwake's . . . *her dark hair threaded with the flowers of the cornfield . . . her pale yellow gown . . . lace trimmed with a deep décolletage. . . .*

'Demme, it's the amorous damozel,' he muttered, and started forward.

But she vanished in the throng. She was an illusion! Then he saw her again, paused on the stairs leading to the gallery. He made his way there as quickly as he could, escaping those that would detain him, his eyes ever concentrated on the stairway. She had disappeared from view once more. She must be in the gallery, he thought. He sprang up the stairs, two at a time, and entered the gallery. She was tripping along it with a dancing step. He followed her, his heart thumping in his breast. Suddenly, she stopped and turned to face him. Then, to his surprise, she entered his study and closed the door behind her!

He slowed his pace to quieten his approach and, for a moment, listened with his ear to the door. All was silent. He entered quietly. Central in the room was a round table. Set upon it, illuminated by a large candlebranch with a taper burning in every holder, was the complete ensemble of "The Amorous Damozel". He gasped. It was more beautiful than he had imagined, the porcelain reflecting a million lights in the candleglow. He walked round the table, admiring it from every angle, dazed by it.

'Where are you?' he shouted into the dark corners of the room. 'Have I you to thank for this wonderful gift?'

Then he saw, set in front of the porcelain lovers, a perfectly pressed rose. Aridity had not caused it to disintegrate. He recognised it as 'Constancy', the rose he had sent to Prue.

'Prue,' he called. 'Taunt me no more. Come to me!'

The window curtains parted and, unmasked, she stepped towards him out of dappled moonlight. He gave a faint cry, then a shuddering sigh of joyful relief as he rushed to take her in his arms. 'My darling girl, what magic brought you here?'

'A little plotting with your mother, your brother and the damozel,' she answered softly.

Time stopped as his eyes coursed her face. A hair's-breadth separated him from her lips, and he kissed her, a subdued kindly kiss of greeting. 'It's a miracle of timing for I was soon to depart for Harrogate to find you.'

'That would have been unfortunate. James is here with Agnes and Lady Wainflete. All are eager to see you, but none more than I.'

He kissed her again, lingeringly, then smiled and led her back to the porcelain ensemble. 'Where did you get that beautiful creature, and how did you know I was seeking her? Did Fittiwake tell you? I knew you were interested in his porcelain.'

She laughed. 'I was seeking the courtier.'

He laughed with her. 'A perfect combination.' He paused. 'Do you realize we are living portrayals in our present dress?'

'Of course,' she murmured, 'but my courtier is more handsome, more sophisticated' – she drew off his wig and smoothed his fair curls – 'and seductive.'

His eyes engaged hers and held them. 'And my damozel the more desirable.' He tossed his wig to a chair. His voice lowered. 'I'm jealous of all you have done before, of every person to whom you've spoken. Cure me, Prue. I'm suffering with love.'

She sighed. 'I share your affliction, for I adore you, Esmond.'

He held her close, excited by the urgent rhythm of her breathing. Moments passed. He pressed his lips upon her hair. 'I love you. I worship you. Why are there no words more expressive than these? There is in you a spring of grace. It lifts my heart.' He pulled her closer and kissed her violently. His kiss was returned with as much zeal as given. Breath intermingled, and emotion shaded her cheeks with a tender rose colour.

'To speak after such kisses is tedium,' he whispered, tremblingly, 'and to let you from my arms is agony. Yet, I have something to give you.' He gently released her and went to his desk, taking something from a drawer which he opened by a secret spring. Returning, he took up her left hand and placed upon the third finger a gold ring which flashed with sapphires, emeralds and diamonds.

'Esmond!' she gasped.

He took her ringed hand and crushed it to his lips.

Her eyes filled with tears of joy.

'I bought it in Bath the day after that never-to-be-forgotten piano recital. The looks we exchanged convinced me that those dire days of separation were not the end. This, my darling, is the end – when we begin our life together. You do agree, don't you? We are betrothed, aren't we?'

'Yes, yes, yes,' she whispered. 'Are you aware it will be announced at the ball tonight at the stroke of midnight?'

He smiled broadly. 'So that is why I am summoned. I had thought to be well on my way to find you – but this is a tryst I cannot miss.'

He lifted her with tender deliberation, turning in a dance-like motion, kissing her the while. Then he set her gently against a cushion on a *chaise-longue* near the fireplace and took her hands in his. He loved the shining eyes that raised to his, and knew himself enslaved.

'We shall marry before Christmas,' he said, looking down at her. 'A Grand Tour in the spring, if Boney allows, then a voyage in the new *Sydney Prudence*.'

'We'll voyage in every respect,' she replied dreamily, 'for to remain at the same point in love, is regressive.'

'That will never happen,' he said, seating himself beside her and drawing her to his heart. She was here in his arms, living and palpable. Her shoulders were uncovered and he had never seen any so beautiful. His eyes moved over her, the décolletage of her dress revealing her exquisite form. He brushed her lips with his and continued down to her throat, neck and bosom, his sensual kisses the precursors of possession.

She whispered his name.

'You are perfection,' he murmured, enraptured.

'Only for you, Esmond,' she smiled, succumbing to the sweetness of his wooing.

Ardour returned as they clung together. He crushed his mouth upon hers and her lips opened to his demand. Moving to the pulse throbbing in her throat, he whispered, 'There's an alphabet of love, my darling, in which we'll instruct each other.'

She sighed in a stupor of happiness. 'I must warn you, Esmond, that once the floodgates of my sensibilities are opened, you may be drowned and—'

He kissed her to silence. 'You forget, my love, I'm a seafarer and able to navigate your inestimable treasures, if you'll permit.'

'Then I'll permit.' Smiling and radiant, she nestled closer into his arms.

He had never known happiness like this. He regarded her lovingly, then gently kissed her eyelids and cheeks. 'Honour First, my darling. Even when there's proven intent and desire afflicts the will, I'll not dishonour our ultimate coming together.'

She quivered, clinging to him.

The marriage of moonlight from without and candleglow from within the study created a rare light, full of bewitchment as the midnight hour approached. Esmond glanced again at the porcelain lovers, pitying their static state in the confines of paste. Reality lay in his arms, her green eyes tenderly regarding him and features ready to undulate in such kindling love as to dazzle and astound him evermore.

She was his amorous damozel and he her lover, in place to kiss and caress the intimate softnesses he knew were waiting for him.

Epilogue

From *The Court Companion*, June 1817.

It would appear that Heberlein's exquisite eighteenth-century porcelain ensemble, 'The Amorous Damozel', has become a unique piece.

Our correspondent reports that the Most Honourable Marquess and Marchioness of Lydney, accompanied by their firstborn, the young Henry Godwin Aumerle known as Viscount Dunnestor, stayed for some time near Dresden on their Grand Tour. While visiting Meissen they arranged for the figures of the damozel and her lover to be expertly joined, thus rendering them inseparable.